The Rancher's Return

JILLIAN HART

Copyright © 2011 By Jillian Hart

First Published 1999
By Zebra Books Kensington Publishing Corp.
Originally titled *Sunlight and Shadows*

Cover art by Kimberly Killion, Hot Damn Designs

Book formatted by Jessica Lewis
http://www.Author'sLifeSaver.com

All rights reserved.

ISBN-13: 978-1490345543
ISBN-10: 149034554X

CHAPTER ONE

"No!" Nettie felt the skin prickle on the back of her neck despite the heat and the sun. In a flash she halted the wagon, harnesses jangling, and hauled her two-and-a-half-year-old son onto her lap, shielding him from the sight before them.

She recognized her neighbor, Jake Beckman, his big frame silhouetted by the bright red-orange disk of the harsh sun, his head bare. Nettie watched in horror as he drew his strong leg backward, his gaze trained on a downed man in the middle of the road, and slammed his boot into the fallen man's midsection with all of his oxlike strength.

"Stop it!" she demanded. "Stop this right now."

Jake jerked his gaze to her. Several other men stepped into view on the rise above, dark figures outlined by the bright glare of the sun and the deep cloudless blue of the sky.

"This ain't none of your business, Nettie." Jake mopped the sweat from his brow with a swipe of his arm. "Come on, boys, let's get this worthless piece of crap off the road so the lady can pass."

Nettie's ears burned at the venom in Jake's voice. She felt her spine straighten with the need to remind him of her and her son's sensibilities, but now her gaze focused on the man lying so still on the ground. He was dirty, hatless, his shirt torn. Yet even with his back to her, something skidded through Nettie's nerves. Like fear.

Like the time she heard the gunshot and knew her husband was dead.

One of the men on the rise dragged the man from the road. "Come on, Nettie," Jake instructed her. "Pass on by."

Silence roared through her ears with the strength and speed of a train so that suddenly, she knew. She *knew*. The man who lay hurt and bleeding and broken was the same man who had killed her husband.

"Come on, Nettie," Jake's voice called her forward.

It was as if the great expanse of the sky was her heart. Unable to feel, Nettie shook the reins, aware of Sam's wide-eyed fear as he cuddled against her on the seat and Old Bessie's protesting groans as they lumbered up the side of the slope. The wooden slats of the wagon rattled. One wheel squeaked. Nettie stared at the passing patch of earth between the tongue of the wagon and the horses' tails.

"Just go on to town," Jake said as she approached. "We'll be along in a few minutes." He spoke casually of the funeral and of his delay as if he were about to tie up his horse or run an errand, not beat a man to death.

Memory slammed through her head with lightning speed. She remembered the threats, two years before, and how her neighbors had taken a stand behind her. Jake had threatened to kill the man if he ever showed his face in the county again.

Nettie pulled the reins hard. Bessie squealed in protest at the pressure on her mouth, but it was a distant sound compared to the heartbeat so loud in her ears. Nettie turned to study the man in the dust. Blood ran from his brow and mouth. His leg lay at a strange angle.

"You men ought to be ashamed of yourselves," Nettie chided as if she were scolding Sam for a misdeed. She left the child on the seat and hopped down from the wagon. Five men stared at her, their eyes dark, their mouths curled into frowns.

Anger. It burned in her breast as fiercely as the sun overhead. It emboldened her now as she halted before the strong, burly men. Men she knew. Men capable of violence. Her hands trembled, but she didn't think of it now. She knelt down next to the man on the ground.

Hank Callahan opened one eye as the woman's shadow threw relief over his hammering body. He had heard Jake Beckman speaking to a woman. He had heard a wagon stop, a horse's complaint, and a woman speak.

Nettie Pickering gazed down at him with concern in her wide brown eyes. Green threads wove through those dark irises like grass on the plain. He opened his mouth to tell her to go, to leave him be, but it only roused up more pain. Pain struck through every piece of him with the force of an ax and it didn't stop.

She was dressed for a funeral. A black straw hat shaded her soft oval face from the sun, and a dusty black dress hugged her from chin to wrist. Ebony fabric skirted her as she knelt, leaning closer, brushing at the cut above his eye with the lightest touch of her small hand.

The ground beside his head shook with little earthquakes. A small tow-haired child grabbed Nettie's arm. Concern frowned across the boy's brow as he leaned close. "Mama, why's he got so many ows?" he asked.

Nettie's soft mouth compressed into a tight line. Hank watched as she brushed a lock of flyaway hair from the boy's innocent eyes. "Sam, tell me why you aren't waiting in the wagon."

The boy shrugged, and Hank drew in a tentative, painful breath as the boy scampered away. Nettie moved from his side, the crisp black fabric rustling around her. Hank watched her slender body rise with a spine-straight dignity. The sun glared around her and heat burned right into the pain in his guts, doubling it.

A boot nudged him hard in his tender right side. Hank snapped open his eyes to stare up at a black-shirted man, who was also dressed for the funeral. Harv Wheaton nudged him hard with his pointed boot's toe. "You're a dead man, son."

Hank swallowed. He understood the quiet certainty in the man's frank statement. Hank was a murderer in many men's eyes, even his own. When the men he'd called neighbors ran him out of town that dark night over two years ago, Hank knew he could never come back. But here he was.

A shadow slipped across him, blocking out the harsh burn of the sun like cold water. He could smell the cinnamon soap scent of her and hear the rustle of her skirts as Nettie knelt beside him again.

"Jake, Harv, Thomas, help me get him into the wagon." Her

voice sounded as firm as the earth beneath his head.

"Now, Nettie. This here is none of your business." Jake's boot stopped within kicking distance. Hank knew the big man's placating voice would urge her away, insist that she continue on her journey to town, and leave them to finish this. It was what Hank expected.

But Nettie stood up, the rock-hard confidence in her voice unmistakable. "This man needs a doctor."

"This man needs a hanging," Harv argued.

"If you don't lift him into the back of my wagon, then I'll do it myself."

Hank felt a small hand catch up each of his wrists and begin pulling him across the rocky, rough earth. Pointed stones bit into his back. His head banged with each small dip and rise.

His leg felt as if someone were ripping it out of his knee joint. Darkness buzzed in Hank's brain until he was hardly aware of the beating sun and the abuse of the ground upon his body. He couldn't even hear the men arguing.

Then a white blast of pain careened through his body as several rough hands ripped him from the ground and tossed him into the back of a wagon.

Pain battered him until he welcomed the comforting blackness.

"You're asking for trouble, Nettie," Jake Beckman cautioned her. "He killed your husband."

"I know that." Nettie's grip on the reins tightened. She couldn't explain her actions, but she knew in her heart she'd done the right thing. "If I had allowed you to beat Hank Callahan to death, then you wouldn't be any better than a murderer."

She clamped her mouth shut She didn't owe Jake Beckman any more of an explanation than that. If she closed her eyes she could still see his vicious and powerful kick to a barely conscious man unable to fight back. Her chest filled with angry sparks of rage.

"Mama." Sam stood up in the wagon bed behind her, his little fingers gripping the wooden seat back. "The man's bleedin'."

"I know, tiger. He's hurt." She unclenched her jaw enough to speak. "Now come sit back down beside me.

"Justice isn't murder, Nettie," Jake spoke with unfailing certainty.

She closed her eyes, counted to ten. For a day that had begun as uneventful as any, her troubles had sorely increased. A funeral to attend. Jake Beckman hovering over her. Now Hank Callahan beaten and vomiting in the back of her old wagon.

Nettie glanced over her shoulder. Blood-tinged spittle clung to the beaten man's lips and chin. A wet patch had darkened the boards, but most of it had already dripped between the slats.

She reached into one skirt pocket and handed Sam a handkerchief. "Can you be a big boy and wipe off his mouth for Mama?"

"Okay." Sam took the piece of plaid cloth and crawled the handful of inches to Hank's head. Nettie watched as he wiped the man's mouth hard. Triumphant, he grinned up at his mother.

"Good boy," she said, and Sam was satisfied.

"That murderer oughtn't be near your boy," Jake pointed out, his hard-featured face harsh beneath the dark brim of his hat.

That hard anger tightened like a fist inside Nettie's chest. "I know you've been a wonderful neighbor and friend to me since Richard's death, but I don't like this. You did this to him, Jake, and I'll expect you and the men to pay the doctor's bill."

The man riding beside her wagon shook his head. "You're too kind for your own damn good, Nettie. I don't care if you like it or not, I'm not leaving you alone with a known murderer. We'll get him to town, and that will be the end of your worries."

Nettie sighed. "Today is Mr. Callahan's funeral. Don't you realize Hank came to town to see his father buried? Surely you could have left him alone."

Jake spat a wad of tobacco juice away from the wagon. "I've known you a long time, Nettie. You won't marry me and you won't marry anyone else around here that's tryin' to help you. Now you just gotta trust that a man knows how to handle this."

Nettie opened her mouth, her angry protest already a string of words in her throat, but she hesitated. She did not agree with Jake Beckman, but he had been more than a good neighbor to her. She couldn't afford to anger him even if she would never agree with his way of thinking.

She snapped her mouth shut, her jaw muscles aching.

"Mama." Sam grabbed the board behind her and leaned into her ear. "Looky."

Nettie glanced over her shoulder past the sun-blond head of her young son to the man lying prostrate on her wagon floor. His strong, masculine body trembled, shivering as if he were in a frigid wind.

She pulled the horses to a stop, set the brake because of the incline, and hopped over the wagon seat. Her skirts fell around her ankles as she hurried to the man's side.

He looked like death. A bright red cut slashed the skin above his left eyebrow and wet blood trailed down the side of his pasty white face. Dark eyelashes fanned the bruises of his eyes; the soft, sensual line of his mouth was swollen in several places, and the split skin bled.

"He got lots of owies." Sam stared down at the injured man.

"Yes, he does." Nettie sighed. "Where is your hat? Put on your hat so you don't get sunburned."

While Sam grabbed up his small hat made just like Jake's, Nettie grabbed a folded blanket from beneath the seat and tucked it around the shivering man. In her heart, she feared he was close to death. Dead for nothing more than coming home to his father's funeral.

Jake had pulled his horse up to the wagon bed, and his shadow fell across Nettie's feet. The man's dark eyes were unreadable beneath the brim of his hat, and she frowned at him, meeting his gaze for a second longer than necessary.

"I'm sorry, Nettie." His voice came gruff but not apologetic.

She said nothing. What was there to say? She condemned what he'd done to this man. She condemned violence of any sort. Perhaps it was because her father's love for whiskey had driven him to abuse his wife and his family and to land him in jail for brawling in the streets. Perhaps it was simply because striking someone never solved one problem that she could see. Either way, Nettie snatched up Sam's hand in her own and lifted him gently over the back of the seat.

"Sit still and watch for gophers," she instructed the boy as she climbed over the boards herself, careful of her skirts. "I bet you can find two or three before we get to town."

With Sam busy, there were no more innocent questions begging to be answered. Jake rode silently beside the wagon. And Nettie settled into her own thoughts, troubled, afraid the man in the back would die before they reached town.

Walla Walla boomed dirty and noisy as Nettie carefully negotiated the main street. Tall brick-and-wood buildings faced her, and movement swirled around her. Shoppers jammed the boardwalks. Horses and buggies stood tethered. Freight wagons crammed the streets, and Nettie waited impatiently until she could nudge around the slow-moving traffic and off the main street.

She pulled up before a tidy white building and told Jake to find someone inside. Sam chattered on about what he'd seen, and Nettie tried to answer him as she glanced at their passenger in the back. The shivering had ceased. He lay like a corpse buried beneath the dark wool blanket. Nettie distracted Sam, her heart heavy, and lifted him down from the wagon.

The grass was cool in the dappled shade, and Nettie sent the boy to pick clover. She watched his gentle footfalls and his little-boy innocence with a tight throat. He would grow up to be gentle like his father, wouldn't he? Troubled, she remembered Jake's behavior today and shivered.

At least the question that had been troubling her for three weeks was answered. She would not marry him.

A serious, solid man wearing dark clothes and spectacles burst out into the sunlight and raced toward the back of the wagon. Nettie wanted to help, but feared there was nothing she could do. She was not a nurse. She could not breathe life back into Hank Callahan if he was dead. She could only pray that he was still alive, or pray for the state of his soul.

"Mama?" Sam held up a fistful of white-and-brown clover flowers.

She smiled at him. She could protect her son. Kneeling down, Nettie accepted the flowers.

Sam stared, worry deep in his brow, watching as the doctor and Jake hauled Hank out of the wagon.

She was told by the doctor to wait. She pulled out Richard's pocket watch from her reticule and studied the time. Although she'd arrived plenty early for the funeral, Nettie had been counting on running errands before the service. She thought of the horses, hot and thirsty, and wandered outside hoping to find a water trough.

There wasn't one close. She boosted Sam onto Emmanuel's broad back. The placid horse stood patiently in his harness while the boy squirmed excitedly. Nettie placed one hand on his leg and led the horses into the dappled, pleasant shade. Out of the direct sunlight, they would be cooler.

"Nettie." Jake strode toward her, his eyes dark. A ring of sweat gathered below the band of his hat, matting his hair and beading along his brow. "Doc says it'll be a long wait. Why don't you go on over to the funeral. I got me a few errands to run, but I'd be happy to escort you."

Nettie stared at him, unable to speak. She'd known this man for years. He'd been a friendly neighbor when Richard lived, a helpful neighbor after Richard died. A friend whenever she needed one. Now, in the span of hours, he'd become a stranger to her.

"I want your word there will be no more violence against that man in there." Nettie swallowed, her throat dry and raw. "Promise me, Jake."

She watched him set his square jaw and some glimmer of doubt twisted through her like a snake in the tall bunchgrass. She couldn't see what he intended to do. She wasn't sure she could trust what he would do.

"I can't trust a man who'd lie to me."

The stiffness in his strong shoulders ebbed. "You have my word. I'll see that he's left alone."

Nettie studied him, weighing the sincerity of his tone against the steady firmness of his eyes. "Is that the truth?"

Jake sighed. "It's the truth."

Nettie pulled Sam down and balanced him on her hip. He was heavy to hold, but she clung to him despite the heat. "I have errands of my own," she told him plainly as she set her son on the wagon floor. "I'll look for you at the funeral."

Jake tipped his hat, clearly displeased with her. With her stomach so twisted up in knots, Nettie didn't care how unhappy he was or what he thought of her for not harboring the same hateful vengeance he did. She only hoped she could trust him to keep to his word. She only hoped Hank Callahan would recover, leave town, and never return.

CHAPTER TWO

Nettie hadn't attended a funeral since she buried her husband. So much felt the same as she sat in the pew in the hot, stuffy church, and yet everything was different. She had her small son beside her, and she'd lived over two years without Richard. But the scene in the small church seemed the same with the mourners somberly dressed, with grief buzzing in the air like flies, with silence as serious as death.

Sam squirmed on the pew, so Nettie reached inside her reticule and handed him his father's watch to keep him occupied.

"Nettie. Bertha said you needed to see me."

She gazed up into the wizened, regal face of Emmalouise Callahan. The deceased's widow. Hank's mother. Mrs. Callahan was of a better class, as evidenced by her pampered lily-white skin and her smooth, jeweled hands. Even in old age, her fashionably plump body was straight and graceful. Shimmering black silk whispered as she moved.

"I'm terribly sorry about Mr. Callahan." Nettie managed to squeeze the words past her dry, tight throat. "Perhaps this isn't the best time, but I wanted you to know straight away. As I was driving into town, I came upon your son beaten and unconscious along the side of the road. He's now at Doc Sutherland's."

Emmalouise Callahan sank to the plain board bench beside Nettie. Horror rounded her clear eyes and slackened her jaw. "Oh my Lord. Robert's been hurt?"

"No, Mrs. Callahan, not Robert. Your oldest son."

As if a gunman had burst into the vestibule and shot her straight in the heart, Mrs. Callahan couldn't have been more surprised. Nettie sat feeling her own heartbeat drum in her chest and watched the unreadable display of emotions play on the older woman's face.

The sounds of the church remained. A horse neighed somewhere outside. Calls on the street rang in through the wide-open door. A fly buzzed. Whispered greetings among neighbors shimmered in the hot, still air.

Finally, Mrs. Callahan pressed her bejeweled right hand to her heart. When she spoke, her words sounded choked and compressed. "You should know better than I, Mrs. Pickering. I have no oldest son."

The woman rose, her movements stiff and jerky, the only betrayal of her emotions. Nettie listened to the crinkle and swish of her clothes as the woman moved away with measured steps.

Nettie closed her eyes. Too much swelled in her heart. Memories of Richard's death. Grief for Mr. Callahan, who had been kind to her. Sadness for Hank Callahan, whose single bullet had not only ended one life but changed three other lives.

She gazed about the packed church. She spotted Harv Wheaton standing against the back wall looking as pious as a preacher on Sunday. She remembered his words on the dust-thick road. She remembered the hate in his eyes.

She remembered the same hatred she once held in her own heart. The same hatred that had been fueled by her grief, by her huge sense of injustice, by her dead husband's body laid to rest in the cemetery. She had been the catalyst of that ugly, violent, emotional night when Jake and Harv had beaten Hank Callahan out of town.

Guilt overwhelmed her, tasting like bile in her mouth. She lowered her gaze to the little boy beside her, his yellow-blond head bent industriously over the gold pocket watch. He, in his innocence, was too young to know such harm, too gentle to hate. Yet she'd not only approved the violence done that night when he was just a baby, she'd been the cause of it.

The ceremony began. A few busy flies circled low around the church while Reverend O'Neil preached. Nettie hardly listened. She kept the gold chain tight in her grip, her gaze on Sam, and tried to push down the emotions balled tight in her throat.

Many women waved fans in the oppressive heat, but Nettie had no fan. She could feel perspiration bead on her forehead and trickle down her spine. Someone had closed the door, muffling the street noise and the fresh breeze-stirred air.

Sam sat, near tears from the heat. It was time to go. Nettie nested the watch inside her reticule, scooped him up in her arms, hugged him to her with a few comforting kisses, and slipped down the aisle.

Jake Beckman opened the door for her and followed her outside.

Fresh air, while unbearably hot and dusty, felt good on her brow. Nettie carried Sam into the shade of the church and set him down in the cooler grass. Swiping at his eyes, he sat sobbing in the grass, too tired. When Jake returned with a dipperful of cool well water, Nettie rewarded him with a troubled smile.

"Thank you." She took the dipper from him and held it in two firm hands. Sam climbed into her lap and drank thirstily, hardly spilling a drop.

Jake knelt beside her in the grass. He was a strongly built man, tall and lean. He'd removed his hat to reveal his sand-brown hair darkened with sweat. She could see the same familiar features she'd come to know so well—his square jaw, his chiseled cheekbones, his straight, too-thin nose that had been broken once, and his dark caring eyes.

Nettie pushed away any other images. She didn't want to remember what she'd seen today, not now when her heart was so troubled. Or what she had learned of the man beside her.

Refreshed, her son climbed over Nettie's skirts and stood in the cool grass between them and rubbed his tired eyes. "Don't see any more gophers."

"Sam." Nettie set her hand on his small arm. "I think it's time for your nap. Come lay down here on the grass."

"I don't wanna nap!" True protest rose in the boy's voice. "I don't wanna."

Jake reached out with his calloused hands to tuck the boy's hot, sticky fingers between his own. "Come on, let's lie down and rest our eyes."

Nettie felt as if the world had tilted. Jake led Sam into the coolest part of the shade and laid him down on the grass. She watched the small boy yawn, watched Jake rub his hair with steady affection. Finally, Sam's back rose in steady breaths and Jake stood, walking quietly toward her.

"Are you still mad at me?" He sat down beside her on the cool grass. Nettie watched him stretch out his denim-covered legs and cross them at the ankles. His dusty black boots gleamed in the sun.

Nettie's dry throat felt like sand. "Yes. I'm still mad at you."

Jake sighed. He took out his pouch and tucked a pinch of tobacco against his cheek. "I suppose I oughtn't be chewing this in the churchyard."

Nettie made no comment.

"Look, I done what I thought was right. He killed your Richard, Nettie. Your husband and my best friend."

Nettie's throat felt like dust. "I know."

"He oughtn't be coming back here stirring up people's feelin's."

Nettie closed her eyes at the grief raw in Jake's voice. She wished she could close off the rest of the world as easily as she closed her eyes. That way she couldn't feel so sad at Mr. Callahan's death, feel so sorry for Emmalouise Callahan, who had lost her youngest son by her own choice, feel confused at the sight of Hank Callahan beaten unconscious at the side of the road. If she could turn off all those things, then maybe her choices would be more clear, more easy to make.

"Still, a man has a right to see his own father buried." Nettie opened her eyes, unable to close off the world. "You saw your father buried, Jake."

"That I did." As if troubled, too, Jake fell silent, chewing tobacco thoughtfully.

The service had ended. The doors opened and mourners somberly descended the few steps and passed Nettie and Jake for the cemetery just beyond.

She watched the sway of fancy dresses as those fine ladies passed.

She averted her eyes at the coffin leading the way to the gravesite. It made her wonder about Hank Callahan. Made her wonder if he was alive or dead, if he was conscious enough to realize he'd missed his father's burial. He'd missed his last chance to say good-bye.

Nettie knew how important good-byes were. She tried not to

think of the beaten, bloody man she'd hauled to town in her wagon, but her mind drifted back to him nevertheless.

Hank opened one eye past the swollen flesh surrounding it to stare up at a white ceiling. Pain split him like an ax from head to toe. He was immediately aware of how thirsty he felt, and immediately aware of his nauseous stomach. He dared to move his head and was rewarded first with a bone-splitting jab of pain and the sight of a row of empty beds freshly made. The room was empty.

Hank couldn't remember what had happened, why he was here. He was in some sort of a doctor's office; he knew that by the look of the place and the deathly quiet of the room. He blinked, trying to remember, but his brain hurt when he thought. An image flashed into his mind.

Nettie Pickering.

It all came back to him like a bobbin of thread unspooling. Of his brother's visit to his mine, of how Robert had talked him into seeing the old man one last time to find some kind of a forgiveness. Hank swallowed, but his throat was too dry. Like sand. Like dust. Where was a damn nurse when he needed one?

Nettie Pickering's face swam before his eyes. He remembered her. Lord, he would never forget her. She'd been his neighbor once, and he'd envied Richard his new bride, a slender, petite woman whom he had thought too skinny to make a good wife and too young to handle the drudgery of work on a wheat farm, but as the year passed and he'd become acquainted with Mrs. Pickering, he'd changed his mind.

She'd knelt over him in the road. He remembered that. Her face had changed with time and hardship and weather. Fine lines frowned beside her soft mouth and carved into the delicate skin around her eyes. Her hands had been roughened from work and tanned from too much sun.

"He's awake," the woman spoke.

Hank blinked, realizing there was no vision swimming before his eyes. Nettie Pickering in her black mourning dress stood at his bedside gazing over him. A cool distance shone in her earth-brown eyes. She turned her head as if she were speaking to someone else out in the corridor.

Hank opened his mouth, but his throat was too dry to speak. It hardly mattered. Telling her how sorry he was about her husband, about that night and every night she'd been alone since, wouldn't change one thing.

His heart twisted at his own inadequacies.

"Let's get him into the back of the wagon." Nettie spoke, and she sounded so different from the woman he'd known. Her voice, no longer musical, wasn't warmed by her light heart. Now her voice sounded as heavy as his own heart

Hank didn't protest as two men grabbed him roughly, jostling him between them as they hauled him down a long hall and out into the baking sun. The fresh air felt good, as stagnant and dusty as it was, brushing across his face with the heat of an oven. He recognized Jake Beckman's face at his feet and swore the man tugged unnecessarily on his broken leg. He was flung into a wagon bed with little ceremony. His back hit the boards hard, jostling his tender ribs.

His breath flew out with a groan, but he said nothing.

A blond little boy knelt over him, nose to nose. His huge brown eyes stared hard, studying Hank's cuts and swollen knots with a serious frown.

"You gots lots of ows," he said.

Hank knew nothing of children and stared at the boy with dread. As he wondered what he could possibly say to the child, a soft voice called, "Leave the man alone, Sam. Come sit up front with me."

The small boy frowned, clearly unwilling to go. Hank closed his eyes, expecting the worst. A temper tantrum. Tears. Screaming.

"Come up here with Mama," Nettie said in her gentle voice, a kind sound he hadn't heard in years.

The boy stood and tottered on steady legs out of his range of vision. He heard Nettie's gentle murmuring and the boy's confident replies. A man on a horse circled the wagon. Hank recognized Jake's brown Stetson.

Presently the vehicle jerked into motion, bumping down Main Street in the harsh afternoon sun. Hank closed his good eye against the glare and saw orange through his eyelids. He could hear the sounds of the busy town—the shouts of men, the squeak of wagon wheels, the clomp of horses' hooves against the hard-packed earth. Eventually those sounds faded into silent countryside. A breeze stirred the air across him, rustling in the tall bunchgrass meadows and wheat fields as they passed.

The road became more rough, the ruts in the road more pronounced. Rain in the spring had stirred the last of the thaw, mixing mud and ice, leaving wagons to churn through the muck that dried as summer came. Now Nettie's wagon wheels rolled over every ripple, rut, and rock in the Nez Perce trail. Hank bit back deeper groans as the jostling grew worse, shaking the very stuffing right out of him. It felt as if the jarring alone could re-break his broken bones.

Hank fell in and out of consciousness. The orange glow of his eyelids swirled to black as if he were being sucked under by the strong current of the Columbia River. Time passed and he would open his good eye to view the crisp blue sky overhead and the sinking red-orange blaze of the sun. Pain accompanied these wakenings, swinging through him with the sharpness of an ax blade. Hank much preferred sleep.

"Look!" he heard the little boy shout.

"Sam! Sit down," Nettie scolded him, and he felt the wagon jerk to a stop. "Don't ever stand up like that when Mama's driving. Do you understand?"

Hank closed his eyes. This was what he didn't like about children. Innocence alongside experience. Helplessness matched with greater size and strength. He willed himself not to hear what came next, but no resounding smack filled his ears. Only Sam's single, heartbroken sob.

"I's sorry, Mama."

Nettie's quiet response was snatched by the wind and so lost to Hank, but he did feel the jostling of the wagon and heard the squeak of the seat. He lay still, afraid to move, trusting Nettie would come back. A shadow fell across him and he opened his good eye.

Jake Beckman stared down at him, his dark face as hard as granite. Something mean and cold lived in his eyes. Something as powerful as hatred. Jake spit and the brown juice splattered on the floorboards next to Hank's cheek, splashing him.

"Don't want you around here," Jake threatened, his voice low enough so that the wind couldn't carry it. "You mend yourself up and you get the hell out of this countryside as soon as you can walk. If you don't, I'll do it for you."

Hank felt the splashed juice dribble down his cheek, past his ear. He felt helpless to move, helpless to stop Jake, unwilling to do anything to fight him.

"You watch how you treat that lady," Jake warned, glancing past where Hank lay in the wagon bed, checking on Nettie's whereabouts. "We're all gonna be watchin' you."

Hank closed his eyes, hearing the man's truth in his voice. Jake Beckman was a strong, hardworking man who meant what he said. His shadow moved away, and Hank lay there feeling his own heart pound in his chest.

The wagon shook slightly, and small pounding footsteps rattled the boards beside him. The little boy in a blue shirt and trousers toddled toward him, his fair face shaded by the brim of his little hat. In his small, tight grip he carried Hank's battered black Stetson.

"Looky what I saw!" Sam said triumphantly. "I seen it in the dirt. I got your hat!"

Bright eyes smiled at him in that round, button face. The little boy grinned, inordinately proud of himself. Hank's heart twisted at such an innocent soul. He tried to find his voice, which was rough and raw and shaky. "Th-thank you."

Grinning widely, Sam placed the dust-covered battered hat on Hank's head. The brim covered his eyes rather than his forehead, but it did supply shade from the sun. Sam laughed, and Nettie called to him. Hank listened to and felt those little footfalls pattering away.

Jake circled the wagon, impatient to be off, but Nettie vowed to ignore his willful pout as she hauled the water jug out from beneath the seat. It was small and half empty, and so it was not difficult to fill a tin cup and hand it to Sam. The boy, dusty and sweaty and tired, sucked down the sun-warmed water without complaint. When he was finished, Nettie poured a second tinful and caught Jake's gaze. He shook his head.

The warm water tasted stale and slightly of the soap she'd used to wash the jug, but it did wet her throat and chase down the dust. Savoring the wonderful sensation for just a second, Nettie sipped slowly.

"We gotta share," Sam informed her.

She smiled. Sharing was a concept Sam understood after he'd already had what he wanted. Nonetheless, she granted him a small smile and emptied the last of the water into the tin cup. Setting the jug back in place, she climbed over the seat into the wagon bed. Sam sat obediently on the seat and watched as she knelt down beside Hank Callahan.

She feared his eyes had swollen shut. Bruised skin crowded out both sockets so that all she could see were his night-dark eyelashes. One eye flicked open staring up between the bruised, swollen flesh. Only now that the blood had been wiped away did Nettie realize the extent of the beating. Perhaps before she hadn't wanted to know, hadn't wanted to become involved. Now, it was too late.

"I'm afraid the water's warm. It's been sitting in the sun all day." Nettie wished she could keep the coolness from her voice, but how could she forget who this man was? She could look upon him as an injured man, but it was his face she remembered at her door that night, his voice that had explained how Richard had died.

Hank parted his swollen mouth, his bottom lip split in several places. Nettie realized he was in too much pain to take the cup himself even as he lifted a trembling hand to try to take it from her. Knowing he had been baking in the sun for the last few hours, she reached down to gather his head carefully in one arm. She could feel the swollen lump crowning the back of his head and the crusted blood in his hair.

Again, those hot embers of rage smoldered in her chest. This man had been outnumbered, beaten, hit on the back of the head.

As if he sensed her anger, Hank struggled to speak, his voice raw and choked sounding. "I'm sorry. I know it doesn't do any good, but I'm sorry."

He was talking about killing Richard. Nettie studied this man, remembered Emmalouise Callahan's words, and said nothing.

"You shouldn't be doing this," Hank told her.

Tears pricked behind Nettie's eyes. She knew he was right. She should have left Jake and Harv and the other men to dole out justice, but that didn't make it right. That didn't mean she had to waste her life being stuffed with hate.

Nettie cleared her throat, working hard to speak normally past the thickness in her throat "Let me tilt your head up. I'll try not to spill."

She could feel his weakness as she lifted his heavy head. He struggled to help her. She saw his trembling hands clasp about the bottom of the cup as if unable to accept her help, but he spilled the water onto his chest, staining his torn shirt. As she steadied the rim of the cup against his mouth, she took care not to bump against the open gashes in his lip but realized it was impossible. Hank sucked down the hot, stale water as if it were cold and fresh.

When the tin was empty, she lowered him gently to the floorboards. Only then did she realize the lump crowning his head rested directly on the hard wood. Unable to keep from caring, Nettie tugged the folded blanket from beneath the seat and laid it like a pillow beneath his head.

As she moved away his hand caught hers. He gazed up at her, his one good eye bloodshot but conveying a sincerity that sliced like the sharpest knife.

"Thank you for your kindness, ma'am," he said.

His words weighed heavy in her heart the rest of the way home.

* * *

Dusk fell in a webby veil of blue-gray as Nettie halted the horses in front of the sawed-board shanty. Home, as ragged as it was, never looked so good. Exhausted from the heat and the long, jostling ride, she sagged in relief.

Jake dismounted, left his black gelding standing, and without meeting Nettie's eyes lifted Sam down from the wagon. She watched, her throat tight, confused by his gentle treatment of the small boy. Again, he was the Jake she knew and trusted, and not the violent man she'd seen today.

Old Bessie complained loudly, staring pointedly at the barn, but Nettie set the brake and climbed down. Jake turned to her as he set Sam down carefully on the dust-thick ground, but she lowered her eyes. She didn't feel ready to speak to him just yet. Sam fell to his knees on the ground and began to cry.

Nettie bent to scoop him up in her arms. Tired and hungry, he cried while jamming his thumb in his mouth. She didn't bother to stay his hand but sympathized with the hot, sweaty little boy. She was exhausted and starving, too.

She faced Jake. "Would you like to stay for supper?"

"I'd like that." He turned away, his jaw stiff, staring hard at the wagon bed. "I can't stay long. I have stock to tend."

Nettie hurried Sam inside, buttered him a slice of bread and sat him down on a chair. She untied her bonnet, the straw hat damp and wilting from the heat. The dark fabric had absorbed the sun's heat all day, and she felt as wrung out as a dirty old mop. She longed to change into something cooler and cleaner, but she didn't trust Jake outside alone with Hank Callahan.

She stepped out into the hot, dusty evening. A peaceful scene stretched out before her. She could see Jake's wheat rippling in the wind, dark like a shadow in the fading light.

"I'll help you get him inside," Nettie said.

Jake stood silhouetted against the last long-reaching rays of the setting sun. He turned at the sound of her voice, his face pensive, his silence typical. He grabbed Hank by the boots and pulled. Then he instructed Nettie to take over as he grabbed the man about the ribs and hefted him from the wagon's bed. Together they hauled him into the house. Nettie winced with each groan that escaped Hank's battered mouth.

Sam hurried over to inspect their progress as they crossed the two-room shanty. He reached high to push open the door into Nettie's bedroom. Jake's boots caught on her huge braided rug, and Nettie's back pinched as she pitched forward.

Jake caught his balance and together they laid the man on top of the quilt on Nettie's bed.

"His shoes are on," Sam pointed out.

Nettie tousled his hair. "Then I guess we'd better take them off."

She waited until Jake's footsteps had crossed out of her room before she knelt down on the floor and tucked the boot under her arm. She pulled, and both shoe and sock slipped off.

The doctor's splint had cut away the fabric of his trousers on the broken leg from the mid thigh down. Nettie's first instinct was to avert her eyes from the sight of his bare thigh, but she had to assess the injury. Since the splint hugged his leg from hip to knee, Nettie decided to risk removing the boot. She did so as gently as she could, but Hank Callahan clenched his jaw and a groan hummed low in his throat.

He was in pain. Nettie's breath caught in her chest, trapped like a cornered bird. Trying not to let herself feel, she knelt to tuck his well-worn boots in the corner by the door. Sam's wide eyes stared at the man, captivated, so Nettie took him by the hand and led him away.

Jake stood in the main room near to the table that was tucked into the farthest corner by the door. His dark eyes watched her with something like a question, and she felt her heartbeat stumble in her chest.

"He's not staying long," Jake told her.

There was something hard and possessive in his voice. Nettie hesitated before she spoke, hesitating because she feared Jake was so close to anger. "I don't want him here either. He'll stay until he's recovered and then he'll leave. It will be best for all of us."

Jake raised one dark, questioning eyebrow, and she ruffled at the doubt she saw there. As if he thought she was lying. As if he wasn't sure he could trust her.

Nettie set her jaw, piercing his hard gaze with her firm one. "This is my house, Jake Beckman, and I'll not have you treating me like this while you're in it."

A tightness slipped into his jaw and Nettie felt, as she had this morning when she'd realized he was beating a helpless man, that her whole world had tipped on end and would never be the same.

CHAPTER THREE

The drowning blackness in his brain began washing away, and Hank opened his good eye. He knew where he was without guessing. He was in Nettie Pickering's room, lying on her bed, breathing in the dried-rose smell from the vase on the bureau.

The room was plain, nothing like his mother's. Sawed-board walls had been chinked carefully, but the chinking was old and the boards had aged to a rich, dark brown. Small windows allowed light into the room. In the webby evening night he could see the white calico curtain hanging between the bureau and the door, presumably her closet. An oil lamp sat on a snow-white doily on the small, carefully carved bureau. He could see the door from where he lay without moving his head. It was slightly ajar, allowing a small splash of lamplight in from the other rooms.

Voices murmured somewhere in the house, a woman's and a man's. Nettie's and Jake's. Hank bit back a groan. He tried, but he couldn't sit up. Pain ricocheted through his leg, jerked through his guts, slammed through his head. Nausea overwhelmed him and he sank back the inch or two onto the cool clean quilt.

The straw tick beneath him felt like heaven. If only he could just close his eyes a bit more and rest; then, Hank was certain, he would have enough fortitude to haul himself from the bed and be on his way.

"As long as he's in this house, then I'm stayin', too." Jake

Beckman's rough, deep voice boomed through the thin wallboards separating room from room. Hank blanched on the bed, sensing trouble.

"You are not sleeping here. End of discussion." Her voice, firm and certain, was accompanied by a deliberate bang. The sound of wood upon wood. Like a chair against a table. "Now, I would appreciate it if you'll see to the horses for me. By the time you're done, I'll have supper on the table."

Hinges squeaked as a door opened. Footsteps drummed like anger on floorboards. The whole house seemed to wait without breathing as the silence remained unbroken. Then those footsteps continued out the door, tramping down the steps.

"Mama, why's he yellin' like that?" Sam asked with great confusion. "Don't he know it's rude?"

Nettie sighed audibly. "Come watch me get supper. Do you want cold beans or cottage cheese for dinner?"

"Cold beans."

Hank closed his good eye. Pain beat at him. He didn't move a muscle for fear he would become sick.

Time passed. He had no way of knowing how long he lay there, caught between sleep and something deeper. He heard the door hinges squeak faintly in the dark. A pool of light spread wider as the door separating the rooms pushed open.

A woman stood there dressed in the same dark dusty clothes. She'd removed her hat, and now her head was bare and he could see the thick coronet of her pinned braids. Her teeth flashed in the light, softening the deep shadows of her face.

"Are you awake, Mr. Callahan?" she whispered, as if afraid to disturb him.

He couldn't blame her. She was probably hoping he was asleep and would need nothing from her. But she'd already seen his open eye, and she crossed deliberately toward the bureau, busying herself with lighting the lamp.

Hank stared at her straight back, slim and pole-stiff. Light suffused the small room with a yellow glow, casting shadows into the corners and glowing softly in her dark hair. She turned, her mouth straight and her eyes unsmiling.

"Would you like something to eat?"

Hank shook his head. The thought of food twisted through his stomach, and he dared not move. He waited until his head steadied.

"W-water, please."

"Of course." She spun and marched away, only to return with a tin cup of water. She knelt beside the bed, efficiently catching up his head and pressing the rim to his cut mouth. Raw, torn flesh burned, but the cool, sweet water cleared away some of his discomfort.

Hank eased his head back onto the soft pillow. "Th-thank you." His jaw hurt when he moved it.

Nettie Pickering said nothing. She stood, set the cup on the bureau and unfolded a blanket. She spread it over him, her eyes unreadable, but there was no mistaking the set line of her jaw.

"I want you to understand why you're here," she said, her voice cold and curt. In another woman he might have thought the tone hardness, but Nettie Pickering had complete justification for hating him.

"Your mother wants nothing to do with you. Jake and Harv cannot afford extended doctoring, and so you are here. I'll expect you to leave when you are first able."

Her serious gaze, dark with the lamp's glow behind her, pierced his. Hank's heart slammed against the cracked bones in his rib cage. "Y-es, ma'am."

Nettie said nothing more as she retrieved the tin cup, blew out the lamp, and shut the door firmly behind her. He could hear her moving about in the other room, and he could see the light-filled crack above the door.

A dark, unsettled tick began in his stomach. Hank felt too hot with the blanket covering him, but he did nothing to move it away. He didn't want to move, he didn't want to breathe, he wanted to slip back into a deep dream and awaken to find this had all been a cruel nightmare.

The first lightening of the sky before dawn rousted Nettie from her fitful sleep. She'd awakened beside Sam in his snug bed in the corner of the smallest bedroom. Now he lay so peacefully, breathing in slow breaths. Nettie's chest twisted with her love for him.

She resisted the urge to brush the baby-fine hair from his brow. His bow-shaped mouth was open, his thumb wedged between his lips. Nettie carefully slipped out from beneath the light covers without disturbing him.

The first bit of light rose over the eastern hills, spinning gray into the black sky. Nettie reached for her dress and realized she had failed to change yesterday. Her work clothes were hanging in the bedroom.

Draping the black dress in front of her and wearing only her corset cover and drawers, she eased open her bedroom door. While he still lay on his back, Hank Callahan's head was turned toward the wall. As the hinges squeaked more loudly, he didn't stir.

Tiptoeing on bare feet into the room, Nettie watched him carefully for signs of movement. Hank Callahan slumbered deeply as she tugged open the curtain strung on rope to choose among her work dresses. She snatched the calico with the tiny pink flowers from its peg and, grabbing a pair of socks, backed out of the room. Mr. Callahan continued to sleep soundly. She closed the door.

In the large main room of the shanty, Nettie tugged on her dress and her socks. She pinned up her braid at the small mirror. She would groom herself more properly when she returned from the barn, but with the work awaiting there, a clean face wouldn't soon matter.

She snatched up the milk pail and headed out toward the barn.

Morning's light began to peer over the rim of the earth. Faint yellow light streaked pink and lavender into the wisps of clouds low in the sky. Nettie could see her way as she circled around the well and behind the house. The new day's dawn felt fresh and beautiful, peaceful before the sun began beating harshly on the land, but Nettie's heart felt heavy and as troubled as last night when she'd shut Hank Callahan in her bedroom.

How long might he need to stay?

The doctor had been brief and unhelpful. He seemed only truly interested in Jake's promise to pay him. Unwilling to keep a patient whose wealthy family would refuse the bill, the doctor denied further treatment. There had been no one else to care for the man.

Jake had argued, but there had been no solutions. Harv's wife might nurse Callahan, he had suggested, but Maude Wheaton was an overworked woman with five children, carrying her sixth. In addition to laboring beside her husband in the fields, when might she find the time and the space in their small two-room shanty to care for an injured man?

Nettie skirted her large, growing garden, her booted feet drumming lightly on the hard-packed path. Chickens squawked in protest as she approached and scattered in their house as she brushed past them.

As Nettie pulled open the barn door, she called herself every kind of fool. Nitwit. Imbecile. Simpleton. She didn't have time to nurse an injured man, especially not Hank Callahan. She had a farm to hang on to, and that would take every bit of her strength, every piece of her hope.

Muffin mooed from her stall, quickly joined by the rest of the animals. Bessie whinnied shrilly, demanding her feed. Nettie tended the cow first, carefully measuring out a cupful of oats from the sealed bin and filling her tray. Muffin lifted her face toward Nettie in appreciation and licked her hand with one wet, rough swipe.

"I'm a fool, Muff," Nettie informed the cow as she tugged up a stool. "I brought home a man."

And not just any man. Hank Callahan. Nettie squatted down on the wood stool and leaned her forehead against the cow's warm flank. Hank had blue eyes, deep and searing like the sky in August. Warm brown hair ruffling in the prairie breezes. Powerful strength in muscled arms.

Once, she'd seen him working his field along their mutual section line. He had worn no shirt, exposing his bare torso to the kiss of the brutal sun. His skin had glistened nearly as brown as the dirt he was plowing. She'd been a married woman then, but after all this time she still remembered.

Muffin lowed empathetically, as if she understood all about males, and nudged Nettie affectionately with her warm nose. Amused, she patted the cow's soft belly and placed the clean bucket on the straw beneath the full udder. She tucked her thumb and third finger around the warm teat and pulled. A hot stream of milk zinged into the bucket.

"Mama! Mama!" The barn door swung open, smacking hard against the outside wall. Muffin startled, jostling the milk pail. Bessie whinnied shrilly in immediate protest. The other milk cow mooed, milling about restlessly in her stall.

Nettie tugged the stool out of Muffin's way, grabbed up the milk pail, and hurried out of the small pen. "Sam." She set aside her load and knelt down to comfort her son.

Worry frowned his forehead and widened his dark eyes. His hair, rumpled from sleep, stood tousled, and his little white drawers were askew. Nettie reached to straighten them around his waist.

"What's wrong, sweet pea? You're not supposed to be in the barn."

"The man's leavin'." Sam jammed his thumb into his mouth, and Nettie gently pulled his hand away.

Nettie felt relief slip over her like the calm morning air. He was leaving. There would be no need to feel the hardness in her own heart when she looked at him. There would be no need to worry how she might cope with his presence. There would be no conflict between her and Jake, and no more of his violent promises.

Nettie rubbed her thumb over the frown lines on Sam's forehead. "Maybe he's feeling well enough to leave today. Maybe it's good that he's well enough to

"But he needs his breakfast He needs to wash up." Sam's worries would not abate.

Then Nettie understood. His world had been so predictable with just the two of them. Clean face and combed hair and breakfast before playtime every morning. Jake was the only man Sam knew, and his presence was occasional and mostly involved with fixing the roof or repairing a wagon wheel. Sam's world was tilting as crazily as her own.

"We'll go make us all some breakfast," Nettie decided. It was the least she could do if Mr. Callahan could force himself to be on his way. If he was recovering from his head injury and he had a cane, then perhaps he would be fine enough to leave. Perhaps.

"Come sit still while I finish the milking." Nettie led Sam by the hand back into Muffin's stall. The gentle cow reached down to him with her curious tongue, swiping Sam across his head. The boy laughed.

"Ooh, she spit on me, Mama."

Nettie's heart lightened. Her whole day suddenly felt more promising. She hunkered down to finish up the milking, the thick warm milk streaking down into the foamy bucket, while Sam sat quietly in the straw, letting Muffin rub his fingers with her huge, rough tongue.

When she'd drained Muffin's udder, the bucket was nearly full. Nettie patted the cow, praising her gentleness, and promised to return soon. Lugging the heavy bucket, she listened to Sam chatter on. He wanted the sick man to eat pancakes because it was his favorite.

Nettie opened the door to an empty shanty. For one brief moment she hoped that he was gone, that he'd simply found his way out while they were in the barn. She scolded herself for such a selfish thought as she strained the milk, poured the pitcher full, and set the rest of the milk down in the cellar.

She lit the stove and considered washing up at the basin, but decided she was in a much bigger hurry to send Hank Callahan on his way. She knocked on her own bedroom door and heard a gruff "Come in."

He stood on one leg beside the bed. Nettie's breath caught at the size of him. While the room was small, there was no mistaking the breadth of his shoulders or the strength in his arms. Nettie ran her eyes down the length of his body. Dirt and blood stained his torn clothes. His eyes, set in a face pale beneath the tan and the dirt, appeared glazed over with the deepest pain.

Nettie's conscience bit her. Surely she'd been cold to him last night, inhospitable. He felt compelled to leave before he was truly able. Perhaps he'd heard the argument between her and Jake last night, further persuading him to leave. Nettie did want him out of her house and out of the area, for her own reasons and because she knew it was not safe for him here. Now, she feared she'd been too harsh.

"You don't look well, Mr. Callahan. Perhaps you'd best lie back down. I can make you some breakfast and we'll see how you feel after a good meal." Nettie stepped forward, catching his arm, but he jerked away from her touch.

Surprised, she stepped back, catching the door against one shoulder blade. The door smacked against the wall with a sharp bang. She jumped, confused, not realizing what she'd done to make him recoil from her touch. "Please, Mr. Callahan, I only wish to help, I—"

"No." The single word boomed through the tiny room. "I've done enough to you already. I just need a crutch of some type."

Nettie glanced around. "I don't think you should be up. You're turning very gray."

"I'll be fine." His terse remark would have been intimidating, but Nettie was not fooled, because of his trembling hand and his weak knee.

As much as she wanted him to leave, he was too injured to do so safely. She stepped forward, wishing to help him into bed, but she remembered he would not tolerate her touch.

"Sit down. I've got some coffee brewing. I—"

He held up one unsteady hand. Nettie fell silent, her heart racing. She wanted to be anywhere but here, alone with Hank Callahan. She wanted nothing more than to see him well enough to travel, but he was gravely injured and sick, too, judging by the red flush staining his cheekbones.

His eyes rolled in his head, and Nettie watched, unable to catch him as he crashed to the floor, striking his head hard on the edge of the bureau.

Hank watched the wardrobe door open and gazed up at his younger brother. "Is he gone?"

Robert, not yet thirteen, nodded, straightening his shoulders. "He's gone."

Hank swallowed back the ugly ripple of fear. He wouldn't cry. He wouldn't. He swallowed the questions he knew better than to ask. He didn't want to know the answers. He didn't want to know what had happened.

It was easier to stay hidden in the back of the wardrobe because out of Father's sight meant out of his mind. He could rage all he wanted downstairs about the dinner being burned or late or not fit to eat, but hidden upstairs in his dark, tight hiding place Hank was safe. Father wouldn't think to yell at him here.

The pain pounded through his head, harder than the blow from a man's fist, harder than the force of a hammer. Nausea roiled through him, and he couldn't escape the heat. Then a soft touch, comforting words like the warm, slow song of a creek, and blessed cold water dribbled across his face.

Then there was no soft touch, no comforting voice. Father stood before him, a sturdy man thickening about the middle, dressed for work at the bank. His anger boomed like gunfire. "You filthy, goddamned, good-for-nothing coward. What do I have to do to make you take it like a man?"

Panic. He was only fourteen. He hadn't meant to cause trouble at school, but he'd gone along with the other boys. He was sorry. He wouldn't do it again.

"You're never going to learn unless I beat it into you."

Father's jowls wiggled as he shouted, his face reddening. "I'm not going to have a sniffling coward for a son..."

Pain drilled through him like a knife with a sharp point. His mother's voice, crying now, telling him how he had to stop angering his father.

And then that cool hand, chasing the dark, twisting anger away. Hank leaned into the cool, caring touch brushing along his brow like the gentlest spring rain. A kind voice, a kind woman like he'd been dreaming of for most of his life.

CHAPTER FOUR

Nettie wearily wiped a trickle of sweat from her brow. The choking heat of mid-afternoon was as hot and dry as an oven. The scents of ripening wheat and warm earth puffed through the open window on a lazy breeze.

Hank Callahan sprawled out before her on the bed. Dappled sunlight danced across his high cheekbones and the intelligent cut of his forehead. Asleep, he no longer looked tortured. A shock of hair tumbled over his brow, and the curve of his mouth suggested that at one time he had smiled a lot.

What had become of him these past years? She remembered how she'd treated him and blamed him for a death that had been accidental. It tore at her conscience now. Guilt weighed heavy on her heart as she wrung herbed water from a cloth. Cool liquid sluiced between her fingers and splashed into the enamel basin. Comfrey and the sharp bite of fresh mint scented the air.

"Noooo—" he moaned, his bronzed chest rising with quick, short breaths.

She was wrong. Even in his sleep, Hank Callahan was a tortured man. She brushed the cloth across his brow. This man's suffering was in part because of her. She'd been so emotional after Richard's death that she hadn't stopped to think. And then, when she was able to, it was too late.

At least she could make amends in this way. Even if she had to keep her heart hard and protected to do it. She may have forgiven Hank Callahan for the life he'd taken that dark night, but she had not forgotten.

"He got a lotta hair."

"He sure does." Nettie's gaze stroked the length of Hank Callahan's leg, muscled and powerful despite the splint of wood and cloth that stretched from his knee to his upper thigh. Her heart skipped a beat. "Go fetch me a towel from the shelf. Just one. And don't—"

Sam launched away from the foot of the bed and took off at a flat-footed dash. His steps knelled against hard wood and echoed in the small room.

"—run," she finished, and his gait slowed. She leaned to watch him pull one towel off the low pile.

Her little boy moved with such innocence and a gentle intent to do good. His brow furrowed and his mouth puckered with concentration as he pulled the towel off the pile and another towel hit the floor. He picked it up and tried to fold it with awkward fingers.

How dear he was. "Go ahead and bring me that one, too."

Flashing his most charming grin, Sam sprinted across the room, cowlick flopping with every step. "Here, Mama."

She ruffled his hair and took the towels, so enormous in his little arms.

"Are you gonna read him a story?" Sam tried to climb up on the bed, all innocence.

She knew what he was up to. "Grown men don't need stories. Now, off the bed and out of this room. Go play with your horses."

It took a while to get him settled in the front room. She latched the screen door shut so he couldn't get away from her when her back was turned. She helped him excavate his carved horses—gifts Richard had bought his son even before Sam was born—from his toy box and watched as he dropped to the floor.

His head bent forward and those unruly straight locks stuck out at all angles as he galloped one Appaloosa across the bands of the braided rug. It took all her willpower not to reach out and smooth those untamed bangs.

"Nettie." Jake's voice rumbled behind her. "I worried about you last night."

"You shouldn't have." Nettie whirled around. She'd been so

absorbed she hadn't heard Jake's boots on her porch steps or the clomp of horse hooves on the hard-packed earth. "With the way you've been behaving lately, I'm surprised you didn't come by earlier."

Jake propped one shoulder against the doorjamb and offered a small smirk. At least he had the grace to blush a little. "I meant to, but there was trouble over at the Johnson place."

"Now? What kind of trouble? The Johnson's land borders mine."

That smirk disappeared, replaced by a grim frown. "That's why I'm here. Have you checked your barn this morning?"

"What kind of trouble, Jake?" She felt a chill shiver over her skin and goose bumps gathered on her arms, even in this heat.

"Jake, are you gonna come play with me?" Sam had climbed to his feet, holding a bay and a buckskin in each hand. "I got wild horses."

"I see that, Sam, but I need to talk to your mother." Jake swept off his hat, and the blue muslin shirt he wore brought out the dark blue sheen of his eyes. "How about you and I have a wild horse roundup in a bit?"

"Goody." Sam seemed satisfied enough to kneel back down on the rug, already busy with his play.

Nettie could see by the stance of Jake's firm shoulders and the slant of the frown across his face that whatever had happened to her neighbors wasn't good. Another thief was at work in the countryside. A thief who had shot a rancher who tried to interfere. What would happen next?

She gestured toward the table. "I have some cinnamon rolls in the kitchen."

"Fine idea." Jake hung his hat on the peg by the door and stepped into the cabin. "Does this mean I'm forgiven for yesterday? I want to apologize about my temper."

"I'm not the one you should apologize to." Nettie headed toward the sanctuary of the kitchen. Sunlight danced against the back of blue calico curtains. Warm cinnamon and cooling coffee scented the air.

"I just saw Callahan and that old anger got the best of me." His boots knelled on the wood floor. He was a tall man, strong and lanky, and he moved with a cowboy's confidence. He'd spent years in the saddle working on cattle drives before he bought the ailing ranch not a half mile away. He was a man confident of his abilities, and he moved with that confidence now as he wrapped his strong hands around the back of a chair and pulled it out with a scrape.

"That anger of yours is the reason I'm sure we will never marry." Nettie set the plate of cinnamon rolls on the table. She hated the tightness in her chest. Saying no to a man whose help had been vital to her ranch's existence wasn't easy. "I wouldn't have been able to hold on to my land without your help, Jake."

"After Richard died, I saw you didn't know the first thing about sowing wheat and I pitched in, that's all." Jake bowed his head, hiding his eyes from her scrutiny. For all his strength and size, he seemed vulnerable now. "It was damn tough for me after Abby's death. Helping you out gave me something to do. I had a lot of empty time on my hands. A lot of time."

She set the coffeepot on the table. Silence ticked by. She remembered the grieving man who'd staunchly refused to go home when her fields needed turning. Who showed her how to harness the team and set the plow and turn a straight row. "I owe you a lot, Jake. More than I can ever repay. But—"

She paused. How did she say it? She no longer felt safe with him. He was a man who'd led an attack on an unarmed man without provocation. "I'd hoped you were better than that. That you could have put to rest your anger over Richard's death."

"I have." His lifted his gaze to hers and she saw a bleakness there, a sadness not only of the heart but also of the soul. "Then marry me."

"Marry you?" She missed a step and nearly stumbled. "Why, I—"

"I'm alone, and I can't stand it. I could go find me a wife in town or through the newspapers if I wanted, but I feel strongly for you, Nettie."

The enamel cup she held clinked against the table, and she didn't trust the steadiness of her hand to pour. "I feel strongly about you, too, Jake. You've been about the only friend I can depend on—"

"Friend?" Then his face turned bitter. "I'm not your friend, Nettie. That's not what I want."

"But a marriage without love, Jake, what kind of marriage is that?" She turned her back and grabbed a knife and spoon from the drawer. They sparkled in the slash of light that crept between the edges of the ruffled curtains.

"You married Richard without love. The same way I married Abby. Marriage is a practical agreement." His voice deepened and became gruff and raw. "All I'm asking is for you to be my wife. We can make this work, I know we can. You know I'll be good to your son. I intend to raise him as my own."

Jake's son had died being born, along with his pretty young wife. Nettie set the flatware on the table. "Tell me about Mr. Johnson. Is he all right?"

"Thieves." Jake pulled the sugar jar from the center of the table with a scrape of enamel on wood. "Last night he lost his only team. Someone snuck in, let out all of the animals to raise a ruckus and hide his escape. All Edmund Johnson saw was his cattle trampling through his wheat fields, and he didn't notice a thief was riding away."

"Then there's damage to his crops, too." Nettie caught hold of a chair and settled onto it. "He wasn't hurt?"

"No. This time." Jake stirred his coffee. "That thief could hit your barn next."

"I don't have fine horses to steal."

"No, but a good pair of work horses would bring a fair price." Jake lifted his cup and studied her over the blue rim. "There's no telling who will be next, and you're a woman alone."

Nettie felt the hair on her arms stand on end. "I know how to handle a gun. And I can scare off a thief if I have to."

His gaze hardened. "Half the county knows you're softhearted. No one who knows of you will believe for a minute that you'd put a bullet in anyone. You need protection. You need a man to take care of you and watch out for your safety."

"I see where this is going." Nettie bit back her anger and sprang off the chair. She might owe Jake for his help over the last few years, but she didn't owe him marriage. And she wouldn't be frightened into it. "I can take care of myself. Excuse me, I need to check on my patient."

"Remember what happened to Richard."

His words sent a chill snaking down her spine, but she clenched her teeth and kept walking. She pushed open her bedroom door and stepped inside. Hank Callahan was sitting up, ashen and shaking. The sheet puddled at his waist, showing the bronzed width of muscled shoulders and chest. His throat worked as she approached.

"I'm ready to move on, ma'am." How low those words, soft, like spring thunder. "I just need to find my clothes."

"In my laundry basket." She couldn't help staring at him and noticing the unflinching line of his jaw and his steady gaze. He looked straight at her as if neither ashamed nor guilty, and it flustered her.

She knelt and drew a small chest from beneath the bed. She could feel him watching her as she unclasped the lid. Her fingers trembled as she reached inside and shook out a light cotton shirt, blue like his eyes, and a pair of denim trousers.

"Maybe these will fit." She stood and laid the clothes on the edge of the bed. "I can help you out to the front room, if you'd like to sit up for a while."

"I want to leave." His hand shook when he reached out for the clothes. A muscle jumped in his jaw. He must have guessed these were Richard's clothes. His eyes were as dark as nightmares when he met her gaze. "How much do I owe you?"

"Not a thing." She moved away. "Will you need help dressing?"

"The doctor bill. How much was it?"

"Jake and Harv are responsible." She might be willing to help this man, but looking at him made her remember. She wanted out of the room. She found the door with the back of her hand and took another step away from him. "I'll fix a meal for you."

"No, I—"

She pulled the door closed behind her. The image of strong shouldered Hank Callahan on her bed was burned into her memory.

"You shouldn't have to do this." Jake's voice spun her around. He stood cradling a saucer in one hand, the cinnamon roll halfway eaten. "Go outside and take a walk or something. I can get him out of here."

"He stays, Jake." Her chest felt so tight she could hardly breathe. "Don't make this any harder on me."

His face twisted. "I can't stand to see you do this to yourself. I'll be out in the fields. I want to see how your corn is coming along."

"It's fine, Jake." She watched him give Sam a wink and then swing his hat from the wall peg. Muscles corded beneath the span of his cotton shirt, and dark hair ruffled his shoulders as he punched the screen door open and loped out into the day.

"Mama? Jake says he's gonna be my pa one day."

She gazed down into those wide, innocent eyes, a warm brown just like her own, and didn't know what to say. Why had Jake said such a thing to him? Was he trying to use any means he could to pressure her?

"Lizzie has a pa."

Lizzie was the Wheaton's little girl, Sam's age. Nettie's heart twisted. She had misgivings, but Sam needed a father. How could she disappoint him? "Jake misses having a family, and that's why he says things like that. He won't be your father."

"Ever?" A frown creased his brow.

"Ever. You and I are doing fine all by ourselves." She smoothed some of those flyaway locks from his eyes, but Sam knelt to the floor, away from her touch, intent on the wild herd sprawled across the rug.

Behind the closed door, she heard a shuffle and a muffled curse. Hank must be managing to dress on his own, and she worried about that. Should she let him leave? She remembered the sight of his leg, less swollen today. Maybe he was strong enough to go.

She remembered the good neighbor he'd been, and that only made it harder. If she could hate him, then maybe the pain in her heart would go away. But she knew it wouldn't be that simple.

Like a drowning man struggling for air, Hank fought to keep from fainting. Pain began, low and dull, and then struck in sharper punches, thudding through his left thigh and pounding through his head. Hot, dry air had beaded sweat across his forehead.

He had to get up. He had no notion how long he'd been lying here, comfortable on that soft bed with the sweet, line-dried sheets. Swallowing a groan and clenching his sore jaw at the pain, Hank swung around and put his feet on the floor. He took a few deep breaths and struggled to stand.

The room wobbled a bit. The slant of sunlight through the curtains hurt his eyes. Light splashed against the side of a carved bureau and onto the worn leather of his billfold. He reached for it and ran his thumb across the braided edges.

All his money was there. Five hundred dollars. He pulled out a twenty to see him home and left the rest where it lay, to reimburse

Nettie for her trouble.

He made it to the door. He slumped against the door frame. He could see the main room of the small house from where he stood. Cozy, the way a home should be. Bits of blue and green in cushions, wall hangings, and rugs warmed the honeyed woods.

The outside door seemed a mile away. He took a small step and felt the splint around his thigh strain with his weight. He needed a crutch if he wanted to go much farther.

He wasn't about to lie another moment in this house, in Richard Pickering's bed, and see the look of pity on the young widow's face.

"You up." A childish voice broke the stillness.

Hank heard a hop and a chair's leg scrape against wood, and he felt the small patter of Sam's feet on the floor. Through his one good eye, he watched the small boy toddle toward him dressed in short white drawers and no shirt The heat had flushed his fair face a soft pink, and his earth-brown eyes shone like buttons. He gripped a carved toy horse in one hand.

"This here's my bestest one." Sam planted his feet and tipped his head back. "You wanna play horses?"

Panic set in as Sam jolted to a stop directly before him. Hank opened his mouth. He didn't know what to say.

"I watchin' ya," the boy confessed.

Hank swallowed. His throat felt parched and his mouth dry. What he'd give for a drink of water. But he wanted out of this house more. Spots spun across his vision. He leaned back against the wall as if that could chase away the dizziness and the pain.

"You got lots of hair." Sam sighed, impressed. "Why's your face rough?"

"I need to shave. Where's your mother?"

"In the cellar. I'm not s'posed to go down there." Sam dropped to the floor where a herd of horses raced along the hand-braided tracks of a rug.

As he gazed down into the child's innocent eyes, something tightened inside Hank's chest. He took a step, and then another. He gritted his teeth and headed for the door. He didn't want to see Nettie Pickering at all. Or see the devastation he'd done to her life.

"Your eye's stuck together."

"I know." He kept limping, half dragging his leg as he went. He could stand on it, and that meant the break wasn't all that bad. He just had to make it to the door.

The little boy trotted after him. "Are you sure you don't wanna play horses?"

"No, Sam." He sounded hard and he knew it. And regretted it.

Somberly, those wide eyes asked an innocent question. And gazing down at that little boy face, seeing that little boy's heart, Hank understood.

Feeling deeply inadequate, he bowed his head. "I'd like to, but I have to go."

He pushed open the screen door and stumbled out into the sunshine. Heat fanned across his face and bore through the muslin shirt. The air tasted like dust, and the ripening wheat in the fields emitted the aroma of baking bread. A lazy wind kicked up dust eddies in the circular driveway, and finches chirped and played in a small bucket of water set beside the porch steps.

The outside yard was more barren than he remembered it. Wild roses still bloomed in pink splendor against the side of the house. But the flat expanse of dusty earth had replaced the rows of bright flowers Nettie used to clutter her yard with. Now there were few flowers.

Dizziness finally claimed him, and he settled on the middle step. He shook from the inside out with weakness and pain. He was never going to make it out of here. He didn't think he could bear looking at Nettie's face one more time and seeing all that he'd done.

Memories of that night breezed into his mind, bold and dark like a bad dream. It had been dismal with rain, and he hadn't been able to see a thing. But the high warning neigh of his stallion brought him with gun drawn to the barn. Something was wrong. Maybe the thief who'd been hitting local ranches had taken a notion to try to steal from him.

He'd cocked the rifle and held it, palms damp because he didn't like confrontations, and headed out through the night. His barn was dark, the animals agitated, and his matched pair of bays were missing, a five-hundred-dollar team of horses. He heard a twig snap and then the sound of a cocking gun. He spun around and saw a man aiming a rifle at him—

"Mr. Callahan." Nettie knelt down to set a cup and a plate of food on the step above him. The breeze brushed dark curls across the delicate cut of her brow and the curve of her cheek, drawing his gaze to her face. Her skirts rippled against her slim body as she straightened, taking a backward step away from him. "You shouldn't be putting weight on that leg."

"It's holding." He stared down at the plate she'd brought him. Lord help him, his stomach twisted with a hard hunger. He couldn't remember when he'd last eaten.

"That doesn't mean you should stand on it. Stay there until I get you a pair of crutches."

"If it's all the same, I'd rather make them myself." He listened to her steps fade back into the cabin.

She didn't want him here, any more than he wanted to be here. He couldn't understand why she would take care of him. Chest tight, he tried to take a breath. He had no answers, except that he was grateful.

He lifted the cup and drank. Cool water sluiced over his tongue and wet his mouth. He watched the seed-heavy tips of grass at the fence line sway with the sluggish wind, and beyond that the spread of golden wheat shimmered like sunlight for miles. He couldn't help wondering what had happened to his land.

The little boy wandered out and sat on the top step, bringing with him two of his horses. Hank tried not to look at the boy as he ran those horses along the floor of the porch, talking to them in a low, ragged whisper. Hank grabbed up his plate and ate his fill of the fried chicken, cold baked beans, and buttery biscuits. And tried hard not to remember he'd been the one who'd taken Sam's father from him.

But such a thing, it was hard to forget. Hank thought of the money that he'd left Nettie on her bureau. Hell, it wasn't enough to compensate for what he'd done. Five hundred dollars wasn't nearly enough to make amends.

Nettie headed out into the fields. She stood on tiptoe in the tall cornstalks and spotted a dark hat through the waving tassels. "Jake!"

"Hell, Nettie, you about scared me to death. I didn't hear you comin'." Jake pushed his way through the corn. "Things are lookin' good out here. It just might be a good harvest."

"Don't say that yet. I said those very words last year, and the next day we had a hailstorm that ruined all of the wheat."

"I remember." Jake burst through the row of stalks, all rough strength and hard eyes. Eyes that could not look at her. "The grass is nearly ready for a second cut."

"Jake, we have to talk about this. I never asked you to help out on my land, and—"

"No, you never asked. I just did what was right. Hell, all the neighbors have." He marched down the row, shoulders braced, hands fisted, as if he knew what she planned to say. "Everyone around here liked Richard. He was my best friend."

"He was mine, too." The words were out before she could stop them, and she wasn't sorry. Maybe it was time to talk about the past and put it to rest "I've been trying to convince you to stop helping me so much, ever since he died. But you are a stubborn man, Jake, and I can't allow you to keep—"

"Is this because of Callahan?" He spat the words out, whirling to face her, and his mouth twisted. "I admit it. I've got a bad temper. Now and then, it pops up and I've gotta deal with it. But it's Callahan's fault. Seeing him again—"

He clamped his jaw tight and stared off toward the house. "I saw him in the road again, and all that anger from years ago just exploded. The sheriff found him innocent. Innocent. Can you believe that? The sheriff, of all people. It didn't even go to trial. Callahan's father bribed—"

"You can't believe that" Nettie caught Jake's arm. "You have to stop this. The sheriff did his best to find out what happened. I believe him, and I always have."

"You're a woman, Nettie." Jake's jaw worked, and he pulled away from her. "You don't understand."

"You're right I don't know the difference between wrong and right, or between accidental and intentional." She was mad now. Heat popped in her chest and propelled her down the row after him. "This is my battle, Jake. Richard was my husband. I should have stood up when you men drove Hank out of the county, and I didn't I was grieving and part of me was still angry. I was wrong. I should have stood up for my principles. This time, I won't allow it."

"You're in no position to allow anything."

She'd had enough of this side of Jake Beckman. "I don't want you in my fields."

His back stiffened, and he skidded to a halt. Dry plumes of dust rose in chalky clouds. "You need me, Nettie."

"No, I've been paying you. What about the steers I make sure you take at summer's end? I made sure you keep a portion of my harvest to sell."

"Now, Nettie, you know you insisted on it—"

"That's right. I'm not beholden to you for marriage or for anything else. I don't like the man I've been seeing in you lately, and I don't want you around my son right now."

"That's a low blow, Nettie. I told you, it's Callahan's fault—"

"Your temper is yours." She shouldered past him and peered through the low rows of corn. Beyond the lush green of the garden, she caught sight of a man limping with a slow, obviously painful gait toward the barn. "I'm never going to marry a man with that kind of temper, Jake. I've been uncertain ever since you proposed, and now I know why."

"Aw, Nettie. C'mon now, you need me—"

She kept walking and felt the heat of Jake's furious gaze on her back, twice as hot as the sun. A pair of chickadees sprinted past, and a garter snake hurried out of sight as she put as much distance between her and Jake as possible. A hard, cold feeling settled in her stomach. What if he showed her the same type of anger?

She caught sight of Sam dashing after Hank Callahan, toys clutched in both hands, kicking up enough dust to choke a horse. The little boy disappeared into the barn. She shouldn't have left the boy with Hank. She bypassed the garden in need of a good watering and swung open the back door.

The barn was hot but shaded. Sunlight seeped between the cracks of the sideboards and lit dust motes that hung in the air. The sweet high scent of hay and the warm smell of animals blended together. Bessie gave a low nicker, and Nettie stopped to rub her velvety nose.

She spotted Hank seated on a molasses barrel, head down, broad shoulders braced, and breathing hard. The muslin shirt fit snug around his arms, shoulders, and chest but hung around his middle. Richard had been a bulky man and not made only of muscle. The trousers were two inches too short and sagging around Hank's hips. But at least he'd gotten the garment over his splint.

"You look ready to fall over." Nettie saw the gray sheen to his face, with a hint of green. "You can't leave yet, Hank."

He didn't look up at her. His entire body seemed to stiffen. "I'm going to do my damnedest."

"Then rest right there for a bit." Nettie grabbed the reins of

Jake's big black gelding. "You don't have to be in such a hurry to leave. You have to be strong enough."

"Here I am!" Sam dashed around the corner. Pieces of straw stuck out of his flyaway hair and clung to his clothes. He held a tiny gray tabby in both hands. "I found my kitty, Mama."

"I see." The sight of her gentle little boy holding that delicate kitten made her forget her anger and her problems. She dropped to her knees to run a single finger over the blinking feline's head. "Are you sure this is the kitty you want? Maybe you'll change your mind after they get a little older."

"Nope." Sam shook his head once, his chin set, happiness flickering in his eyes. "This one's mine."

"Can you go put him back now? Look, he's starting to cry. He misses his mother." Nettie brushed a few of those bits of straw from Sam's hair.

"Okay." The little boy cradled the kitten and walked with careful steps around the corner to the first stall that the mother tabby had claimed as hers.

"You're raising a good boy." Hank's voice rumbled low, leaving much unspoken.

"He is." She led the horse toward the double doors. "Sam, come with me."

"Aw, Mama. I wanna play with the kitties."

"Later." After a few more requests, he trudged out of the barn. She found Jake gazing out at the horizon, where the golden hills yielded to the distant purple-blue mountains. "I brought your horse."

His dark gaze pinned hers. She read anger in those shadowed depths. He reached out with a gloved hand to take the reins from her grip. For a brief moment, she saw the same man who'd taken pleasure beating Hank Callahan on the road.

Then it was gone, and Jake managed a half grin. "I can take a hint, Nettie. I know I'm in trouble with you. But trust me, you'll come around."

He nodded toward the barn. "Watch him. If you have any trouble, make sure you ask for help. Johnson is closest, but you know I'll take care of you."

"Jake! There's more kittens, and Mama says I get one." Sam laughed as the big man swung him up into the air, and then back down again.

"You be good and mind your mama." Jake ruffled his hair, then mounted up, a man in black against the shimmering sky. He rode away without a goodbye.

Probably because he didn't intend to do as she asked and stop courting her, stop making her obligated to him. Nettie sighed, the burdens on her shoulders doubling.

CHAPTER FIVE

Hours later, she brought supper to Hank Callahan in the barn. More cold chicken, beans, and biscuits, but this time she added a bowl of coleslaw.

"The cabbage is fresh," she said, without meeting his gaze.

His gratitude stuck in his throat and he watched her hurry from his presence. Her step was quick, rustling her calico skirts at her ankles. Without a petticoat, the skirt hugged her slim legs and hips. The nip of her small waist was real, not from a corset, not in this heat, and the gentle sway of her breasts when she stopped to give the milk cow a pat set his blood on fire.

It would be far better if Nettie treated him with the vengeful anger Jake Beckman did. Ashamed, Hank looked away. He heard the soft fall of her step on the hard-packed floor, the snap of her skirts and then only the whisper of the wind tunneling through the barn. In the rafters overhead, baby swallows chattered and chirped as their parents returned.

Hank set down the saw and brushed the dust from his trousers. The scent of newly cut wood lingered in the air as he reached for the plate Nettie left for him. It had been a long time since he'd had a decent meal. Sure, he'd learned to cook after he'd retreated up into the mountains. There'd been no one else to do it for him.

He'd first bought canned goods from the little store not far from his shanty and lived on beans for a good while. Then, when he realized he wasn't having much luck drinking himself to death, he started figuring out how to fry up salt pork and ham.

His cooking skills snowballed from there. He'd tried to work himself to death, too, but that had failed. He'd only managed to pull a small fortune in gold from the solitary mountain, and the physical labor had built up his strength even more than when he'd been on his ranch.

He took a bite out of a chicken thigh and wondered what Nettie used to make it so crispy. It wasn't as if he felt comfortable asking her. She might not hate him, but she didn't like him. She didn't like looking at him and seeing the man responsible for changing her life.

It wasn't easy for a woman alone to hold on to her ranch. He wasn't blind—he could see the row after row of empty stalls. His family's fine-blooded horses had been Richard's pride and joy, and he wanted nothing more than to bring in a few winning crops so he could afford to go into horse breeding. Now, those beautiful horses were gone, every last one of them.

Nettie was able to keep her land with the help of her neighbors; Hank knew that. He'd liked living here among these good and honest people. He'd been proud to call them neighbors at one time, before they turned on him in fury, believing he had been stealing from them.

Jake must have made certain Nettie had all the help she needed to get along. Whatever hard feelings Hank had for Jake, he had to give Beckman that respect Not many men would take on work not their own.

Hank had spent a lot of sleepless nights wondering what had become of the young and gentle Nettie Pickering.

It was good to know she was holding on to her land. He thought of the payment that he'd wired to his brother years ago, asking to pay off the Pickering mortgage. At least his gold had gone to some use, and Nettie had never even known the debt existed.

Twilight gathered in the air. The sun's hold on the land eased. Light changed the world from vibrant to subtle. A pink glow brushed the horizon, and shadows lengthened. Hank finished his supper, set the plate out of his way, and went back to work building his crutches.

If he could get these finished, he wouldn't need to spend another night in Nettie Pickering's bed. Or another morning looking at the strain bracketing her pretty mouth whenever she looked at him. Not another day watching the fatherless little boy play so trustingly on the floor with his toys.

Hank picked up the hammer. It felt good to work with his hands. He wasn't a man who liked to be idle. The sawed wood felt smooth and new beneath his hands. The weight of the hammer was like an old friend. He tapped nails into the wood, then sawed a little more.

As he worked he could hear Sam's cheerful laugh out in the yard and then the low mumble of Nettie's melodic voice, as soft as twilight. They were far away, near the house. Their voices faded.

Night fell with a slow hush. Hank sanded his crutches in the darkness. He worked by feel. He'd missed the peace of a summer's night on these plains. The cheep of a bat spreading its wings on a trip through the barn. And the hoot of an owl hunting in the fields. And the contented whoof of air as a horse sighed, settling down for the night.

It was time to leave. Hank gathered the crutches, and the wood clacked together noisily. He stood and fit the wooden supports beneath his arms. He tested their strength, and they held his weight. He took a tentative step and then another. Good. These would do, and he could be on his way.

He hobbled to the back end of the barn and wrestled a bridle from a high peg. He hung the straps over his arm and then swung a saddle and blanket onto his shoulder. Sweat poured off his brow as he took one wobbly step and then another. The weight of the saddle threw off his balance, and it was no small feat crutching all the way to the end of the barn where the two draft horses drowsed in separate stalls.

He'd relied on no one for so long, he didn't think he could stomach asking for help now. Or putting Nettie through having to see him one more time. No, it was better to leave this way in the dark and without a word.

The mare seemed friendlier than the old gelding, and Hank opened her stall. She shied at the sight of the crutches, jumping sideways into the barrier of the wall. But he soothed her and soon she was investigating the lengths of wood with her lips and tongue. He slid the bridle over her head and the bit into her mouth. Well, that was half the battle. Now, to saddle her up.

That took more ingenuity, since the mare refused to let him

crutch close enough to reach beneath her belly to cinch the saddle tight. She kept shying away. He finally laid the crutches against the wall and hopped on his good leg. She allowed him to tighten the buckle. He climbed up on the rail and eased into the saddle.

The angle hurt his thigh and spots swirled in front of his eyes. He took a deep breath and waited until the dizziness passed. It wouldn't be easy, but he could make it to town. His dependence upon Nettie Pickering had come to an end.

He grabbed his crutches and hung them over the pommel. The old mare started for a minute, but after she realized that the long lengths of wood weren't hurting her, she obediently headed out of the barn and into the night-swept yard. A crescent moon cast a bold glow, lighting his way to the house.

The windows shone with warm, lemony lamplight. He could easily see her through the glass. Her hair was down in a single braid and her oval face was relaxed, pink with happiness. Tendrils curled at her brow above eyes that crinkled as she laughed. She bent down and swung Sam up into her arms with a graceful ease that left him breathless.

He was glad to know that Nettie had found her own happiness. He would always regret his thoughtless act that night long ago, but maybe his guilt and his nights would be easier knowing that she still laughed and smiled, just as she always had. Even if her life was harder.

He nosed the old mare toward the road, turning his back to the lighted window and the brief glimpse of domestic bliss.

"Hold it right there."

Hank recognized the voice even above the click of a Colt .45 being cocked. Chills slid up his spine as a tall man stepped out of the shadows made by the cottonwoods at the edge of the road. "Don't shoot, Beckman."

"I've been waiting for you, Callahan." Beckman's voice rang low and as dark as the night. "It was only a matter of time before you started thieving again. Couldn't help yourself, could you?"

"I'm borrowing the horse, that's all." Hank could taste the hatred in the air, one made stronger through time. "Nettie wants me gone."

"With her horse?"

"I can't walk to town." Hank's fingers itched for the gun he used to wear, the walnut-handled Colt that was always strapped to his thigh.

"Stealing a horse is a hanging offense in this territory. Too bad for you, Callahan. I think the sheriff is going to see things my way."

The irony beat at him. "I've been dead for years. Hanging me now would only be a formality. Stand aside, Beckman. I have nothing to lose." Hank nosed the mare toward the shoulder of the road. He wasn't afraid of a bully like Beckman.

"Don't be so sure."

With a flash of fire and the clap of thunder, a bullet bit into the dust in front of the horse. The old mare cried out, rearing up. Without the strength in his injured thigh to hold on, Hank slipped from the saddle. He hit the ground on his injured leg. The shards of pain left him shaking.

Footsteps thudded on the earth behind him. The cold nose of a revolver bit into the underside of his jaw. The scent of old cigarette smoke and cheap whiskey tainted the air.

"You shoulda left him on the horse, Jake. Unless you plan to drag him to town." Hank recognized Harv Wheaton's voice.

"Now there's an idea."

Hank's stomach turned. He couldn't fight two armed men, and he wasn't armed himself. He couldn't run. Hell, he could hardly stand up.

Harv holstered his revolver. "Stop shooting. Nettie's bound to hear. We're lucky she hasn't heard that gunshot of yours and come out to see what's goin' on.

"I can handle Nettie." Beckman's mouth twisted. The moonlight sheened across his face and revealed eyes that were hard and cold. The eyes of a killer.

Hank knew with a cold certainty that he was in deep trouble. Jake was responsible for this broken leg. Hank tried to reason out a way to fight, to win.

"Nettie isn't going to press charges, and this is her horse." Hank stood with a calm ease, disregarding his pain. "She's going to figure out what kind of man you are, if you're not more careful. Think about it. You want to marry her, and beating up on me must have changed her mind."

"The lady hasn't decided yet." Jake's hand trembled and he bolted forward. He jammed the gun at an angle beneath Hank's chin.

He'd pushed him too far. Hank braced, waiting for the boom of the gun. The cold metal pinched the skin beneath his jaw.

"This ain't none of your business, Callahan. She'll marry me. She has to. Who else can keep her safe from thieves like you?" One corner of his mouth twisted into a smirk. "Get the rope, Harv. We're gonna collect a nice fat reward."

That sounds like a gunshot. Nettie closed the book in her hands. In her arms, Sam breathed slow and steady, fast asleep. She set the book on the sofa next to her and stood, careful not to wake him. Sam's head lolled to a rest against her shoulder and he didn't stir.

Outside, Bessie squealed. Remembering that a horse thief was roaming loose, Nettie laid Sam down on the bed in his room. Moonlight slanted through the window and onto the sleeping child. As if brushed by magic, he slept peacefully, untouched by the violence outside.

Nettie closed the door with a quiet click. Then she lifted Richard's rifle down from the pegs over the door in case she needed protection. The gun was kept loaded. She turned down the lamps before she stepped outside.

The world was dark but not completely. The silvered moonlight brushed the surface of the road, and she studied the shadows. With the gun held tight in both hands, she followed the low rumble of voices coming, not from the barn but from the road. Behind the grove of cottonwoods that shielded the cabin from the view of the road.

With every step she took nearer, those voices grew louder and more threatening. Why, that sounded like Jake's voice. Still too far away to make out the words, Nettie started running. She rounded the corner and saw two men huddled over a prone form in the middle of the road. Silvered light illuminated Jake's sharp profile and Harv's rough face.

What were they doing? Bessie nickered and trotted down the road toward her. Nettie saw the reins trailing and the empty saddle. Had Hank tried to leave? She remembered the day of old Mr. Callahan's funeral when she'd come across Harv and Jake beating Hank in the road.

"No! Stop!" Fear clawed in her chest. She took off running, her skirts flying, air burning in her chest. Hank was badly injured and to be attacked again— oh, she hated to think what would happen.

"Jake! Harv! Let him go."

"This ain't no business of yours now, Nettie." Jake stepped in front of the man sprawled on his back in the road. He planted his hands on his hips and braced his feet apart. He looked ready for a fight.

"Not my business? This is on my land, and you have no right to be here." She kept running, using both hands to keep her gun steady, one on the stalk and the other on the butt. Her skirts nearly tripped her once, and she caught her balance. "Leave him alone."

"This is a public road." Jake motioned to Harv, who knelt to bind Hank's wrists behind his back. "And this dispute is between Callahan and me. I can't understand why you've got yourself all worked up over this. You of all people ought to hate this man worse than I do."

"And what has hatred ever gained anyone? Nothing but heartache." She couldn't bear the sight of Hank on the ground, hunched in the darkness. Blood spotted his bottom lip. Nor could she stand the sight of Jake, so certain of his actions. It hurt that he wasn't the man she'd hoped him to be.

Her grip tightened on the Winchester. "You have to let this anger go, Jake."

"What I have to do is get you back into the house. This is a matter for the sheriff. Lower the gun and head back down the road."

"Not without Hank." The rifle felt heavy in her hands. "I know what you're going to do to him before you take him in to the sheriff. I won't let you harm him anymore."

"C'mon, you ain't gonna shoot me. You know it and I know it." Jake motioned toward the man Harv Wheaton pulled to his feet. "We just caught us our local horse thief. He stole from his neighbors years ago and now he's returned to do it again. First Johnson—"

"Hank wasn't well enough to walk to the neighbors, much less steal any horses." Nettie circled around Jake and stared hard at Harv. Wheaton backed away and she cradled the rifle over the crook of one arm while she worked at the knot.

Jake towered over her, imposing and intimidating at her side. "It's my sworn duty to watch over you, and by God, that's what I'm gonna do. One of these days, you're gonna thank me. You're going to realize how much you need me. You can't keep your pretty little ranch and your cozy little house on your own." Jake circled around the horse's flank and swept off his hat "Without me, you'll lose your land. How are you going to take care of Sam then?"

"I'll have a clear conscience, and that's of value, too. This is the last time I'm asking you, Jake."

In answer, he thumbed back the hammer and placed his revolver against the back of Hank's neck. "I want that reward money, Nettie."

"You shoot, and I will, too." She nudged her rifle against his side. "Bessie is my animal, and I won't press charges. You know it. You're just using this as an excuse to avenge something you have no right to. Put your gun away."

Jake released the hammer and holstered his Colt "It's a five thousand dollar reward. Enough to get both me and Harv out from under our mortgages."

Out of the corner of her eye she saw Harv reach for his gun. She swung and fired. The Winchester kicked hard against the curve of her shoulder and knocked her back. But she kept her balance and saw dirt fly up an inch in front of Harv's shoe.

"Holster your guns, both of you. If you draw on me, I won't shoot the ground next time." She cocked the hammer, careful not to take her eyes off Jake and Harv as they complied.

Surprise flickered in Jake's eyes. He hadn't guessed she was that good a shot. "I want that money, Nettie."

"I don't care. Now mount up and ride out of here."

Jake grabbed his gelding and Harv pulled his horse out of the middle of the road. Both men mounted up and, keeping an eye on them both, she lifted the crutches off Bessie's saddle.

"Are you all right?" She handed them to the bruised and battered Hank Callahan.

He looked her in the eyes, not with guilt or that sorrowful regret, but with a sturdy respect. "Thank you, ma'am. Without a gun, I didn't stand much of a chance."

"Judging by the scrapes on your knuckles, you tried." Her whole chest warmed. "It's twice now that I've saved your life. I guess that means you owe me."

"I guess that it does." But it was with dignity he smiled, a genuine smile, that stretched the corners of his mouth and dazzled his eyes. He crutched down the road at her side. "I haven't carried a gun since the shooting. Maybe it's time I started."

"This is tough country and getting tougher." Nettie knew Jake wanted to blame last night's theft on Hank. She walked backward down the road. Jake stood in the shadows of the broad-leafed maple, head up and jaw set. His fisted hands hovered at his hips, and she figured he was just itching to go for his gun.

"The courting is over." She shouted the words on the night breeze so he would be certain to hear. "You are no longer welcome on my ranch or near my son."

"Hasty words, Nettie." Jake whistled for his gelding, and the horse trotted to his side. He caught the reins in one gloved hand. "You'll see otherwise, trust me. You need me more than you'll ever know."

A chill raced down her spine—from fear or a warning, she didn't know which. She didn't relax until the grove of cottonwoods separated her and Hank from Jake's view and the range of his gun. Nettie held open the cabin door for Hank, but he hesitated at the bottom of the stairs.

"I don't want to take your bed, Nettie. It doesn't feel right." His shoulders squared, he gazed up at her. A hank of hair fell over his forehead. He looked both rugged and vulnerable, unbowed by his injuries or Jake's assault.

She couldn't help noticing how handsome he was. "You could come in. I'll fix—"

"You've done enough for me."

"But you—"

He held up one strong hand. "I'll be more comfortable in the barn for the night. Don't worry. I've been living in a claim shanty. It's what I'm used to."

She didn't know what to say. He'd been through enough with his father's passing and the trouble from people he used to call friends. Maybe he needed to be alone. She watched to make certain he made it to the barn all right; then she stepped inside the cabin.

Silence met her. She lit a lamp and then drew the curtains shut over the glass. She couldn't help wanting to make things right for Hank. He didn't deserve such treatment. She didn't understand why Jake would try to turn in a completely innocent man. Maybe it was for the money. She knew he had a note on his land coming due and stood to lose it.

Another reason she had been wary all along of his one-sided courtship.

She checked on her son, who slept sweetly with his arms tucked around his stuffed horse. She closed the door tight and began gathering up a pillow, a set of sheets, and a blanket. She added to the pile fresh bandages and the crock of salve from the upper shelf in the kitchen. With gun in hand, she headed back out into the night.

The warm breeze smelled of the cooling earth and felt welcome on her face. Was Jake out there watching? She hesitated on the stairs and listened for any sound out of place. Owls hooted, and one dived low to the ground, searching for prey. Somewhere a coyote howled, and another answered. No sign of anything amiss.

She headed for the barn, walking fast but not running. Dust puffed up like chalk and she could taste it in the air she breathed. Her heartbeat quickened, but she didn't feel watched. She found the barn doors closed and pulled one door open just enough to slip inside.

A single lantern hung on a hook in the center aisle and cast light across the straw-strewn floor. Hank had unsaddled Bessie and put her in her stall. Fresh corn scented the air, and the big mare chewed contentedly.

Goodness, had he carried the saddle all by himself? She set down her supplies only to see him crutch out of the tack room. Muscles corded and bunched in his arms as he approached. The tips of his crutches bit into the hard-packed floor.

"I brought you makings for a bed."

"That's mighty thoughtful of you, Nettie. You shouldn't have come out in the dark alone." Hank's gaze searched hers, and in those deep eyes she read his genuine concern. "Your friend, Jake, isn't too happy with either one of us."

"There was a time when we were all friends." It hurt to remember what had happened tonight, and she turned away. "Come sit and let me take a look at your injuries. You're bleeding again."

"I'm tough." He lifted one powerful shoulder in a slow shrug. "Just cracked my lip, is all."

"What about the leg?" She curled her fingers around the outside wooden supports of the crutches and tugged. He let go, balancing his weight on one leg.

"Sit down here in the light so I can tend your wounds."

"I never remembered you being this bossy." An easy grin

softened his well-cut mouth and teased a dimple into his cheek.

"I've had to learn to be assertive with a valuable piece of land and a lot of men looking to increase their assets." She laid the crutches against a stall door and caught his elbows in both hands to help him.

He smelled like pine and her mint scented soap. She was close enough to see each individual stubble that darkened his jaw. His arm beneath her fingertips was solid and warm. It had been a long time since she'd touched a man and she'd forgotten how good it could feel.

He sat down on the bench with a small sigh. He was in more pain than he wanted to admit. "Jake was in his rights, technically. I did take your horse."

"What were you going to do with her?" Nettie reached for her small crock.

"Pay a boy at the livery in town to return her to you."

"That's what I figured." She uncapped the crock. "When you were our neighbor, you returned everything you ever borrowed in better shape than it was when you took it. You're an honest man, Hank Callahan. I would never believe you tried to steal my horse. Jake was way out of line tonight."

"He wants to marry you."

"And I said no. I'll never marry a man who enjoys harming someone else." She pressed a cloth to the salve and rubbed a thin layer over the cut on Hank's lip. "Stings a little, I know. This will help heal it faster. Now, take off your trousers. I need to look at your leg."

"Not a chance. I think you've seen too much of me already." He blushed a little, and on such a big, rugged-looking man it was endearing. She couldn't help noticing the handsome cut of his face and the fullness of his bottom lip. "Leave the salve and I'll tend to it. I'm used to looking after myself."

"Fine." The awkwardness was back, as was the remembrance of who he was and what he'd done. She tightened the lid and set it next to the bandages. "I'll just carry the bedding to an empty stall—"

"I'd rather do it" His hand covered hers to stop her from taking the sheets, and his touch was male-hot and liquefying.

She jumped back, not startled by his touch as much as by the spark that raced up her arm.

"Sorry." His voice dipped low. "I shouldn't have—"

"It's okay." She stepped back, her heart aching in her chest. She didn't know how to tell him what had happened. That she wasn't shying away from contact with a man who'd repulsed her but from the surprising flash of her attraction to him.

She'd been around long enough to recognize it. It was a frisson of sensation she'd not felt once in all her time working side by side with Jake. It was something she'd had with Richard, but not this sharp or bright. She laid her hand over her chest and could feel her heart skipping fast and hard.

"Should I leave you with the rifle?"

Her question hovered in the air. Bessie nickered, begging for more corn. Hank stared long and hard at the barrel of the gun. "Yes."

She laid it, barrel up, on the far side of his crutches. "It's loaded and ready, just so you know."

He didn't say a thing, and she wondered what he was thinking. He had said that he hadn't carried a gun since Richard's death. In this sometimes rough territory, now and then a rifle was all that stood between a man and death. And yet he remained unarmed. He made no move to touch the Winchester.

She cleared her throat. "Jake tried to hurt you tonight. You have the right to defend yourself."

"How do you do it?" His eyes pinched, and he studied her with such a quiet curiosity he didn't even appear to breathe.

"Do what? Oh, handle a rifle." She stepped away from him and the obvious question, choosing both safer ground and distance. "My mother taught me. When my father died, we moved back with Grandmother on a farm not far from here. This was a while ago, when this territory was lawless and wild. I was the oldest and had to protect us when we were alone."

"How old were you?"

"Eleven." Nettie remembered those good years spent with Grandmother, better without Pa's drunken rages. "I practiced until I was good enough to stop a charging bear or a sharpshooting outlaw."

"Did you ever stop one?"

"Never needed to. I threatened a drifter once, but that was all." Nettie couldn't help the bubble of laughter. "I scared Jake half to death when I shot at Harv's foot."

"You scared me to death, too." He stared hard at his hands, big strong tanned hands made calloused by hard work. "You are the last person who should wind up being my guardian angel."

She turned, hearing the somber rumble of his voice and the heavy notes of emotion. "I don't want to talk about the past, Hank."

"Then we'll talk about now. Like how you can look at me and not hate me for what I did to you."

"That's easy." She took a step toward the door. "You're an injured man, that's all. Someone who used to be a good neighbor."

"I did something unforgivable that night. Something I haven't been able to forgive myself for." His voice cracked once, and she heard the guilt.

She wondered what he'd been doing with himself these last few years, lost to his family and friends. "It was an accident. And that's all I'm willing to say." She kept walking, and the dark expanse of the closed double doors felt like they were a mile away.

She wanted to get away from him. She was tired, and the gossamer-thin strands of forgiveness were starting to fray. "Lock the door after me. I don't think Jake will be back—"

"He'll be back." Hank's voice came with a firm boom, and she heard the rattle of his crutches.

She walked faster toward the door. "Jake Beckman is not allowed on my ranch again."

"Then how are you going to bring in the harvest?" The plunk of his crutches and the soft pad of his step trailed her. "You need him to help you with the crops, don't you?"

"I don't need a man like Jake." Nettie caught hold of the door to throw it open. "I can hire it done."

"You don't have that kind of money." Hank's hand curled around her wrist, warm and sustaining.

"How do you know—"

"You wouldn't have relied on help in the first place. I'm not afraid of Jake. I'm not afraid to stay." His gaze met hers and she read the strength of the man. He did not blink or flinch, just as he hadn't, kneeling before Jake in the road.

"To stay and do what?"

"Make amends." Shadows drew down the corners of his mouth. Little sparks of heat danced along her skin as his touch continued. "To make up for what I've done to you."

"To me? It wasn't me you wronged. It was Richard." She jerked her hand away. Anger flared first, hot and energizing. It gave her the strength to throw open the door and storm out into the night. Shadows moved as wind kicked up plumes of dust between the barn and the house.

Stay? She didn't want him to stay. And yet, what merit would she be giving to Richard's memory if she let Hank leave? If she left him a victim to Jake Beckman's brand of justice?

She ran into the house and locked the door.

Hank watched her dash up the steps, nothing but a ribbon of shadow in the growing darkness of the night. He heard the slam of a door and imagined her flicking the bolt into place, shutting out the memory of him.

He locked the door and leaned against it. Exhaustion and pain battered him, but that wasn't the worst of it. He'd seen the dislike in Nettie's eyes and her quick withdrawal when they'd touched. She might have brought the gunfire he needed to chase off his enemies, but it rankled his pride at what her brave action had cost her.

He crutched down the aisle, stopping to pat Bessie, who was still interested in another few cups of corn. He obliged, only because he had a soft spot for pretty-eyed females. He gave the old gelding some, too, and then chose a stall for his bed. Close to the door, so he wouldn't have to crutch far. And not far from the rifle. He forked an extra layer of straw into the stall and spread out the blanket and sheets.

He turned down the wick before he settled into bed for the night. His leg hurt with a sharp thudding ache, and he gritted his teeth. After a while it eased, and he relaxed into the cool muslin sheets.

The fresh crisp scent of the straw was comforting and crackled with his every movement, reminding him of happier days spent in his own barn. The scent of sunshine and lye soap clung to the sheets. He imagined Nettie scrubbing them on a washboard, then hanging them up to dry in the fresh summer breezes.

A movement in the dark gave him a start, but the intruder gave a welcoming meow. The kitten must have been from a late litter last year, judging by her size. The calico hesitated, then ventured close. He knew she had her eye on his blanket.

"Oh, go ahead." He pulled the length of wool out from under

him and laid it out on the straw.

The feline accepted his invitation, curling into a ball and bursting into a full-fledged rumbling purr.

He didn't mind company for the night, no matter how small. The dreams that came in his sleep were ones he did not want to face, and so he lay for a long while, listening to the cat's purr fade away and the horses shift in their stalls.

Sleep came, but it was fitful, full of dark nightmares. When he opened his eyes at first light, it felt as if he hadn't slept at all.

CHAPTER SIX

Jake watched first light glint through the front windows of the saloon with an irritating brightness that shot pain straight through his eyes. The dealer called, and he laid down his cards. And lost another damn hand.

"Lady Luck ain't favorin' you, Beckman. Go home, why don't you?" Wayne Brady scooped the winnings into his hands and swept them to his side of the table. "Your playin' stinks. Maybe some sleep'll do you good."

"It ain't sleep I need." Thinking of Nettie and how she'd held a gun on him rekindled his anger. "C'mon, Harv, we've thrown away enough money for one night."

The newly rising sun reflected off the windows and shot straight into his eyes. He could no longer deny that the night had ended. It was time to head home and face that empty house, push open the front door, and walk into the same parlor Abby had lovingly decorated.

Why, she'd spent the better part of a year stitching cushions and curtains, making rugs and lacy things. And it hurt even more to lie down in their bed and try to sleep, knowing the place beside him was empty.

Hell, he hated going home.

"The baby's probably squalling about now." Harv gathered his chips and shoved his chair back from the table. "Time to start for home and do the chores."

Jake cast a glance around the bar. He didn't see the saloon's owner anywhere. It was a good time to head for the door. Pulling his hat low on his head, Jake cut through the saloon hoping no one would say a word about his long-standing debt.

"Beckman." Tailor-dressed as always, the owner of the saloon stepped out from behind the polished counter, bringing with him the scent of fine cigars and even finer whiskey. "You weren't trying to slip by without making that payment you owe me, now were you?"

"No, Denton." Lying came easier than telling the truth these days. He wondered what Abby would have thought about that, too. And it sickened him. But she wouldn't have turned against him the way Nettie had. Remembering that gun aimed at his chest fueled his anger. "I'll get your money today."

"That's what you said the last time you were in here." Denton's eyes flickered with a nasty gleam. "I'd hate to send my boys after you. They'd rough you up pretty good. So, I guess the choice is yours, Beckman. My money by noon or you'll get a nice long stay in the doc's clinic."

Triumph lifted Denton's chin as he stalked away, a man too big for his britches and thinkin' he was a step above a common rancher. Acid soured Jake's mouth. He punched through the door and out into the morning.

The town was practically abandoned. A teamster's wagon slowed to a stop in front of the grocery across the street, loaded with crates of fresh vegetables. Finches chirped on the tailor's awning, and a scrawny dog sniffed its way down the boardwalk.

Jake loosened his reins from the hitching post and swung up on the big black horse. The gelding knew better than to protest a long night standing without food or water, and it picked up a well-trained trot.

"Wait up!" Harv's call echoed against the tall storefronts.

Jake just kept going. Maybe Harv was to blame for his unlucky spell. Maybe Nettie was, for upsetting him like this. She'd turned on him, and all for a no-good pansy-ass like Callahan. A rich banker's son who didn't need a good crop to survive. Oh, no, Hank had his papa's money, and come hailstorm or grasshoppers, a drought or a prairie fire, it didn't matter. He wouldn't lose his land.

"I almost had that bastard." And enough money to pay off

Denton and Callahan's bank. Plus, if he played his hand right, all the evidence would point to Hank. It would be handy to have someone else pay for his own crimes, especially since the federal marshals were taking an interest in the string of thefts.

That's the way a man got caught. Yes, it was better to set Callahan up than to find himself swinging from a rope. A man couldn't always count on luck, and judging by the look of things lately, his luck was running out

"Callahan hasn't accused you of stealing his horses the night Pickering was killed. Or he would have thumbed you by now." Harv chugged back a mouthful of whiskey. "I don't think he remembers nothin'."

"That doesn't mean he won't." The image of Nettie holding that gun and firing a skilled shot remained with him. And it troubled him. "I didn't know she could shoot a rifle like that. She said she doesn't want to see me again."

"She'll change her mind once her temper wears down. Nettie's too softhearted for her own good. She'll take you back."

"She'd better." He'd thought that the lonely nights would end. Now, he wasn't so sure. "Her land is richer than mine. Better soil and more water. I could mortgage her land to pay off mine and sell it."

"If she can defend that no-good Callahan, she can forgive you, Jake. After all, she'll need help with the harvest and soon."

"I haven't forgotten that." Jake leaned back in his saddle, studying the lay of the land, and he noticed a small ranch tucked between two rolling knolls. "Look at that. Doesn't look like anyone's up and around yet"

"Pity. Wonder what they've got in their barn."

"Some good stock, judging by all the fresh whitewash." Harv pulled his repeating rifle from its holster. "Are you ready?"

"Hell, yes." Jake tugged the bandanna tied loosely at his throat over his chin and across his face.

They took off at a dead run, already counting the money they would make.

Hank watched Nettie work. Despite the sun's scorching touch, she appeared calm and cool, soothing as a gentle breeze. She knelt, and her little, slender hands brushed over the beanpoles. With gentle tugs, she picked pods and slipped them into the pail on the ground at her knees.

Sam played in the dirt just behind her, mixing dust and water. Mud smeared his forehead, his white drawers, and the browned skin of his hands. He chattered merrily to himself, the battered felt hat shading his face from the sun.

Hank's chest twisted as he watched Nettie shine a loving smile down on her son. Perhaps this was what interested him most about her. This alien, honest loving, this affection that moved through her like the sun through clouds.

It was something he'd never known in his life.

No, Nettie Pickering was one woman he had never wanted to hurt. His conscience ached like an old wound. He hobbled toward her, not knowing what to say after last night.

"Looky." Sam pointed a muddy finger at him. Delight lit up that button face. "Howdy."

"Howdy, partner." It was hard not to like the boy. Hank watched as Nettie twisted around to get a look at him, a fat pea pod clutched in one slender hand.

"I'm glad to see you're up. You do look better today." She smiled, but it didn't reach her eyes. She looked beautiful in a blue-checkered dress, the soft cotton skirt twisting gently around her ankles as she worked. The breeze lifted a lock of satin curls from her brow. "How does the leg feel?"

"Not too bad." He could see it in her eyes—she didn't want him here. She was too polite to say it, but he'd caused her more trouble than she'd bargained for. "I used your salve and the pain is better."

"Good." She stood, and her skirts swished around her slim legs.

He could see water spots on her dress and a smudge of dust along one soft cheek. "You left your billfold in my room. When you're helping yourself to breakfast, why don't you retrieve it? Or I can bring it out to you."

"You know good and well I left the money for you."

Her chin hiked up a notch. "I don't want your money."

"I know. That's why I left it there. I figured I'd be long gone and you'd have to keep it." He shifted the crutches beneath his arms. "I've been a lot of trouble for you."

"Yes." She nodded without judgment or emotion darkening her earth-soft eyes. "But money isn't the solution."

"I never said it was." Hank reached down to ruffle Sam's hair as the tike grabbed hold of Hank's knee.

"I got somethin' for ya." Sam held out a clover, the purple flower fragrant with the sharp scent of pollen.

Hank accepted the gift with thanks and was rewarded with the boy's wide grin. Sam announced he had to go make more mud and dashed back to the mud puddle he'd created at the edge of the garden.

Nettie, without another word, sank to her knees and continued to fill her pail. The pods snapped as she picked them, her movements more jerky than before.

Hell, he'd offended her. "I just meant to help."

"I'm aware of that." Another pea pod snapped from its vine, then another. "I don't want your guilt money. I don't *need* it."

She crept down the row, her back turned firmly to him. Hank stared at the tensed line of her shoulders and the jerky movements as she continued to pick peas. He just wanted to help her hire someone for the harvest. He was responsible for the hardship in her life. He couldn't just let that go without giving her what he had.

"There has to be something I can do for you. To make up for what I've put you through."

"How can you do that, Hank? You've got a broken leg, and besides, I don't want your pity or your charity. I don't blame you for what happened."

Well, maybe a little. He could see the hard pinch around her eyes.

"If you want to leave, I could drive you to town." At the end of the row she stood, straightening her back. The little pail was full, but her work wasn't done. She didn't look at him as she lifted a heavy water bucket and emptied it in the irrigation row. The water crept across the hard ground. "I don't think Jake would bother us if we're armed. After last night, he wouldn't dare."

"I appreciate the offer, Nettie, but I don't need a woman to fight my battles for me. You have enough burdens."

Her jaw clamped shut. "Then fight your own battles alone. That's what you do best."

She grabbed another empty water bucket and stalked away to the well, her angry steps hard on the sun-baked earth.

"She's very mad," Sam whispered.

"I can see that."

With her words still stinging, he watched her lift the well cover. She worked with a determined focus, probably because he'd made her so angry. He felt bad about that. The breeze flicked the scent of roses from the front of the house and reminded him of her, of how she smelled like flowers and sunshine.

Behind her, the fields undulated in the wind and shimmered beneath the golden sun. Ripening wheat, corn, and hay stretched as far as his eye could see— Nettie's land and Nettie's crops. Both were valuable. It wasn't hard to guess what Beckman wanted.

Alone, Hank crutched along the beaten path to the house. The sun shone warm on his back as he hobbled up the stairs.

She needed help, and he had no place to go, not really. He had a shanty far up in the mountains he didn't even think of as home. Something in his guts, something cold and unsettled, told him not to leave.

He crutched to the kitchen and found a plate warming on the stove. It touched him that she would think to leave him a meal. He grabbed a couple of biscuits from the basket on the counter and headed for the table. The coffee was cold, but on a hot morning like this it tasted just right.

He could see her through the window. She was a petite woman, hardly more than a willow in the wind as she knelt to empty another set of water buckets. Sam chattered to her, his fingers gloved with mud. Then he returned to his work, pouring a ladle of water onto the dusty earth. He bent with childish innocence to stick both hands in the muddy goo and squish it between his fingers.

Nettie looked up from her bean picking and said something to her son. Love shone in her eyes and lit her face. For a moment there, she looked like the woman he remembered, soft and pretty and always smiling. The shadows were gone from her eyes and the sternness from her face. Then she grabbed her empty buckets and headed back to the well.

She was alone out here, vulnerable and looking for a man to raise her son. Jake Beckman was the kind of man who didn't stop until he got what he wanted. Hank remembered the man's ugly words last night, and a quick hatred flashed in his chest. *She'll marry me. She has to. Who else can keep her safe?*

I can. Hank considered that thought. He knew the last thing she needed was to look at him every day, a reminder of all she'd lost. But he had nowhere to go and he had a chance to set things right.

His gaze found Nettie in the garden, this time plucking carrots from their rows.

For the first time in years, his life had a purpose.

"Mama." Sam padded through the rows of carrots. Mud was everywhere—on his feet and on his hands and splashed across his britches. "I gonna go watch him."

"No, we might need you to make more mud." Nettie caught him before he toddled after the man who was in their house. She asked Sam how many mud pies he'd made, and he was momentarily diverted from his growing interest in Hank Callahan.

A part of her wanted Hank out of her life. Another part was glad he was safe here and had a chance to heal. The problem was that he'd changed everything and made her feel things she'd thought impossible.

She felt a keen awareness of him as a man, and that troubled her. She wasn't ready for these changes. But she needed a father for her son. Now she knew that she needed to love someone again, too.

It hurt to admit it. She hadn't realized how much she wanted love in her life.

The rattle of a wagon broke the morning's stillness. Nettie brushed the dust from her apron and prayed it wasn't Jake come to apologize. She didn't trust him, not now. She feared being alone with him. She glanced toward the house and saw Hank's face in the window. He'd heard the approaching wagon, too.

A bay mare circled around the cottonwoods and into sight, drawing the Wheaton wagon. Maude perched on the seat, a child at her side and three more in the back. Her faded sunbonnet shaded her face, and an apron almost hid the roundness of her advancing pregnancy.

Relieved, Nettie saw Hank step back from the window.

"My goodness, you look a sight." Maude drew the wagon to a stop and set the brake with a creak. "I've been worried near to death about you ever since I heard from Jake Beckman that you had Hank Callahan in your house. Goodness, that man is dangerous. You oughtn't to be alone with him. Harv told me just last night he tried to steal your horse—"

"There was a misunderstanding. Hank borrowed Bessie." Nettie had to wonder what Harv had told his wife about last night's events. "I'm not in any danger. Hank is staying with me until he's strong enough to leave."

THE RANCHER'S RETURN

"You're far too generous, Nettie."

"Generous? No. It's just that his own family wouldn't claim him, and there is no one else."

"Of course not, not with the way he shamed that fine family." Maude checked on her baby cradled in a basket on the floorboards, then climbed down. "I've come because Jake asked it of me. We've been friends a long time, you and me, and I owe it to look after you."

Tightness cinched around Nettie's chest. "If this has to do with accepting Jake's apology, I won't do it."

"Now, he's a fine man. Don't you go judging him." Maude caught hold of Nettie's hand and squeezed gently. "I know you and Jake had some kind of argument. He's a man with a temper, but he's a hard worker and a good provider. Believe me, a woman with a child ought to be grateful for a man like that to look after her."

Nettie knew the truth behind Maude's unspoken words. Harv had not been a dependable provider for his family. It was no secret that he had a weakness for alcohol. "I'm doing just fine as I am, Maude."

"You'll need a man for the harvest. You know the neighbors will help, like they always do, but they don't have the same kind of time to give as Jake does. He's devoted to you. He'll make sure you bring in a good crop."

"No one can make sure of that." She stepped away, glancing behind her shoulder at the house. "I have fresh biscuits if you and the children would like to come in—"

"Nope, we have to get going. I wanted to check on the Johnsons after their awful scare. I heard their fields are a mess. It's a sad thing, the kind of vermin that prey on good and decent people." Maude's gaze arrowed to the cabin's open front door.

"I'd be happy to get you a drink of water. It's hot as the dickens this morning."

Maude shook her head, but the ardent movement could not dislodge that rigid bun crowning her head. "I mean to take him with me."

"Who?" Nettie already knew. Sam leaned against her knee and curled his fingers around hers, mud and all.

"It isn't good for you to have that man in your house." Maude's eyes darkened with true sympathy. "He killed your husband and stole from his friends, and now he's at it again. I'm on my way to town, after checking with the Johnsons, and I don't mind. After all, you can't up and leave your work this time of year, and I'm headed to see the doctor anyway. Go on. If you don't ask him, I'll tell him."

A hard knot gathered behind Nettie's breastbone. It would be much easier if she could let Maude take Hank Callahan. But the exhaustion on the pregnant woman's face was unmistakable. Besides, it wasn't the right thing to do. "He has nowhere to go, and he can't ride far with his injury."

"I know you have a kind heart, Nettie. You take in every creature that needs a home in these parts, but that man doesn't deserve your mercy, of all people." Maude patted her hand, then stepped back. "If he can't move on his own, then I'll have my oldest boys come in and drag him out. Either way, he can't stay here with you. You don't need that heartache."

"Heartache or no, he stays." Maude was wrong— this had nothing to do with her soft heart. If they moved him, she feared for what would become of him. It was as simple as that.

"Have some sense, Nettie. You're a woman alone. Jake and Harv say the marshal's put up a reward for the horse thieves. Another ranch was hit early this morning before the family was even out of their beds—"

"I won't let you turn Hank in to the sheriff." Nettie clamped her jaw. "He's one of the wealthiest men in this county. He doesn't need to steal."

"That was before his father cut him off—"

"Maude! He didn't do it. Hank was right here all night long with me—"

"*With you?*" Outrage sharpened those words. "Have you lost all sense of decency—"

"In my barn."

Maude shook her head sadly. "I know you're trying to do what's right, but this isn't it. You need a man at your side. Someone who can protect you. You know I worry about your safety, Nettie. It isn't good, you living out here by yourself."

"I'm not alone—"

"I'd best be headin' out." Maude turned toward her battered wagon and climbed up onto the wagon seat. "Maybe it's no coincidence this trouble starts back up again about the same time Hank Callahan returns. You're a woman alone, and you need to think about your reputation."

"My reputation? But—"

"If you change your mind, you let me know, Nettie. And think about what I said. Jake cares for you."

Nettie bit back any argument as Maude gathered up the thick leather reins and released the brake. The tired-looking mare ambled off, pulling the squeaky wagon and kicking up chalky plumes of dust.

Nettie felt suddenly alone and vulnerable standing in the yard, squinting into the morning sun. She still had chores to do and the day's work to begin, but she felt too overwhelmed to start. She wouldn't be pressured by her friends or by anyone to accept Jake's apology. There was no excuse for what he had tried to do last night.

She turned toward the house and saw that the door was open. Had Hank heard Maude's words?

He killed your husband and stole from his friends, and now he's at it again. Maude Wheaton's words echoed in his head as he retrieved a dishpan from the bottom shelf. He'd never had anything against the woman. Hell, he'd barely known her, but he was rapidly developing a dislike for her. Especially since she'd urged Nettie to reconcile with Beckman. He suspected Maude Wheaton had no idea what her husband had tried to do last night.

Hank dropped the basin on the counter. The stove poured out heat and the fresh scent of buttermilk biscuits and baking beans. He lifted the water kettle from the heat and filled the dishpan half full. The big pot sitting on the stove began bubbling, and he added a half dozen ears of fresh corn to the steaming water.

He heard the screen door squeak open and Nettie's light step on the floor. "What on earth are you doing?"

He covered the kettle and looked at her across the room. The wind had whipped wild tendrils around her face, and the sun had brought out the freckles across her nose. That smudge of dust still marked her skirt and bits of grass clung to her hem.

"What does it look like? I'm cooking our meal." He set the hot pads on the edge of the counter and hobbled to the hutch. "It's almost noon and I thought I'd better make myself useful. Are you thinking of starting your second cutting of hay?"

"It's just about ready." She swept up beside him smelling of sunshine and the soft, sweet perfume of her skin. "Let me get the plates. I don't know how you managed to do all this on those crutches."

"All it takes is patience." He let her take the plates but pulled open the drawer to count out the flatware.

"It can't be good for your leg to be up on it so much." Nettie moved away with a swish of skirts and the flick of her long braid. She kept her back to him as she passed the plates around the table.

"My leg is fine." He joined her at the table, but already she moved away. "I can't just lie around, Nettie. I'd hate to think what Maude Wheaton's opinion would be on that."

She leaned out of the screen door to check on Sam, playing with his toy train in the yard. A calico cat wandered over from the barn and plopped down to rest beside the boy in the shady grass. "You did overhear us talking."

"I couldn't help it Maude was loud enough for the entire county to hear."

"Maude gets a little harsh in her opinions now and then." When Nettie faced him there was softness in her eyes, a blend of compassion and understanding for her friend.

He laid out the forks and knives. "Did you hear what Jake is trying to do?"

"He still thinks I'll forgive him." Nettie grabbed a hot pad and lifted the kettle's lid. "Hmm, these are almost done."

"You will forgive him."

"No, not this time." She replaced the lid and knelt to open the oven. "These smell wonderful, I'm going to have to get the recipe from you—"

"He hurt you, didn't he?"

"He almost did. I almost—" She paused, never finishing her thought. She bent at the waist and lifted the fragrant beans from the oven. The pot steamed as she set it on the nearby trivet. Heat curled the tendrils at her brow and pinkened her cheeks.

She closed the oven door, careful not to look at him. "I could never allow a man like that near my son. I'm just grateful I saw this side of him before it was too late. I almost married him. In a way, I'm grateful to you."

"For breaking my leg?" He managed a small grin.

"Yes. Your injury has been a good thing for me." The corners of her mouth twitched in the smallest of smiles.

"Then I'm glad I could accommodate you." Hank felt something tighten low and deep in his abdomen. A powerful ache thudded in his groin.

Nettie pushed open the screen door and called Sam in for the meal. The little boy came running, always eager for food. His train clattered to the floor as he dashed into the kitchen.

"Corn, goody!"

"It's my favorite, too." Hank pulled out the chair for the boy to climb up into it

"This is such a treat, Hank." Nettie grabbed a pair of forks from the hutch.

"No, you don't. This is my meal to serve." He took the utensils from her sun-browned hands, calloused from work, but long and beautifully shaped. His heart kicked powerfully at the brush of her skin on his. Pulse racing, he jerked away. Did she feel this, too?

Blushing, she ducked her chin and circled around the table and tugged napkins out of another drawer. Embarrassed by his response to her, he grabbed a hot pad and lifted the lid from the kettle. Corn-scented steam heated his face. He scooped the bright yellow cobs onto a platter. He heard Nettie swish around the table, and she appeared at his side. Her shoulder bumped his arm when she reached for the platter.

He tried to swallow, but his throat was suddenly dry. He opened his mouth to speak, but no words came.

She looked up at him, an echo of desire dark in her eyes. Small tendrils twisted about her soft face, contrasting richly with her sun-browned skin.

His gaze fell to her lips, pink and lush, and his blood heated. Shame swept through him, because he had no right to think of her like this. He had no right to dream about kissing her mouth. No right at all.

She carried the platter away and the moment was lost. Hank spooned the steaming beans into a serving bowl and carried it to the table, awkward because of the crutches.

"I'll get the rest, Hank." She breezed past him, her rose and sunshine scent driving his pulse faster.

He still couldn't speak. He grabbed a butter knife. "Which one do you want, partner?"

"That one." Sam pointed to the brightest ear of corn.

Hank slipped it onto the boy's plate and buttered it for him. He felt Nettie's gaze and saw her smile. This time it reached her eyes and lingered there, genuine and as wonderful as the first star of the night. And it didn't fade. He liked that.

Sam tugged on Hank's sleeve, and he had to add more butter to the corn, according to Sam's instructions, and salt. He was amused, but he didn't like having to take his gaze from Nettie.

A boot knelled on the porch outside. Hank turned to see a man dressed in dark blue, a badge glinting on his chest.

Sheriff Larson curled his hand into a fist and knocked on the door. His wary gaze pinned Hank's through the wire mesh. "Mrs. Pickering?"

Nettie dropped her fork with a clatter. The chair scraped against the wood floor as she bounded to her feet Concern drew brackets around her mouth. She opened the door. "How can I help you, Sheriff?"

"I have reason to suspect Hank Callahan is responsible for a few robberies in the area." The lawman tipped his hat politely, but his gaze never left Hank's. "I heard he tried to steal your mare last night."

"That's not true." Nettie's voice sounded taut as a frayed rope.

Hank crutched past her to the door. "Sheriff, I did take Nettie's horse, but only to get to town. You know who I am—"

"And what you've done." Grim, the sheriff laid his hand on the holster of his polished Colt. "You can come in for questioning, nice and friendly-like without handcuffs or force. Or I can drag you to my jail the hard way. It's your choice."

"I'll come—"

"No, Hank." Nettie caught his arm, refusing to let him go. "You didn't do anything wrong. Sheriff, I'll be more than happy to testify that Hank couldn't have been responsible for the local horse thefts—"

"I'm sure you will, Mrs. Pickering." The sheriff's words silenced her and made her blush.

"It's all right." Hank wished he could take her in his arms and hold her until the hurt in her eyes faded. "I'm innocent. I'll answer the lawman's questions, and then he'll know it, too."

"In my opinion, a man who can ride a stolen horse can steal others." The sheriff caught Hank by the elbow and spun him against the outside wall of the house. "Are you carrying any weapons?"

"Not even a knife." Hank let the man search him. "Nettie, don't let Sam watch this. Don't come after me, you hear? I don't want you in the middle of this."

"I already am." Her small hands splayed against the screen mesh, and her eyes filled with a heartbreaking sadness.

Even during the past few years banished to his mountain cabin, he had never felt so lonely as he did when the sheriff led him away from Nettie Pickering's sight.

CHAPTER SEVEN

Made of brick and stone and shaded by tall trees, the jailhouse was cool even though the afternoon was hot. Nettie's back ached from the hard-backed chair in the sheriff's office. Sam curled up in her lap, drowsing. It was well past his naptime. Earlier, he'd been cranky, and she'd walked him down the street to the ice-cream parlor for a special treat.

Hank was still inside, and the sheriff refused to tell her how much longer she had to wait. Or if they would be pressing charges.

Jake's done this. She knew it with a sick certainty. There were little things over the years that had made her uncertain, but Jake had always been steady and reliable. He just had been able to hide this irrational animosity for Hank during the years Callahan had been gone.

Nettie understood grief and she understood the resulting rage. But anger was one thing—violence was another. She would not stand by a second time.

The inner door opened and the sheriff emerged. He didn't look her way as he crossed over to his paper-piled desk, the reward poster for the local horse thief prominent on the wall behind him.

Hank crutched into sight. There was a new cut on his mouth and a fresh bruise against his jaw. His shirt was torn at the collar and un-tucked from his trousers. He looked pale, and she wondered how much his leg was hurting him.

Sam stirred and then hopped off her lap. "Hank!"

He dashed across the small room and threw his arms around the big man's knees. He clung tightly. "Mama said you was talkin' with the sheriff."

"I sure was." Hank reached down and ruffled the boy's hair. The affectionate gesture softened his rugged face. He looked like the man Nettie remembered once—strong, sure, gentle. He'd had a good hand with horses, she recalled, and a steady, quiet humor.

"You're free to go, Callahan." The sheriff didn't look happy as he leaned one hip against his desk, arms crossed over his broad chest and the revolvers gleaming at his belt. The threat was clear. "Don't go thinkin' you should leave this county. If I find you heading toward the border and Idaho Territory, I'll arrest you on the spot."

"I have no reason to run." Hank didn't flinch as he met the rough lawman's gaze. He stood straight and tall, and the width of his muscled shoulders and the span of his chest made him look invincible. He ruffled Sam's hair one more time, then bent to speak with the boy. "Did your mama tell you there was a candy store just down the street?"

"I get candy, too?" Sam clapped his hands.

"Yep, partner, you get candy, too." Hank leaned on his crutches and stepped forward with an easy grace, one built of power and strength.

"I took him for ice cream earlier," Nettie said, to fill the silence between them. She could feel the sheriff's harsh scrutiny and it made her pulse quicken. She held open the heavy door, and Hank thanked her with a nod of his head and a quick tip of his hat.

"You shouldn't have come, Nettie." Hank squinted against the low sun as she closed the door behind them. "This isn't safe for you. Not after what happened in there."

"Tell me." She ran after Sam, who raced ahead of her down the walk, and caught him by the arm. "They hurt you, didn't they?"

"They were just trying to get some answers." Hank stared off at the horizon, past the low buildings at this end of town to the crisp purple blue hills far away. "I can't fault them for that. Someone led the sheriff to believe I was the thief."

"Jake."

"That's my guess." Hank's muscles bunched beneath the soft cotton shirt as he crutched at her side. Serious and grim, he winced a little with each step.

Had they beaten him? Nettie glanced back at the jail and saw the sheriff in the barred window, watching Hank Callahan. What had Jake said to convince the lawman that Hank was guilty? She could see the sheriff believed that, although he had no evidence.

If only old Sheriff Joe hadn't retired. Nettie ushered Sam in front of her as Hank tugged open the shop's glass door, awkward on his crutches. The scents of sugar and cinnamon and mint warred with the dusty air.

"It was good of you to care what happened to me." He followed her inside. "Even though I don't want you mixed up in my problems, thank you for coming."

Her throat tightened, and it hurt to speak. "You don't deserve how Jake is treating you."

"He's jealous. That's why he's doing this. Jealousy can make a man insane. He's had you all to himself for the last few years and figured you'd be his wife one day. And now he sees me as a threat." A smile stretched his mouth and erased those tired lines. "He's in love with you."

"He has a hard side to him that scares me." Out of the corner of her eye, Nettie saw the candy maker's wife stare hard at Hank, then duck behind the counter and rush out of sight.

"Mama, I want lic'rish." Sam tilted his head back to grin up at her with dazzling charm. Dark eyes sparkled with happiness.

She couldn't help brushing a hand over that unruly cowlick at the crown of his head. "I do, too."

Mr. Tobias burst out from a back room, his apron powdered with sugar and streaked with chocolate. His wizened face hardened and he cleared his throat. "Hank Callahan. You're not welcome in my store."

Strong and steady, Hank's gaze pinned hers. She read the apology there in eyes pinching with regret His throat worked. With a quiet dignity, he nodded and took a step back. "It's your store, Mr. Tobias. I'll wait outside."

He reached into his pocket. The old man held up his hands, refusing even to take Hank's money. Outrage sparked in Nettie's chest and she nearly gave the old candy maker a piece of her mind, but Sam stopped her. There hadn't been a lot of extra pennies for candy lately, and now Hank was holding out a twenty-dollar bill.

"You can buy your own candy, partner." Hank ruffled the boy's hair and earned a full-hearted grin.

"Thank you, partner." Sam backed against his mother's skirts.

"I'll wait for you outside. It's all right, Nettie." Hank crutched out of the shop and onto the boardwalk. The bell above the door chimed as he closed it.

"Ain't Hank stayin'?"

Nettie didn't know what to say, so she clamped her jaw shut. Sam studied the greenback with great interest and then the door where Hank could be seen, sitting down on a bench in the shade of a tree.

"What will you have, little man?" Mr. Tobias asked kindly, and she could see the old man was simply scared. Scared of the rumors of a horse thief who harmed the people who crossed him.

Had the news spread so fast that everyone knew Hank had been brought in for questioning?

Sam wanted lots of licorice, and the old man filled a white paper sack but refused the money.

"My treat," Mr. Tobias told Nettie. "I know I offended you."

She bit her lip, hating the harsh words that sat on her tongue. But harsh words rarely made a difference in this world; she believed only the gentle ones could do that. So she made sure Sam thanked Mr. Tobias before they headed out to join Hank on the boardwalk.

"I got lotsa lic'rish." Sam hopped up onto the wooden bench, a red rope already dangling from his hand. He offered up his bag. "You want some?"

"I sure do." A slow smile tugged across Hank's mouth, and Nettie nearly missed her step watching the dimple tease its way into his cheek. He tugged out the end of a red rope from Sam's sack and broke it off midway.

Nettie watched as he bit into the piece of candy. His mouth looked supple and firm. She wondered if his kiss would feel the same way.

Now, where did that thought come from? She could feel a blush heat her face, and she stared hard at a passing wagon loaded with freight.

A sharp whistle shrieked above the clatter and din of the busy town as the train announced its arrival at the station.

"I wanna see the train, Mama." Sam clutched his paper sack tightly in one hand and his red candy rope in the other.

"It will be gone before we can see it, sweet pea." She pressed a kiss to his cheek. "Hank, what are you planning to do now?"

His eyes narrowed. "Is this your polite way of wanting me gone?"

"No." His frankness surprised her. And his words. "You know I don't think you're guilty."

"I know. But hanging around a suspected criminal like me isn't good for your reputation. You have a lot at stake, Nettie. Your little boy, for one."

The responsibility of being Sam's sole support weighed heavily on her shoulders, she couldn't deny it. "I'm not going to lose my ranch because you stay with me while your leg mends."

"You still look at me and see Richard's killer, don't you?" A grim frown tugged at his mouth, and even though he sat there, straight-backed and strong, he winced, as if it mattered how she saw him.

"Sometimes." She hated those words to be true. "I know it was an accident Hank. I know it. But these past years haven't been easy. The hardest thing I ever did was bury my husband."

"And I'm responsible for that."

She nodded, hating the simple truth. "But I also see someone else. An honest man who deserves a good life. Who has been kind to my little boy. You've reminded me that there are good men in this world."

His throat worked, and he stared hard at the street, where dust devils chased ahead of the wind. "If I've done that little bit of good, then I'm glad. It's time for me to leave. I thought maybe I could stay and help you out, but with the sheriffs suspicions and the threat of charges hanging over my head, it's better for you if I go."

"What will you do?"

"Well, I don't dare head back to my shanty. I'd have to cross into Idaho Territory to do it, and the sheriff already said he won't take kindly to that." Hank lifted one brawny shoulder in an easy shrug. "I'll probably have to get a room at the hotel and wait until the sheriff figures out I'm not his thief. Then I'll head back to the mountains."

This was her chance to finally be rid of Hank Callahan. Except now it wasn't what she wanted, not really. Despite the injustice and the cruelty shown to him today, he didn't lash out, didn't swear revenge. He faced all aspects of life with a determined steadiness,

THE RANCHER'S RETURN

and it made her heart ache. "I'll miss you, Hank Callahan."

"I doubt it." Another dimple flashed in his chin. "Don't worry. It's time for me to go. Thank you for all you've done for me." He turned away and began crutching toward her wagon tethered not far away.

She took Sam's hand and followed after him. Old Bessie nickered in greeting, both to her and to Hank.

"You might need this." She reached into her reticule and withdrew his leather billfold.

"No. I meant for you to have it."

She lifted Sam up onto the wagon seat. "I don't need your money."

He stood a step back, shaking his head. His throat worked and his eyes narrowed, and so much seemed unsaid between them. "Keep it for Sam. It's what I want."

He turned and crutched away, and she watched the play of muscles beneath his shirt. He put as much distance between them as he could, as fast as he could.

"Hank gettin' more candy?" Sam asked.

"No, sweet pea." She climbed up onto the seat next to him. The reins felt hot in her hands, and she released the brake. "Hank is going to stay here in town, where he belongs."

"He comin' home for supper?" True worry crinkled those concerned eyes.

"No. He's going to get a room here in town. But we can come visit him if you'd like." Nettie flicked the reins and her team stepped out into the street, pulling the wagon into the stream of traffic.

"No!" Sam stood up on the seat, and Nettie grabbed hold of him before he could try to get away. The ground was a long way down for such a little boy, and so she pulled him onto her lap and held him tight.

Hot tears stained her bodice, and she kissed his brow. But nothing could ease the pain of his loss.

Hank Callahan was nowhere in sight as she turned the wagon toward home.

His father's bank loomed above Hank, blocking the light of the setting sun and casting a gigantic shadow across the boardwalk and street. The white-trunked beeches out front rustled in the cooling breeze like the sound of greenbacks rubbing together. The brick building rose three stories, the second-tallest building in Walla Walla, its gleaming redbrick front visible from a quarter mile away.

Hank studied those polished oak doors until he found the courage to take one step forward and then another. He shouldered his way inside.

A pleasant cool dimness met him. He smelled the familiar scents of money, leather, and wood polish. Low murmurs hummed in the air as business was transacted. Even with Father gone, there was still a faint aroma of his expensive cigars and the same controlled tension snapping through the bank. Employees stood stiffly behind highly polished counters, hardly daring to smile for the customers.

The polished wood walls shone in the bright light. The deep green carpet contrasted richly with the dark woods and fragrant leathers. It felt odd to think his father was gone. Odd to think the bank ran efficiently and normally without him.

Hank had spent two years in this bank trying to step into his father's shoes. Years that had not been the best, but at least he discovered he had no love for banking. That's when he bought the land next to Nettie's and became a rancher. He liked being out-of-doors in the sunshine and wind.

Blinking, Hank forced himself to move forward toward a waiting clerk, both hands braced hard against the grips of his crutches.

The somberly dressed clerk offered him a dignified smile. "May I help you?"

"I need to transfer funds."

"From this bank?" The man's eyebrows lifted. His skeptical gaze traveled the length of Hank from his battered hat to his worn boots, noting the simple cloth shirt and trousers. "Come right this way."

Hank sat down in a wooden chair before a neat desk. No one occupied it. He glanced around and recognized familiar faces, but no one recognized him. He'd changed in the last handful of years. He didn't look like the same man. Little wonder nobody knew him.

"May I have your name, sir?" a different employee asked, striding ardently toward him. Then his step faltered. Recognition widened the man's eyes and surprise pushed up his bushy, silvered eyebrows. "Hank, is that you? I can't believe it. I didn't see you at the funeral. Do you know about your father?"

Hank stood, offering his hand. "I know."

Barnaby Matson, Father's partner, clasped his beefy hand around Hank's. It was a sturdy grip. "I suppose you didn't come here to dredge up the past."

"No." Hank's throat felt full, and he cleared it. It didn't help. "I want to transfer funds. The last time I did this, I had my brother's help."

"Let me guess. To Mrs. Pickering's account." Matson was a sharp man, unbowed by his advancing years. "Sit down, Hank. I hear that nasty business has returned to haunt you again."

His leg throbbed without mercy and sitting did little to alleviate it. But he gratefully sank into the hard chair anyway, braced. It looked like the past wouldn't stay buried today, so he matched Barnaby's bird-eyed gaze. "Have you also heard I was just questioned by the sheriff and released?"

The old man froze. One bushy eyebrow arched with a question. "A man is innocent until proven guilty by law, but not by public opinion. That can't be easy, because you are your father's son. Everyone assumes that you're just like him. And he wasn't the most honest of men."

"I came to transfer funds and get a little cash for myself, that's all. I don't owe you any explanations." The bank had quieted, and he realized his voice sounded loud and gruff against the strained stillness.

"Of course." Barnaby's gaze sharpened, slicing as neatly as a butcher's knife. "Mrs. Pickering closed her account here about a year ago. She's no longer a customer of this bank."

"I see." Hank leaned forward, closing the distance over the desktop. "I didn't expect your courtesy—after all you were devoted to my father. But if you're lying to me—"

"I'm not lying." The old man studied him hard, and a muscle jumped along his jaw. Something glittered in his birdlike eyes. "I'm not your father."

That stubborn lump in Hank's throat swelled, blocking his air entirely. He couldn't breathe. He couldn't speak. He could only look away.

"You are welcome in this bank, son." Barnaby stood, cornered the desk, and halted beside Hank's chair. "By the looks of you,

you've paid hard for a mistake."

When Barnaby's age-spotted, blue-veined hand curled around Hank's shoulder, he felt as if a boulder had lodged itself in his throat.

He was in danger of feeling again.

"If you need a job, then I'd like you to work here with me. All you need to do is ask."

The weight of so much pulled at Hank, forcing him to breathe, forcing him to feel. Barnaby's sharp eyes swept over him with gentleness.

Then he removed his hand. "You said you wanted to withdraw money for yourself?"

Since Hank couldn't speak, he nodded. Barnaby strode away, powerful in his authority, and more powerful yet because of his kindness.

It took nearly an hour to calm Sam down. Not even the excitement of looking for gophers or the beautiful hawks and eagles soaring overhead could distract him from his tears. She comforted him the best she could, cuddling him in her lap and promising corn on the cob for supper. He finally cried himself to sleep, head resting against her chest, his cheeks tear-stained.

She pulled the horses to a stop in front of the cabin. With the doors locked and the curtains drawn to keep out the afternoon sun, it looked lonely against the background of the enormous plains. Lonely, just like she was. If Hank's presence had done nothing, it had shown her how isolated her life had become.

She set the brake and hopped to the ground. The air had turned muggy as thunderheads gathered in the sky. The sun's rays felt muted as she cradled Sam in her arms and managed to spread out a blanket in the shadow of the cottonwoods.

Fragrant grasses rattled with the force of the wind as she laid Sam down on the blanket. It was cooler here in the shade. She knew the house would be far too hot after being shut up all afternoon.

Sam rolled onto his stomach without waking, and his back rose and fell with each peaceful breath. Tear tracks still stained his cheeks, a testimony to how much he liked Hank Callahan. He needed a father. There was no denying it Sam needed a man to look up to, someone to butter his cobs of corn and buy him candy.

Could it be possible? Could she be missing Hank already?

Leaving Sam to sleep, she led the horses to the barn and unhitched them. Bessie and Emmanuel, drained by the heat and humidity, ambled without halter or bridle to a patch of grass in the shade of the barn. She grabbed the picket ropes from inside the tack room and caught sight of the rifle set high above the door on brand-new pegs. Hank had done that.

Chores awaited her, and the fields lay ready, ripening more day by day. The fragrant corncobs were almost mature. The golden wheat was nearly ready to be harvested. Another gust of wind blew, and she stepped outside to study the sky. She could smell a storm in the air, and judging by the brilliant purples and crimsons along the horizon as the sun began setting, it was going to be a powerful one. Not a good thing for the wheat.

She watered and picketed the horses, checking over her shoulder to see Sam still asleep on his blanket. She opened up the house so the oven-like heat could dissipate. Rain scented the air but did not fall. She turned around, and the blanket in the grass was empty except for the indentation from a little boy's body and a few straw grass seeds. Sam was gone.

The first flash of lightning split the sky. Thunder crashed once and then again overhead. Hard, cold rain hit the ground with drumming force, swallowing up her voice as she called his name.

She ran down the road but saw no sign of him. She checked the house and barn, and he hadn't gone inside. That only left the fields. The crops were tall enough to hide one small boy and stretched out in every direction for as far as she could see.

The storm hit with fury. Hank hobbled out of the tailor's shop, pleased with the clothes he'd purchased and had delivered to his hotel room. Along with the purchases he'd made at the mercantile, it was enough to keep him decently covered for a while. He had no idea what had happened to his horse and his saddlebags, but he had his suspicions.

His stomach rumbled with nearly the same fury as the thunder overhead, and he spotted a diner a few doors down. He remembered it was a decent place. The wooden door swung open easily, and he chose a booth in back near the window. Thunderclaps rattled the windowpanes. Rain and then hail pounded the streets. A weathered-face waitress arrived to take his order. She returned with iced tea and a plate of chowder. He ate while he waited for his steak.

"Hiding out, Callahan?" Black-gloved hands splayed across the edge of the table. Beckman smelled of cheap alcohol and even cheaper cigars. Revolvers were strapped to his hips. "Keeping out of the sheriffs sight? I thought you'd be hiding behind Nettie's skirts, or at least in jail where a thief like you belongs."

Hank sank his spoon into the rich chowder and did his best not to look ruffled. He wasn't really. He could handle Beckman. "The sheriff let me go."

"The hell he did."

"Ask him." Hank kept eating. "You wouldn't have anything to do with the accusations against me, now would you?"

"Me?" A slow pleasure flickered in those eyes. "Now, I only told the sheriff the truth as I saw it. You did try to take Nettie's mare. Who's to say you didn't do the same at the Johnson ranch? Or the Glover's? Or the Long's?"

"Right. I could have been prowling these plains for a good couple of months stealing honest men's horses when I have enough money in the bank already."

Hank knew it wasn't his solid alibis that had kept him from a cell tonight. Being injured and living in Idaho hadn't been good enough for the sheriff. It was the lack of motive. Stealing twenty-, even hundred-dollar horses made no sense. None at all. "Still gambling these days?"

"All of life's a gamble. Surely you know that better than most, Callahan." Jake helped himself to a chair and spun it around. He sat with his elbows propped on the wooden back, blocking the aisle. "Sometimes you win, and sometimes you lose. What's important is that you keep playing, because one day you're bound to land on top of things."

"Or run into debt and have a pack of hired thugs after you." Hank stirred the chowder to find a chunk of potato. A hot cold rage burned in his chest, one that left him shaking. But he didn't act on his anger, figuring that's what Jake wanted—to provoke him. To prove Hank Callahan was a volatile outlaw.

Beckman's fist hit the table. "I won't be happy until you're hanging from a noose, the way you deserve. I want you out of my way."

A chill iced the back of Hank's neck. "Killing a man is illegal in this territory."

"Maybe that's a bet I'm willing to make."

"You want Nettie, is that it?" Hank shook his head, staring out at the driving hail. "You had your chance and lost it. There's no way Nettie will want a man capable of brutalizing others to raise her son."

"She might not have much of a choice. Look at that hail. Why, that can ruin a good crop. Drive the wheat to the ground so it's not salvageable. It's a shame ranching is a big gamble. Nettie needs a good crop if she wants to keep a roof over her son's head."

"And you think you can back her into that corner of choosing you or homelessness."

"You just never know what events will conspire to aid a man in his quest. Look, even the weather can lend a hand. I figure Nettie will need someone to help out, now that you're out of the way. Don't think the sheriff is going to let you leave this town an innocent man. Mark my words, by this time tomorrow you could be standing before the county judge."

Hank watched Beckman go, his threat lingering in the air. The waitress brought the rest of the meal and he ate it, weighing Jake's words. The man was no fool—he'd come by to provoke not just a fight but a battle. Over Nettie, over freedom, over Hank's life. It was one battle Jake Beckman would lose.

CHAPTER EIGHT

Nettie had never been so frantic in her life. She called for her son as she searched the yard and barn. Hail drummed to the ground, draining the last of daylight from the darkening sky. The endless acres of wheat whipped and rustled, and there was no sign of her son anywhere.

She couldn't do this alone. Finally giving up, she bridled Emmanuel and galloped him hard down the muddy road. Lightning flared and touched the ground with a blinding jolt. Thunder cracked immediately overhead.

Emmanuel panicked, and she shortened the reins to keep him from bolting. Hail bit her skin and sluiced down her face. It collected at her collar and melted as Emmanuel raced up Edmund Johnson's driveway. She jumped off and charged up the steps. She banged on the door with all her might.

Hank guided the horse he'd purchased back in town down the muddy road. The hail had turned back to rain, and water rushed in currents, gaining strength. Creeks, the water gone underground for the summer, now rushed over their banks. Twice he'd had to back the palomino up a hill and find a way around a gully that now gurgled and churned.

He saw Harv and what look liked two of his oldest boys riding ahead on the road to Nettie's house. Lightning cracked, and rain beat the earth with punishing force. He lost sight of the riders ahead, but as he neared the grove of cottonwoods he saw the flash of lanterns through the black curtain of rain.

"Is that you, Hank Callahan?" Edmund Johnson padded close, pushing back the hood of his slicker just enough to see. He held up the lantern and nodded a quiet approval. "I'm glad you came. I'd hoped we could count on you. It's going to take all of us to find that little boy of Nettie's."

"Find him?" Panic beat like a drum in his chest. The bottom fell from his stomach, leaving him reeling. "What happened?"

"Don't you know? Nettie only turned around, but the boy must have taken off mighty quick." Edmund gestured with his lantern to the barn where his wife stood just inside the door, lighting lanterns for Harv and his sons. "Head over and get yourself a light. I've got the south fields covered behind the house, but we need men to walk due north on the other side of the road. I'm asking each man to search a twenty-foot strip. My boy will show you where to start"

"Nettie must be frantic. Thanks for pitching in, Johnson." There was no accusation in the man's eyes, and that felt good. "I'll get started."

Harv was not as generous. He turned his back and drew his boys away. Hank thanked Mrs. Johnson for the lantern and guided his horse through the rain. He couldn't see Nettie anywhere, and the house was lit, but no one was inside. Through the windows, he could see a young girl making sandwiches on the kitchen table.

No, Nettie would be out here in the rain, searching for her son.

A cold, eerie call rose above the crash of thunder and the hard rain. An equally chilling bark answered.

Hank shivered. Coyotes could kill a child as defenseless as Sam. They didn't usually hunt on a night like this. Another howl split the night. Hank gave his mare a firm heel and drove the tired horse back down the road and through the Fields.

"Nettie." A lantern jostled in the dark as Maude Wheaton fought the rain, mud, and slowly flooding fields to catch up with her as she headed back for the house.

"I don't have a lot of time right now, Maude. I've got to get started searching the other side of the road." Nettie slowed down when she wanted to walk faster. Not to evade her friend, but all she could think about right now was Sam. He could be hurt, afraid, and needing her.

"I wanted you to know we have hot coffee and sandwiches for everyone." Maude, clutching her slicker tight, stepped carefully through the rows of corn.

"You're a good friend." Nettie choked the words out. Hardly more than a whisper remained of her voice because her throat was raw from shouting Sam's name over the last few hours.

Rain sluiced down her face, and Nettie swiped it out of her eyes. "Are you sure you should be out in your condition? Come, I'll walk you to the house. Feel free to use my bed if you need to rest."

"I wanted you to know Hank Callahan rode in from town." Maude lowered her voice, her words nearly lost on the gusting wind. "Edmund Johnson didn't have the good sense to send him away."

"Hank came?" Nettie heard the clomp of a galloping horse and knew before her eyes found the shadowed rider that it was Hank, riding hard down the road and straight out into the fields. His light bobbed with the horse's fast gait.

Then she heard why. The eerie cries of coyotes howled with the wind and made her shiver. She dropped her lantern and ran. Emmanuel still stood bridled in the covered corral where she'd left him. She swung up and sent the gelding loping down the road.

"Nettie!" Jake Beckman skidded his mount to a stop as she charged around the grove of cottonwoods and nearly collided with him.

Emmanuel shied, but she calmed him with steady hands and a low voice, and the horse kept running. Mud splattered as the gelding churned down the straight stretch, and then jumped the rapidly rising creek. Water splashed her legs and skirt, and then rain-heavy wheat slapped her bare ankles.

If she squinted, she could just make out Hank's light in the distance. She nosed Emmanuel due north and rode him hard over the rolling hills and rain-soaked fields.

More howls and barks resounded, closer now. Nettie counted ten, maybe twenty. Excited yips that filled the night and iced the blood in her veins.

She could never live with herself if anything happened to Sam. She urged Emmanuel into a full-out gallop despite the dark and muddy ground. For three hours she'd searched without stop and she'd screamed until she was hoarse. She tried to call her son, but she could only manage a low rasp.

A gunshot rang out in the night, and the coyotes barked and yapped in protest. She heard the cries moving away, growing fainter as she skidded Emmanuel to a stop. Hank stood, leaning on his good leg, revolver gleaming darkly in the rain.

"Did you find him?" She slid to the ground, afraid of what she might see. "I can't lose him, Hank. I only turned away for a minute. Just a minute. He knows better than to run off like this—"

"I know. All I found was a shoe." He hobbled toward her, without his crutches, and lowered his gun.

Nettie cried out at the sight of Sam's left shoe dangling from the tip of Hank's forefinger. Agony knifed through her. Not her little boy! "No, it can't be—"

Hank folded her against his chest. Although he was wet through, he felt warm and safe. He smelled of autumn rain and thunder. One hand settled on the upper curve of her back and stroked small circles across her spine. His chin rubbed the top of her head, and then she could swear he'd pressed a kiss to her hair.

"We haven't found him yet, Nettie. Either way. Good news or bad news." His voice rumbled in his chest. How substantial he felt. His comfort wrapped around her like a wool blanket, warming her against the coldest of fears.

She needed a friend like this—no, she needed more than a friend. She needed a partner, a man to walk this path through life with her. To warm her. To comfort her. To stand beside her.

Although she ached for the sound of his warm, cello-smooth voice, she knew she could not linger in the shelter of his arms. She stepped away, struggling to keep a tight rein on the panic spinning through her.

"Let's search the creek bank." Hank took her hand.

Her son was out here somewhere, and no matter what, she was going to find him.

She took a step . . . and whispered a prayer.

Jake watched them search the creek where the coyotes had been hunting together. Sometimes Callahan reached out and took Nettie's hand in a squeeze of comfort. Sometimes he laid a hand on her shoulder or on the back of her neck and rubbed her gently. Jake hated the way Hank touched her as if he owned her.

Jake ground his teeth, fighting back his rage. He'd let his

impulse rule him the night he'd caught Callahan taking Nettie's horse, and look where that had got him. It was just like Nettie to get high-and-mighty instead of seeing the crux of the issue.

Hank Callahan had to leave this county, one way or another. Better feet first. Dead men couldn't talk or remember. Jake had seen it in Hank's eyes today— the bastard knew the truth. That Jake was the man the marshals were after, and he had no intention of swinging from a noose.

If he found the boy before Callahan did, then Nettie would owe him her gratitude. She would have to forgive him. She would have to see he was a decent man inside. It was just the times that were hard, that's all. He hadn't been like this when Abby lived, and he knew that when he remarried, when he could drive the demons of loneliness and grief from his life, he would be all right again.

As midnight passed, a crescent moon nudged above the horizon. The muted light silvered the land, creating more depth and more contrast to the night shades. The rain and wind had stopped. Creeks gurgled, and water droplets plopped to the earth from heavy stalks of wheat and grass.

Hank's leg ached and he shivered in the cool breeze; even if exhaustion battered him, he didn't want Nettie to know. She'd risked her reputation for his sake. If only he could do that much for her.

She rode at his side, alert as he called for the boy. Her hair had tumbled out of her single braid and had dried in the wind in light, airy curls that trailed out behind her. He could feel her keen fear. He could sense her growing panic. He didn't know how to reassure her.

Now and then he dismounted to study a track or a broken sagebrush that caught his eye. He didn't know what to tell her. He didn't know if the faint trail he lost more than once would lead them to disaster or to a little boy alive and safe.

Hank saw another print, only the side of a small toe in the thick mud. He squinted through the stalks of wheat and the thickness of bunchgrass bordering the muddy road to town. They must have traveled two miles through rolling hills and muddy fields, just to find the road again.

He drew his mare to a halt and surveyed the landscape, trying to decide where to go. The road reminded him of his life, of how it stretched before him lonely and half traveled.

What would the last half of that road be? At the bank, Barnaby had been right. Hank was like his father. He might not have killed Richard on purpose, but he had destroyed a life. No matter how sorry he was, the destructive violence inside him was his father's. They were alike despite the distance of time and miles and death.

How much control did a man have over the darkness inside of him? Was his future like this road, predestined? Did he have to walk this one road or could he abandon it for another? Could a man control what lived in his heart?

Emmanuel pricked his ears and scented the wind.

His low nicker gave Hank hope. "Loosen your hold on the reins, Nettie. Let him have his head."

"Can he scent Sam?"

"Maybe." Hank didn't dare allow even a seed of hope to take root in his chest. He watched, unable to breathe, as the powerful horse stopped in the road and turned his head. Before Hank could urge him on, he heard it too.

A small sniff. The sound of a little boy's cries.

Hank scanned the darkness. He couldn't see a child anywhere. But Emmanuel began walking, and Hank nudged his palomino after the big workhorse. Emmanuel walked up the road, then angled down the bank and into the ditch.

"Sam! Sam!" Hank called out, cupping his hands to his mouth.

A deep sob answered, and a shadow moved amid the weeds. Sam climbed to his feet, a fist rubbing his eyes, so small and dwarfed by the waning night. "I couldn't find you, Hank."

"Sam!" Nettie dropped to her knees. Tears shook her. She flung her arms around the little boy and cradled him against her chest.

Hank felt as brittle as old glass. He slipped from the horse and landed with a jolt on his good leg. Too much tangled in his throat and ached like tears.

"Hank!" Sam tore away from Nettie's grip and crashed hard into Hank's knees. Those little arms held him tight, and Sam pressed against him with need. Hank folded his arms around the boy and held on tight.

"You left me," Sam sobbed. "You left me."

Hank felt the burn of tears behind his eyes, and in that moment he knew his life could have meaning again.

"I finally got Sam to sleep." She closed the door behind her with a quiet click. The neighbors had all returned home with her thanks, although that hardly seemed adequate for all they'd done for her and for Sam.

Hank stared up at her from his place at the table, and she couldn't read his gaze. Exhaustion bruised the skin beneath his eyes but did not touch his invincible shoulders. His hair was tousled from the wind and rain and had dried into a tangle of roguish locks.

"I didn't realize he'd try to come after me." Hank wrapped his hand around a tin cup and sipped.

"I didn't realize it either." Grateful tears burned in her eyes. "Thank you for finding him."

"Emmanuel found him."

"You didn't give up."

"How could I?" He set the cup back on the table and stared into it. His silence said more than his words.

Hank Callahan was a good, honest, hardworking man who had been a friend to them those years ago. Who had helped Richard with the harvests. Who had lent a hand to roof the barn and dig the well.

Yet he was a different man now, too. Time had changed him, forged a strength in him like iron in a hot fire. He sat straighter, spoke with more command, moved with a steadiness that made her heart cinch tight.

She couldn't help noticing the man he was, handsome and rugged and beautifully made from the span of his shoulders to the hard cut of his legs. She remembered how he'd looked stripped down to his drawers, injured and asleep in her bed. Those images of bronzed skin and delineated muscle taunted her now.

Nettie snared the pitcher from the counter and filled Hank's mug. The sweet apple cider smelled so good, she poured a second cup. Maybe it would soothe her raw throat. "I owe you the moon now."

"Just the moon?" He quirked one brow. "For saving your son's life, I'd think you'd give me more than that."

Warmth bubbled inside her, a sweetness of affection that hit suddenly, like tonight's storm. Her gaze fell to his lips and remembered the moment in this kitchen when she'd sworn Hank was going to kiss her. Her lips tingled, and she realized Hank watched her mouth.

Did he want to kiss her, too? She saw the shine in his eyes and ached to know the feel of his mouth on hers. Then she shivered and realized the curtains were still open. She walked in front of the lamp and drew the ruffled pieces of calico together over the dark glass.

"It doesn't feel as safe around here as it used to." She crossed to the door and turned the bolt. "Nothing in my life has been the same since the day you came back."

"Neither has mine." He stood, the chair scraping, the cup clinking in its saucer.

"No, I guess not." She looked at him with wide eyes. Then sympathy filled them and softened her kissable mouth. "I saw Jake's horse tethered along the street as I rode out of town. Did he track you down?"

"He sure did. He seemed surprised to find out the sheriff released me." Exhaustion hung on his shoulders, heavy like hundred-pound weights. But when he looked at her, he forgot his weariness and pain. "He wasn't too happy to see I was still free to roam the streets."

"He turned you in to the sheriff."

"He wants me away from you, Nettie. For some reason, I spark his anger. I always have, I guess." Father had not been so different from Beckman. When he was in a good temper, he was charming, solid, and dependable. But when he was in a bad mood, anger and violence seemed to swallow him whole. "No man is entirely what he seems."

"I suppose no one is. At first glance." Nettie laid her small, work-rough hand over one of his.

He started at her touch but didn't pull away. He couldn't. Everything about her was so small—everything but her heart. As Hank studied the difference between her hand and his, all the reasons why he should bolt out that door seemed clear.

Gazing into the softness of her face, pretty and kind and radiating an integrity he so ached to know, Hank wanted to stay and knew he shouldn't

"It's nearly dawn." He removed his hand from Nettie's touch. "Do you want me to do the morning chores before I catch some sleep? I don't mind."

"You've done more than enough already. Besides, you looked

exhausted." She swept past, and her arm brushed his.

Lightning jolted through him, but she kept right on going. With the grace of a gentle breeze, she skirted the table and drew out the chair farthest away from him. She settled down to the table and curled her hands around her cup.

"You look exhausted, too." He cleared his throat, but the gruffness remained in his voice. "Maybe I'll just head out to the barn now."

"If you want. But after tonight, maybe you don't need to sleep out in the barn. I think for such an honored guest I can find you a more comfortable bed." She nodded toward the horsehair sofa beneath the window.

"Sleep here?"

"I would feel safer. Jake might return, and it would be better to have a locked door between us." The lamplight burned a honeyed softness into her hair and warmed her ivory skin to an attractive peach.

Hank's blood turned to fire in his veins. Even though the night had been a long one, he saw only the beauty in her. Her curls were a wild tangle of satin that made his throat go dry and his pulse race. The vulnerable tilt to her head and the shine of warmth in her eyes made him ache for more than a night spent alone on her sofa.

Hank fought the urge to reach out and comfort her. To hold her in his arms and inhale the fragrance of her hair and feel her heart beat next to his.

Lamplight caressed the side of her face as she sipped her cider, watching him with an unmistakable interest in her earth-soft eyes. She needed a man to stand by her side, to hold her all the night through, and to help her raise Sam.

But he was not the man who could.

"I'll still do the morning chores, Nettie." He hobbled to the door and opened it. Already the night grayed along the eastern horizon. "I won't be long. You go to bed. Sam will be up before you know it, and you're going to need your rest."

"You're a good man to have around."

"I'm not as shabby as some men in this world." With a wink, he stepped out into the silence. As he made his way to the barn, he felt watched. He was glad the rifle was still on the pegs above the tack room. Hank vowed to take the gun with him when he returned to the house.

"**D**o you need any help down there?" Hank's voice overhead startled her, and Nettie nearly dropped the pan full of milk.

"No." It was impossible not to remember how much she'd wanted to kiss him last night. And more impossible to make her voice sound normal. "I'm nearly done."

"I'll start cooking, then." He gazed down at her from where he knelt on the kitchen floor. His dark hair was tousled and a night's growth shadowed his jaw. "Sam has informed me that he wants pancakes."

"Pancakes, Mama." Sam's face peeked over the edge of the cellar's doorway.

"How about some fresh eggs to fry up? If Hank knows how to fix eggs."

"You're in luck. I make only the best sunny-side-up eggs this side of the Continental Divide."

"Says who?" Nettie handed up a half-dozen fresh eggs still warm from the hens.

Hank reached down and his fingers brushed hers. Shooting sparks licked her skin and she tried to ignore them. "Sam, have you washed up yet?"

"No." A guilty grin slashed his round face. "You helpin' me?"

"I'll help." Nettie grabbed the butter crock on the way up the steps.

She felt Hank's gaze on her as tangible as a breath, and she herded Sam to the basin. Her skin tingled with awareness as she began scrubbing her son's hands. Sam seemed extra needy this morning and she didn't mind giving him more hugs than usual.

Hank's pancakes were surprisingly light and tasty, and his eggs were very good. Again it was a treat not to have to eat her own cooking. It was a treat to have a man in her house and in her kitchen.

"I've been thinking," Hank began as he gathered the plates after they'd finished eating. "Since the sheriff has ordered me not to leave the county, I'm pretty much trapped here."

"Trapped, huh?" She wrung water from a washcloth and caught hold of one of Sam's sticky hands.

"I had a room in town, but I packed up and decided I like the company here better." He carried the stack of dishes the few steps to the counter. "And since I'm here, I might as well make myself useful."

"That's right. I wouldn't let you stay if I didn't have a use for you." She liked the way humor drew the fatigue from his face.

"Since I'm still hobbling, I'll volunteer to do the household chores. Just until this leg can take my weight better." He grabbed a dishpan from its shelf and filled it from the reservoir. "Do we have a deal?"

"I shouldn't let you do this." She finished wiping off Sam's other hand and then caught both little fists with a clean towel. "I've got to ride the fields and see if any of the wheat made it."

"That was a pretty hard rain, Nettie."

"I know." She released Sam, who took off at a dead run to play with his horses, and she didn't even remind him to slow down. She hung up the towel. "That wheat crop is pretty important to me. I've had two bad harvests in a row. I can't manage a third one."

"There's still the corn and the hay." Hank left the pan on the counter. "It's going to be okay. We can ride the fields together later, after the mud has had a chance to dry up."

"I'd like that." She wrapped her arms around her waist and wondered how long it had been since she'd heard those words—and believed them. "I'll be out in the garden. I've got to see if my peas survived the flood."

She headed outside, unnerved by her reaction to Hank. The fresh morning met her with the scent of a clean new day. The fields looked rumpled and beaten down, and she took a deep breath.

Although she'd only slept a few hours, she knew she would have to find a way to face the day's hard truths.

"I'm real thirsty."

Hank turned from the counter lodged against the back wall of the kitchen, drying the enamel plate in his hands. "You want me to pour you some cider?"

The boy nodded and waved the toy horses in either hand. "You goin' to town?"

"Not today, partner." Hank set the plate on the stack and grabbed a cup from the shelf. He felt awkward tending to the child, but it was an easy thing to do. He poured the cider.

"You like horses, Hank?"

Hank knelt down and offered the cup to Sam. "I sure do."

"Then could you hold 'em?"

"That I can do." Hank took both horses in hand with a clatter of wood and watched while the boy drank. That flyaway hair was plagued by an unruly cowlick.

What would have happened if he hadn't found the boy? Hank thought of the coyotes and rattlesnakes and irrigation ditches, all dangers to such a small child.

"You wanna play with me?" Hope twinkled in those dark eyes.

"Work before play." Hank traded the empty cup for the painted horses. "You wanna help me? If I get my work done, then we'll have time for your herd."

Sam clearly didn't like the idea of work, and what child should? Laughing, Hank straightened. "Tell you what, you play without me. I've got to start the laundry."

"Mama don't like to do that. She gets a hot temper." Sam shook his head once, his eyes wide as saucers.

"A hot temper, huh?" Sounded like he chose the right chore. It didn't hurt to be on Nettie's good side.

Nettie closed the gate. The bull nosed over the corral's top wooden board, his liquid brown eyes eager and begging for more attention. She could not resist scraping her short fingernails across his broad throat one more time. Ike lifted his huge head to give her better access to the spot on his chin.

She headed toward the house and froze at the sight of Hank bending over her washboard. Sam sat on the ground nearby, playing with his wooden horses.

"How did you haul all that water? Are you trying to cripple yourself?"

"Nettie." He graced her with a smile, the slow, mischievous one she was beginning to like. "The leg's mending and I made a cane. And besides, all the clothes I bought in town are wet from last night's storm."

"So, if you didn't haul and heat all this water, then you would have to go around . . . naked."

"Exactly. You should thank me."

But his jesting didn't fool her. Hank wanted to be useful. "I can take over now."

"Once I start a job, I finish it." He shook out one of Sam's shirts to inspect his work. It looked clean, so he dropped it into the rinse water.

The sun bronzed his face, drawing her gaze. His bruises had faded, and only his lip was still slightly puffy. The rich sun-browned tint of his skin contrasted against the flash of his white smile and the snap of his vivid blue eyes. A flicker of warmth skidded through her veins. She wasn't attracted to him. Really, she wasn't.

"How is your old gelding?" He arched one brow, and it softened his chiseled cheekbones and quirked up the right corner of his mouth. "He put in a hard night last night. He's an old horse, judging by the amount of white on his face."

"He's favoring his left fetlock, but I applied a salve and wrapped it. It should take down the swelling."

Hank stood and tugged his shirt over his head. The air whooshed out of her at the sight of his bare chest and shoulders.

As if unaware of her reaction, he tossed the garment into the sudsy water. "Do you need anything washed? I've got the whites boiling. Sam helped me strip both beds."

Nettie couldn't figure out a way to breathe. She opened her mouth, but nothing came out.

"Okay, then. I've got dinner set out on the table."

"Dinner? You're too good to be true." There, she'd figured out how to speak again.

"I want you to know that as soon as my leg will take harder work, I'm not going to be your housekeeper." Hank's mouth curved in a jaunty, alluring grin.

She definitely wanted to know what it would feel like to kiss those lips and that man. Blushing, she headed for the house and a little solitude. Sam was happy playing at Hank's side and hardly noticed when she brushed past him.

The house was perfect. The kitchen spotless. The table set and fresh towels covered the food—biscuits and vegetables and cold beans. The floor was swept clean.

Hank had done this. For her. Not out of guilt, as he'd wanted to do in the beginning, but because he wanted to.

The lonely places in her heart hurt a little less, and she knew then what she could give him in return.

CHAPTER NINE

Nettie watched Hank shake out the rinsed shirts before he hung them from the line. Why her stomach fluttered, she couldn't say. But it wasn't just her stomach reacting to him. Like a warm breeze to her skin, she tingled everywhere just at the sight of him.

"Mama!" Sam abandoned his herd and wrapped his arms tight around her knees. "I stay with Hank today."

"I see that." She lifted him up on her hip. "Hank, are you almost done?"

He looked over his shoulder, and his eyes darkened at her approach. She felt his gaze glide over her curves like a slow touch. "Almost."

"Good."

"Want to ride the fields? I wouldn't mind getting out on horseback." He pinned the blue shirt to the line and plucked another one from the pile.

"Do you miss ranching?"

His hand stilled. "Sometimes I miss it a lot." He grabbed another clothespin from the hanger. "When I found out I wasn't a banker at heart like my father, I bought my ranch. I suppose it's been sold, since I didn't keep up on the taxes. I should have seen to it, but I just . . . let it go."

"Bad memories?"

"Unforgivable ones." He shook out the last shirt. The sheets and petticoats and dresses flapped in the breezes. "Living on my own, I had to learn a few domestic skills."

"I'm glad you did. I don't think there's a rancher in this county who can boast about such clean whites." She liked his easy humor and the determined way he helped her out. Because he kept an eye on Sam, she'd been able to get nearly an entire day's work done in the barn.

She blushed, seeing her drawers pinned at the end of the line. "I have the horses saddled up, if you're done."

"Close enough." Hank secured the last pin. Rich brown locks tumbled into his eyes and brushed his collar. "Can Sam ride for that long?"

"He's done it before." She lowered her son to the ground. "Run inside and grab your hat. We're going riding."

"Goody." Sam ran off, and she leaned to one side to watch him hop up the stairs and into the house. She counted the seconds and then he popped back outside, his dark felt hat clutched in both hands.

Nettie plopped it on his head and took his hand. She shivered with anticipation as she led the way to the barn. The horses waited in the shade. Bessie nickered a low greeting as Sam ran up to her and held out his hand to pet her velvety nose. The old horse lipped him gently, and then Nettie lifted him up into the saddle.

Hank strolled into the barn, his hat shading his eyes and a holster strapped to his thigh. She didn't ask questions as he swung up into his saddle. The fine-blooded palomino glistened like honey when Hank guided him out into the sun. "Which way?"

"I want to see the south fields first. I'll lead." She headed Bessie east beyond the corn to where the wheat lay in acres of devastation. Proud stalks no longer undulated in the gentle breezes.

Hank swung down. His hat hid his face, and the line of his jaw looked grim. "It was a hard rain last night. Knocked a lot of wheat to the ground."

She already knew that. "It never fails. This is the third year in a row. A lot of ranchers won't be able to survive this."

"Will you?" He cocked his head to one side, his gaze riveting hers.

She shivered as if he'd touched her. "I'm not certain. Like you said, the corn is still good. And I've got hay to sell."

"Some of this will be salvageable."

She wasn't alone this time, and that made all the difference. "Mount up, and let's keep going."

He gazed off to the east, squinting against the bright sun. He had to know his land was just over the next low rise. But he turned away. "I need to get back."

She wasn't fooled. He didn't want to see what had been lost and what had stayed the same. "It's still yours. Robert must be paying the taxes on it. He comes out here now and again, just to check on things."

"Robert?"

"He wanted to keep the land for you, in case you ever decided to return."

Hank stared eastward a long time. "He told you that?"

"Yes. One day he stopped by to see if I needed any help." She urged Bessie closer. "I agreed to keep my eye on the place and let him know if there were any problems, like squatters or vandals. Would you like to see it?"

He nodded; it was all he could manage. He swung up into the saddle and urged the mare past Nettie. He couldn't quite look her in the eye. He couldn't find the words to thank her for letting him know that after all this, he hadn't lost what mattered to him the most.

The land stretched out before him, golden and captivating. He loved the smell of it—rain-soaked earth and sage and sunshine. The wind dusted his face, hot and steady. The light burned so bright it hurt his eyes.

"Maybe you belong here, Hank." Nettie's arm brushed his sleeve.

"Maybe." He wanted to draw her against him and discover the taste and feel of her mouth. He wanted to loosen those prim buttons marching down the front placket of her blue gingham dress.

Instead, he gathered the reins and headed his mare toward the gentle rise that divided his land from hers. He urged the palomino into a trot, and air breezed across his face but could not dissipate the strange new feelings snapping to life in his heart.

"I got the reins, Mama." Sam's fingers clamped down hard on the leather straps.

"You sure do." Sun-kissed and merry, Nettie ran a hand over

the boy's unruly cowlick. "Don't pull too hard now, or Bessie won't like it."

Watching mother and son, Hank's throat filled and he had to look away.

"There it is." She breathed, and he felt changed at the sight in front of him.

Bunchgrass had overtaken the fields, and wildflowers bloomed with a rich vibrancy of yellows, purples, and whites against the shivering green-gold grass. A doe lifted her head to study them, frozen and ready to flee. Two fawns huddled at her side.

"Look at the deer, Sam."

"There's three of 'em."

"That's right."

Hank's heart filled, and he was glad that Nettie was at his side. He gazed out at his land, unable to move, breathe, or even think. Too much moved inside him—emotions so long buried.

After two years of isolation, he'd come home.

Nettie lifted Sam down to the weed-thick yard. What was once a neat, cared-for garden had gone wild, and the once freshly whitewashed home was now weathered and forgotten. The look of abandonment was everywhere, but the house was in good shape, left untouched all this time. Sam toddled straight into the waist-high grass, becoming instantly lost from her sight; she ran after him.

"I can't believe this is still mine." Hank cleared his throat but couldn't clear the gruffness from his voice.

"Believe it." Nettie kept an eye on Sam as he ran in irregular circles through the tall grass. "How does it feel?"

"Wonderful." Hank looked away from her. She could only see his throat work. "I've missed this place, the work, everything."

"I know what you mean. I think I would shrivel up without the sun on my face and the wide-open spaces." There was no mistaking the light that glinted in his eyes, and for once he looked like a man at peace. "Will you stay now?"

"I never dreamed that I could come back." He jammed his hands in his pockets.

"You could have stayed in the hotel in town, but you came back to my ranch. I think it's because you missed this."

"No, I came back for you, Nettie." Tension gathered in his jaw, and a muscle quivered there.

She didn't know what to say, and yet she wished Hank would tell her what he was thinking. He was holding something back. Something about Jake. And that was the reason why Hank had returned.

"Come inside with me." He tried the carved door. "It's locked."

"Robert would have a key."

"Not necessary." Happiness flashed in his eyes like sunlight on water, and he knelt beside the overgrown garden. He removed a big rock and withdrew a dirt-caked key. "It's still here."

His grin was contagious, and she found herself following him, just to be close. She called Sam out of the grass.

He emerged carrying a long twig he'd found. He ran past her. "Hank, see my stick?"

"I see." Hank ruffled Sam's head and together they climbed the steps. Side by side they stood, the big man and the small boy. Hank unlocked the door and the hinges creaked from disuse. Sunlight fell through the windows and lighted wide swatches on the dusty floor.

Once Hank's caring hand had sawed these walls and nailed them, had fit the doors and the windows. Nettie could still see that care. Inside, Hank stood with his back to her. She could hear his stunned silence.

She shouldered around him. She saw light, honeyed wood and more dust than she'd ever imagined. "I've never been inside your house before."

"It's just the way I left it." His gaze lingered on the gray stone hearth where a shirt hung beneath the mantel, drying before a fire that had long since burned out.

"Robert came by after you left and cleaned out the pantry and locked everything up." Nettie had never seen such a beautiful house. "You built this yourself."

"Just me and a hammer. I hired a carpenter to help me with the rafters, but that's all." A small piece of pride rang in that voice. He crossed the parlor with slow steps, leaving footprints in the dust on the floor. He looked like a man who'd lost his dreams—and then found them.

The boom of nearby gunfire ricocheted through the house and shattered the quiet. Nettie snatched Sam and pulled him into her arms. Hank whirled around, hand on his revolver, and strode to the door.

"Stay here." His command boomed both with authority and concern. His steps knelled on the porch, and then faded.

"What is it, Mama?"

"The sound of trouble." She leaned out the door far enough to see past the side of the house. She saw Hank standing tall with his back to the sun, legs braced, revolver in hand.

A distant shot fired again.

Nettie stepped away from the door as Hank hopped back onto the porch. "There's trouble over at the McCullen ranch."

"I'm going with you. A thief has never struck in the light of day—"

"You'll be safer keeping away." He nodded at the wide-eyed little boy clinging to her skirts. "I've got a bad feeling. McCullen needs help."

"Be careful, Hank." A shivery foreboding wrapped around her spine, and she didn't want to let him go. But neighbors helped neighbors in this part of the country. "You're not alone either."

"That's good to know." He tipped his hat to her, and when he walked away, her heart lifted.

She couldn't help watching him through the window as he mounted his golden horse and rode into the sun, a man of substance and might.

Hank knew he was in trouble the instant a bullet whizzed past his head.

"Don't shoot!" he shouted, but was met with another bullet that dug into the earth in front of his horse. "I said, don't shoot!"

He could see the old man holding a rifle in the wide door of the barn. Even in the shadows, the barrel caught bright sunlight. McCullen didn't shoot again but didn't lower his weapon either.

That was at least an improvement. Hank urged his mare forward when she balked. She apparently didn't like bullets flying at her any more than he did.

"Is that you, Callahan?" The wizened old man remained in the shadows.

Hank could feel that Winchester trained on him.

"I was over at my place and heard gunfire. Thought you might have some trouble and need a hand."

"Now don't that beat all?" McCullen limped out of the cover of the barn. "I wouldn't have believed it if I hadn't seen it for myself. I could have sworn you were the one who stole my horses. My only matched set. My wife's pride and joy."

"Me?"

"Everyone said you rode to town on a bay. And you left this." McCullen tossed him a belt buckle. The silver rectangle flew through the air.

Hank caught it and recognized it. "Father gave this to me. It has my name engraved on the back. I had it in my saddlebags when I came to town."

"Yep. Figured it fell off when you were runnin' from my bullets. But you rode off that way." The old man pointed in the opposite direction, toward the ragged Blue Mountains cresting the horizon. "Not two minutes later, you come from over there. Now somethin' ain't quite right here."

"I didn't steal your horses."

"Don't see how you could. Thought for sure you were back to your old ways, but this makes me think. Let me saddle up, and we'll see where those tracks lead. My wife wants her horses back."

"Yes, sir." Hank studied the tracks through the tall grass marking Jake Beckman's escape.

Now, all he had to do was prove it.

It was the heat of the day when Nettie returned home. She opened up the house to the breezes, with Sam protesting all the way. He wanted Hank. He wanted to go to Hank. He wanted up on Bessie so they could go find Hank.

"But Sam, it's time to feed the babies. Can you hear them bawling?" It took her a while to talk him into helping her feed the orphaned calves.

Bessie on her picket line in the shade watched with hopeful eyes, for there was always the chance of more grain. Cows lowed to her in the pasture to remind her that the water trough was getting low.

Once inside the dim barn, the calves bleated hungrily. "See? We need to feed those babies."

"Hank ain't here yet." Sam sighed.

Nettie's heart cinched up tight as she filled the buckets in the storeroom. She couldn't forget the image of Hank as he rode away today. He'd been gone a long while. She feared what kind of trouble he'd ridden into.

She hoped Jake had nothing to do with it. She tried not to think of all that could have gone wrong as she tugged open the wooden planks fronting the box stall.

Two hungry little calves stuck their desperate tongues into her skirt and grabbed hold.

"Over here, little ones." She knelt down, careful not to spill the buckets.

The tiny calves, not much bigger than leggy dogs, nudged her hungrily. Sam stuck his hand through the slats of the pen, and the lighter-brown calf's tongue shot out to lick those little fingers.

Sam giggled. "Sugar likes me."

"She sure does." Nettie placed her palm on the eager calf's wet nose, slipped her fingers into his mouth, and lowered her hand to one bucket. The calf slurped the milk, and Nettie managed to extricate her fingers.

"Sam, come help me hold the bucket."

"I comin', but Sugar's kissin' me again." The little boy dropped to his knees as the calf's tongue lashed at his cheek. He giggled.

"Sugar, I have your dinner over here." She waited until both of Sam's hands were splayed around the smooth wood of the first pail before she grabbed the second bucket of milk and helped the other calf.

But Sugar had other ideas and kissed Nettie's chin. A soft, shifting step sounded behind her. "I'm jealous of that little calf."

Tiny tingles danced all over her skin. The calf took advantage of her inattention and dived for her jaw. Wet, warm, whiskery lips found suction on her collar and held on hard. Laughing, she managed to slip two fingers into the calf's mouth and lower her to the milk bucket.

"It's me. Safe and sound, just like I promised."

"Hank! Hank!" Sam jumped to his feet. "I helpin'."

"You're such a big help, too." Hank's low, cello-smooth voice slipped down Nettie's spine.

She grabbed hold of Sugar's bucket just as Spice began slurping the last of the milk from the bottom of his pail. In seconds it was empty. "Sam, take this bucket for me."

Did she dare turn around? No, Hank would see the relief in her eyes. A relief so big she shook with it and so intense her eyes burned. She'd been really worried about him. She nudged the empty pail behind her, but the calf wasn't ready to give up that bucket and grabbed hold of Nettie's collar.

"Here." Hank knelt down beside her, the straw crackling beneath his weight.

His presence shivered over her like a late summer wind—slow and casual and heated. His shoulder brushed hers, and she could smell the sunshine in his hair and the fragrance of warm horse and fresh wildflowers on his clothes.

Sugar began knocking her bucket into Nettie's knee, clearly done with her milk and unhappy about it. An unexpected giggle tickled in her throat.

As one calf began battering her pail, the little bull sank his teeth into Nettie's collar and refused to let go. She started to chuckle, then laugh, and then howl. Tears welled in her eyes. Spice took a step back, releasing his stranglehold on her dress.

Nettie slid her fingers into the little one's mouth and let the grain roll down onto the eager tongue.

Sedated by grain, Spice calmed down and chewed.

Hank brushed a piece of straw from her hair. "Do you always have this much trouble?"

"Not until now."

His mouth was a whisper away from hers. Nettie couldn't help noticing the way his lips looked soft, touched by an alluring grin. Amusement snapped in his vivid eyes, and his gaze caressed the curves of her face like a lover's touch. He stared hard at her lips.

They tingled, and she licked them. "Sam is here."

"I know. It's all that's holding me back." Hank watched her with those intense eyes, making it clear what he wanted.

She ached to lean against the steely span of his chest. But she wanted more than a hug of comfort, as he'd given her before. She wanted the kiss his eyes had promised—sweet and passionate and slow. It took all her willpower to stand.

Hank groaned as she moved away.

Sam giggled with delight as the tiny calves warred with each other for his attention. Nettie grabbed the buckets and set them outside the door to wash later.

"I just came by to tell you, McCullen and I are heading to town to see the sheriff." Hank followed her.

"Why? What happened?" Nettie checked to make sure Sam was busy and couldn't hear.

"Apparently I stole McCullen's horses—"

"You were with me." Anger flared, and she felt more than the need to defend an innocent man. "I'll tell the sheriff—"

"He'll probably want you to verify my whereabouts, but I don't think there will be trouble." Hank curled his fingers around her hand. "Even McCullen could see someone is trying to blame these thefts on me. I might have the chance to clear my name. A man can't ask for anything more than that."

"Do you know who's really doing the stealing?"

"I have my suspicions." Hank's jaw tensed. "McCullen and I followed the trail all the way to the river, but we lost the tracks in the water. Someone is using my old horse, the one I lost when Beckman and his friends ganged up on me."

"You suspect Jake." She hated saying the words.

"It's just my hunch. I won't accuse a man until he can be proven guilty." Hank looked grim. He pulled her close, and she went willingly against his chest. "Now it's in the sheriff's hands."

"I worried about you the entire time you were gone."

His chin grazed the top of her head before he let her go. "That's good to know, Nettie. I thought about you, too. About doing this."

He traced his thumb across her lips, leaving fire burning where he touched. Then he leaned forward and fit his mouth to hers. His kiss was both hot and sweet. He tasted like the wind. His kiss was a quick caressing brush, and when she feared he would end it, he returned with a long tender pressure that parted her lips. He stepped away, leaving her trembling.

"Yep, that's exactly what I was thinking about." His eyes sparkled.

She felt the earth give away beneath her feet. He walked away, leaving her reeling.

After seeing the sheriff, Hank rode his new mare down tree-lined lanes. Regal, proud homes faced the street, distinctive and genteel. He stopped in front of an elegant two-story Colonial brushed white and ringed with a carefully tended garden. Flowers lined the yard and walk, providing bright splotches of color. The yard was neat and lovingly tended. He took a deep breath and guided his horse into the driveway.

He swung down, tethered his mare, and then hesitated on the brick steps. What if Robert didn't want to see him? Hank rapped his knuckles against the painted door-frame and waited. The door tugged open.

A soft-faced woman in a finely tailored sateen dress looked up at him. She held a red-faced infant in her arms. "Can I help you?"

Did he have the right house? "I'm looking for Robert Callahan. I'm his brother."

"You look so much like him. And like your father. Please, won't you come in?" She stepped back, trying to comfort the baby in her arms. "I'll let Robert know you're here."

Hank hobbled over the threshold and into the elegant, dark-wood foyer. His pulse thudded in his ears and he shifted his weight. A movement at the end of a long hallway drew his gaze. Robert strode confidently toward him with steady eyes that revealed little of what he was thinking.

Silence stretched between them. Hank didn't know what to say or how to begin.

The baby cried from several rooms away, a sharp unhappy sound that was quickly comforted.

"You look good, Robert."

"I heard you got hurt pretty badly. I didn't know about it until after—" He shrugged, ducking his chin as if ashamed. "I would have taken you in had I known. Where have you been staying?"

"With Nettie Pickering."

Robert lifted one brow. "I heard some rumors, but you know I didn't believe them. I never did."

"You've been paying the taxes on my land."

"Someone had to." Robert almost smiled. "I figured you might want to come back someday when the time was right."

"Papa." A little boy, younger than Sam, with a head of curly dark hair and a solemn frown toddled into view from the end of the hallway where Robert had come from. His blue shirt matched his eyes.

"William." Robert knelt down to snatch up his son.

"You have a family."

"Yes." Robert's gaze matched his. "This is your nephew. You've already met your new niece."

"Not formally."

His younger brother smiled. "Then maybe you had best come back to the kitchen. I don't believe you've formally met my wife either."

Years of distance stood between them, and yet all felt changed. Hank followed his brother down the hallway past the staircase and into a light-filled kitchen.

Robert's wife sat in a brocaded chair in the corner that looked out on a prolific flower garden, the baby still cradled in her arms.

"Hank, come in and meet Ella, my new daughter, and Marie, my wife," Robert invited with an easy grin. There were no shadows in his eyes or hints of unhappiness.

"I'm so glad to finally meet you." Marie stood, her manner shy but kind. "I was just about to start supper. Would you like to join us?"

"Please stay, brother." Robert's hand cupped Hank's shoulder.

Robert had a family. How could Hank say no?

The early evening light sprinkled cool shadows across the yard as he circled the grove of cottonwoods. The first thing Hank saw was Nettie kneeling in her garden. Sam was a few feet away, in her sight, digging in the dirt with a stick.

"Hank!" Sam hopped to his feet and came running.

Hank swung down, so the mare wouldn't startle, and scooped the boy up in his arms.

"You're mine." Sam wrapped his arms hard about Hank's neck.

He felt a cold patch of his heart melt a little. The boy spotted the calico kitty and wanted down. He dashed away, kneeling to pet the animal.

"How did it go with the sheriff?" Nettie stood, brushing dirt and leaves from her checkered skirts. She cocked her head, searching his face, her concern and interest unmistakable. In the mild evening light, she approached him with the breeze ruffling her skirts and the tendrils at her brow.

She looked like a dream.

Robert had a family. There were no signs of Father's legacy in that house. No tension so stark and loveless. No fear in a little boy's round eyes.

Hank had to wonder. He had to hope. Could he do the same?

Desire for Nettie twisted down deep inside, hard and hot and sudden.

"You're just in time." The tip of her tongue flicked out to brush her bottom lip, a nervous gesture. Her gaze fastened on his mouth.

He cupped his hand around the back of her neck and kissed her hard enough so she knew he had no regrets. So she knew she was the one he wanted— only her. She responded with a tiny moan, and she opened her lips at the brush of his tongue.

"It's Sam's bath and bedtime." She smiled at him, breaking away. Her cheeks were flushed and her eyes dark with want.

His stomach twisted with a strong, sharp need. He didn't want to stop kissing her, but Sam was running toward them, and before he knew it, he'd volunteered to haul water.

"See, I'm dirty." Sam held out two grubby hands.

"You are very dirty," Nettie agreed, laughing down at the dried mud staining his little drawers. She swung him up onto her slim hip.

The night breezes stilled, as did his heart. She swept up the steps, her skirts hugging her slim legs, her voice a gentle melody as she carried her son into the house, leaving Hank alone in the webby twilight.

"One more story," Sam begged, smelling of fresh soap. "Please?"

"You already got one more story than your mother said." It wasn't easy to say no, but it was getting late. Exhaustion shadowed the boy's face. "Go to sleep, and I promise I'll read another story to you tomorrow."

"But I wanna another now, Hank." Sam yawned, already halfway asleep.

"Tomorrow. I promise." He tucked the sheets beneath the boy's chin and turned down the light.

Darkness cloaked the room, and he found the door by feel. Sam was already asleep, so Hank closed the door without another word.

He heard a splash of water and the strike of a match. A small light leaped to life in the kitchen on the other side of the wall. Glass chinked and the light strengthened.

Hank made his way to the sofa, intending to start the book he'd picked up on his shopping trip in town. But the lick of light radiating from around the corner of the room cast eerie, ghostlike images across the simple plank floor.

Then Nettie's silhouette flashed through the light. Heaven help him, but he couldn't force his gaze away from the beautiful shadow of her naked body, brushed by the lamp and cast along the floor.

Her forehead was a soft line and her nose a gentle slope. Her lips were full but delicately cut, even in shadow. Her chin was not too small and gave way to her curving neck. She reached up and released her hair, and it cascaded down her neck to cloak the pebbled peaks of her full breasts.

He squeezed his eyes shut. He heard the whisper of cotton puddling on the floor. He heard a series of splashes. He opened his eyes to see her perfect breasts for two long seconds before she disappeared from his sight with a slosh of water against the brim of the tub.

Desire arrowed through him, and he realized how fast his heart was beating and how quick his breaths. A hot need for her burned, as steady as the surest flame. How he wanted her. Only her. He'd seen the look in her eyes after they'd kissed. Did she want him? He didn't know. But he was about to find out.

He took one step forward, then another. He watched her silhouette on the floor in front of him. Finished with washing her hair, she lifted a pitcher high overhead. Water splashed and chimed. He propped his shoulder against the wall, afraid his knees might give out, and watched.

Her hair sheened in the low lamplight as if laced with diamonds. Her skin wore those same diamonds, winking in the light. She looked satin-soft everywhere, and he ached to kneel down before the tub and touch all of her.

Instead, he snared the towel from the table and shook it out. She did not stiffen, although she didn't move. If she wanted him to leave, she would have said it by now. Blood thickening, he knelt at her side. Water brushed the top curves of her breasts and glistened on her shoulders and throat.

Her eyes met his, a little shy, but the want burning in those dark depths was unmistakable. "You found my towel."

"Thought you might need it"

"Are you sure about that?" Her chin trembled a little when she spoke.

"Yes." He brushed the curls out of her eyes with the palm of his hand to her brow. She felt hot and sweet and looked so vulnerable. "I'm going to have to dry you off to make love to you. Unless you want water all over your floor."

Her teeth caught hold of her bottom lip and she chewed on it; then she smiled. "That would be a terrible thing. I'd better let you dry me off."

"I thought you might say that."

She stood with a splash. Water sloshed over the rim. Light glistened on her wet skin and brushed her soft breasts, pink-tipped and lush. Breasts he ached to caress with his hands and stroke with his tongue. He grew hard as she stepped out of the tub and into the towel he held.

Her dark gaze met his, and she seemed to understand his question. Desire darkened her eyes and drew a mysterious smile to her lips.

They needed no words as he wrapped the towel around her slim body and pulled her into his arms.

CHAPTER TEN

Lamplight cast a soft sepia glow over the dark richness of her curls and her damp skin. Her teeth caught her bottom lip again in a nervous gesture.

It wasn't easy for her to love again or to take this risk. His breath rattled in his chest when she took hold of the button at the hollow of his throat. She tugged and the fabric gave way.

Buttons whispered through their buttonholes once, twice, three times. Her gaze met his with a brazen request that sent fire through his veins, throbbing and powerful.

His fingers bumped hers as he popped off the last buttons and shrugged out of the shirt. He watched her gaze trace the width of his chest. Her fingers splayed out and settled timidly against his breastbone.

"You're so hard." Those fingers spread and began to stroke.

Something warm and sweet exploded deep in his heart. He squeezed his eyes shut, and no matter how much he wanted to touch her in the same way, he fisted his hands and let her fingers roam the lines of his shoulders with her warm damp hand.

He didn't dare move. He was afraid to break the spell. She splayed clever and caressing hands across his chest Her fingers curled into the downy spray of hair there. Want for her skidded through him like a shooting star through the night, bright and lustrous and falling. That was how she made him feel.

He clenched his jaw and fought for control as her hands stroked over his chest and explored the line of his shoulders with tender brushes of her feather-soft fingers.

Her touch was not hurried, and he felt the tension gather in his muscles. Cords strained in his neck. He clenched his jaw tight when her hand snaked down his abdomen in soft, tantalizing circular strokes that ended at the waist of his denims.

"I can take those off," he leaned to whisper.

"Yes." Her cheek brushed his jaw. "But I could do it for you."

"But then I'd lose the little bit of control I have left." His lips grazed her temple. He breathed in her mint soap and sweet woman scent, and desire for her thudded in his groin. He pressed another kiss to her brow, and her arms wrapped around his neck.

"It's been so long for me." She brushed her lips to his. "I've wanted to feel this again. All of it."

There was no better invitation than that. He ran his finger across the top of her knotted towel, against soft heated skin and the top curves of her breasts.

In answer her fingers tugged at the button at his waistband. Desire pulsed through him, hard and rhythmic. Want felt like liquid heat in his veins. Her shy boldness was going to be the death of him.

Her fingers caught the edges of his trousers and drawers and eased them off his hips. His erection sprang free as he stepped out of the last of his clothes. He watched her eyes widen.

Seconds pulsed as he waited, hands fisted and he braced.

Then he held out his hand, and she laid her palm in his. His groin kicked, thrumming with a building need. He could feel the calluses marking the base of her fingers. Despite the hard ranching work she did daily, her skin was silken heat and satin smooth. She was fragility and strength, iron and sweetness.

He caressed her palm with his fingertips. He traced the row of calluses and the length of each finger. He explored the rays of lines cut into her palm and the sensitive spot between her thumb and forefinger.

He brought her hand to his lips and explored those same places with his tongue.

She moaned low in her throat.

"You like that?"

She smiled, so he fit his mouth to hers and tasted her. She

responded with a tilt of her head, bringing them more completely together. Tongues brushed and glided and teased. Her hands curled around his shoulders and held on tight. On a moan, he laved her full bottom lip and then dipped inside he mouth. She met his every caress, and soon her breath came as fast as his. She arched against him. Need curled around the base of his spine.

He moaned as she lifted her mouth from his. Something dark and beautiful shimmered in her eyes. His words came ragged and rough as he cupped the fine curve of her jaw. "We can go to the bedroom if you want. It would be more comfortable."

"I don't care about comfort right now."

"Then you don't mind the table after all."

"No. As long as I'm with you."

He pressed a kiss to her mouth, then nibbled down the column of her throat. He lingered in the hollow between her collarbones where her pulse beat wildly. He cupped the nape of her neck, tangled his fingers in her drying curls, and breathed in their sweetness.

"All I want is you, Hank." She brushed her hand down his throat, fingers splayed, over his chest, and then down his abdomen.

She caressed his stomach and he had to wonder how much more she intended to stroke. He drew in a ragged breath of air. Her knuckles brushed the head of his shaft, and he groaned.

Nettie shivered, aware of the way he wanted her, of how they wanted each other. Want pooled low in her belly. She was breathing hard, and the need to be joined with him thundered through her. He was hot male flesh and iron-hard muscle. She couldn't help the way her hips arched, aching for the feel of him.

"This is driving me crazy." His hand curved over the ball of her shoulder. "You know that."

"Yes."

"I can't wait much longer. Not without taking you in my arms and laying you down on the floor and—"

"Not the table?" She meant to tease.

But Hank didn't grin, didn't even smile. "Why not? It looks more comfortable than the floor."

Her gaze drifted downward to study his erection. The swollen, rounded tip beckoned her. Her throat went dry, and her pulse quickened. She ached to curl her fingers around that part of him. "You can't wait much longer. And neither can I—"

Hank wrapped his big hand around the back of her head and pulled her into another kiss. His kiss was demanding, just short of bruising. His lips caressed and molded, sucked and slid across hers with a boldness that left her breathless.

Heat shot through her at the heady, tantalizing caress of his lips to hers. He stroked and laved and drew her to his chest. She felt the hard length of his shaft nudge the low curve of her stomach.

Sharp, sweet, agonizing pleasure streaked through her abdomen. She pressed against him, until only her towel separated them. She could feel every plane and curve of his body, every detail. She shook with the need to do more than kiss him.

But his other hand cupped the side of her face, holding her captive as he deepened the kiss with a melding of lips and passion. Nettie ached from her scalp to her toes, and burned in between.

And as if oblivious to her need, Hank's silken-damp tongue slipped in and out of her mouth as if they had all the time in the world.

"I want you." She blurted the words. "Please, now."

"But I'm not through with you yet." He moved away, and lamplight burnished his bronzed skin, worshiping every hard plane and curve and his thick, jutting shaft.

Beneath her towel, her skin prickled with anticipation.

"I don't want you to regret this come morning." His thumb caressed the length of one collarbone.

She placed her hand flat on his chest and felt the last of his words resonate beneath her palm. "I've made up my mind, Hank. I want you more than I've ever wanted anyone."

Seriousness glinted in his eyes. "As much as I want you right now, I'm afraid you might regret this. Maybe you want to think over what we're about to do. I don't want you hurt."

"Then stop making me wait."

"As you wish."

Hank ran his fingers across the top of the towel and his thumb slid inside the fabric to brush the dip between her breasts. The tucked ends of the towel parted and eased off her chest. With a slight shrug the linen shivered down over her hips and thighs and out of sight.

Naked, she shivered. Desire twisted tighter, hard and low. How she ached for him. How she needed him. His fingers clamped on her right thigh and drew her leg over his, and she leaned into him.

The root of his thick shaft met her moist heat. Sensation rolled over her in fiery waves. Desire thundered through her until every part of her body felt throbbing and heavy.

He backed her the few short steps to the table. His hands cupped the backs of her thighs, and he lifted her onto the surface. The polished wood felt cool against her heated skin. Sitting up, she parted her knees and he moved between them. He lowered his mouth to hers.

Air rattled in her chest and she traced her fingernails down the length of his chest and over his washboard-firm abdomen. His hard shaft pulsed against her hand. She closed her fingers around its thickness.

"Nettie," he murmured, his voice rough.

She held him boldly, feeling the rock-hard firmness expand with each heartbeat. She moved her fingers down the length of his shaft.

He moaned and kissed her hard. His hands brushed up her sides, and his thumbs lightly grazed the outside curves of her breasts. She trembled with a powerful rush of need and desire. Heat coiled in sharp, delicious anticipation.

When he placed a hot kiss between her breasts, a sharp gasp escaped from her throat. She wanted more. Much more. She arched against him, hungry and asking for more of his touch, and he obliged. He splayed his fingers over her breast, and electricity jolted down her spine. He leaned forward and caught a nipple with his tongue, drawing it into his hot mouth.

Pleasure rippled through her, pulsing low in her abdomen and gathering between her thighs. Lost in sensation, she felt him roll his tongue around her nipple and she gasped again, moaning his name. Her fingers crept over his steely shoulders to cup the back of his head. Moaning, she held him to her breast. Her thighs gripped his hips hard, and not even air separated them.

With a final flick of his tongue, Hank lifted his mouth from her breast, but his hands continued to caress her. His fingers played along the low curve of her stomach, then dipped lower to brush between her thighs. Nettie could not stop the quaking need clenched tight inside, growing more urgent with every breath, and she shuddered at his intimate touch.

White-hot pleasure speared through her in one electric jolt after another. Her head fell back and her eyes drifted shut, battered by the sharp edge of all-consuming pleasure. She lay back on the table, melting at his touch. He leaned over her. His shaft nudged at her inner thigh. His kiss grazed her collarbone and then the sensitive underside of her chin. She shivered, lost and aflame.

She looked up at him. He watched her, and desire sizzled in his eyes. Desire that was enormous and unmistakable and all for her. His hands gripped her hips, and she opened to him. She felt the hot nudge of his shaft against her wetness and then his slow intrusion. Sweet heaven, but it was exquisite torture. She cried out at the way he filled her inch by slow inch. She gripped his low back and pulled him into her. His hot thickness filled her completely.

He pinned her against the table, and she arched into him, pulling him closer and deeper. But it wasn't enough. She wrapped her legs around his hips and crossed her ankles, holding him there. In answer, he started a slow, teasing withdrawal, and his hard heat stroked inside her.

They moved together, and he began a deep, sweet rhythm. She met his thrusts, tottering on the edge of control. She could feel that final, elusive pleasure, just out of reach. He held her tight and pumped harder. She felt a deep warmth twisting there, where they joined, and release hammered through her in great, white-hot flashes. She cried out as her body clenched and released. Delicious spirals of pleasure licked through her in sharp waves, one after another, twisting and aching and glorious.

She saw Hank's face grimace and heard the moan in his throat. His body tensed and he thrust with short, hard strokes. Still breathless from her own release, she felt him swell inside her and spill his seed in one long hot pulse. Trembling with emotion, she closed her eyes.

His hand touched her cheek, soft like morning rain, gentle and welcoming. And loving.

Hank pressed a kiss to her lips, a masculine sweetness that made her want to love him all over again. But he cradled her against him.

Eyes stinging, she buried her face in the crook of his neck and shoulder and held him with all her strength. He was like a balm to the wound of the last few years of hardship and loneliness, and she felt healed. No longer empty, but whole.

She loved him. She would always love him. He had taken a part of her heart no other man could ever claim.

He couldn't take his gaze from her. The soft lamp's glow shivered over her in undulating caresses and brushed her creamy breasts with shadowed light A satisfied smile played along her mouth, and her eyes twinkled with a quiet happiness.

"This table is putting a crick in my back."

"Roll over and I'll kiss it away."

Her smile widened. "I want more than just a kiss."

"That can be arranged." Happiness glowed in his belly, like a buried ember exposed to the air. It crackled to life and burned more brightly with each passing movement. He bent to roll his tongue around her nipple. "Maybe we should try a more comfortable place."

She moaned, shivered, and her tight muscles still gloving him clenched hard. "The sofa?"

"No. I want to make love to you in bed. Long and slow and all through the night. How does that sound?"

"Like heaven." She sighed.

He moved away from her, withdrawing until they were no longer joined.

"Wait." Her fingers caught his, as if she couldn't bear to be separated either.

She led the way across the room and down the dark hallway, moving through the shadows. Even though it was dark, his blood pulsed at the sight of her shadowed back and softly curving fanny. She pushed open her bedroom door, and weak moonlight glowed on the small glass panes.

He heard crisp muslin sheets rustle. The ropes creaked slightly as she settled on the feather tick. She gazed up at him with need-filled eyes. He saw the curling luxury of her hair dark against the snowy-white pillow slip. He saw the rise of her breasts and the length of her thighs as she held out her arms, welcoming him to her bed.

There was no need for words. He went to her and covered her body with his. She was wet and ready, and he was as hard as steel.

The mattress rustled with his weight as he stretched out over her. She was satin heat against his bare chest and abdomen, and softer still against his shaft and thighs. He kissed her lovingly and brushed tangled curls from her eyes.

She tasted like desire, honeyed and hot. She felt more

substantial than dreams. She pulled away, her eyes alight with promises of passion.

"Love me," she whispered, her sweet breath hot against his lips. She lifted her knees, cradling him between her thighs.

He filled her in one thrust. She was hot and tight, wanton and sweet. He balanced his weight on his elbows so his hands were free to hold her face as his mouth found hers. His stomach fell with a twisting sensation. Nettie arched up to match his thrusts, release crashing through her. Like a sudden storm, Hank felt that same thrilling pleasure rush through him.

Love so powerful that it hurt twisted in his chest. She had given him this feeling, this greatness, this love. Unable to speak, he kissed her lips, her face, and her throat. He held her until she was ready to love him all over again.

Hank woke to a soft glow of peach light sweeping through the single window. He heard a rooster crow and the chirp of busy robins. Nettie slept beside him curled on her side, her untamed tresses spilling across her pillow and down her back. The white sheet puddled at her waist, covering the curves of her hips and thighs from view. He smelled the soap in her hair.

He sat up. Memories of last night returned, one after another. They'd made love half the night, and he had no regrets. He hoped Nettie didn't, either. He could hear the quiet rhythm of her breathing, and it tugged at his heart. Suddenly, the first light of day hurt his eyes. Hating to leave her, he stood and pulled on his clothes.

He nudged open the bedroom door and checked on Sam. The boy lay curled up in his bed, breathing gently, his thumb in his mouth. Hank knew that if he stayed and loved Nettie the way he wanted to, then the boy would be his son one day.

The thought thrilled him and frightened him. Troubled, he tugged the door shut and headed out to the barn. Already the arid climate had wrung all the dampness from the earth. Dust kicked up beneath his boots.

The bull watched him with curious eyes. Bessie nickered to him from her stall. He fed the animals and cleaned their pens.

He was just measuring out the grain for the milk cow when Nettie appeared with Sam and the milk bucket in tow. She looked as fresh as morning and twice as desirable. Her hair fell softly around her oval face, tied back with a single ribbon. Small dark curls framed her eyes and darkened their luxurious softness.

She flashed him a wide smile. "It's good to see you up and around."

"It feels good to be doing regular chores, instead of the cooking and laundry." He winked, and he felt so happy.

"Is there any pain in that leg?"

"Not too much."

Sam dashed up, the brim of his cowboy hat flopping. "I gonna help you."

"Me? Not your mama?"

Sam wrapped both arms around Hank's good leg and held tight.

Hank's heart warmed. "Then I guess I could use some help. Here, do you want to help me hitch up the team?"

"Goody. Are we goin' to town?"

"Nope. I'm starting the second cutting of hay." Hank watched Nettie set the stool in the cow's pen.

She tilted her head, her braid falling over her shoulder. He remembered her astride him last night, her head thrown back as she strove toward her release. The memory robbed the breath from his lungs. His blood thickened, and he wanted to love her that way again.

"You're going to cut my hay?" She leaned one slim elbow on the top rail of the pen. "Just you, huh? What about the household chores you said you'd stick to until your leg was stronger?"

"It feels stronger."

She frowned at him, quirking one slim brow in disbelief.

That's when he knew he was in trouble.

"Whose farm is this?" She studied him with a sparkling humor.

Oh, he could see where she was heading. "Yours, and you know it."

"And you just assigned yourself to haying my fields." Her eyes raked his with both amusement and a steady truth. "Maybe you should think about mowing your own fields."

"Maybe I will, but I plan to do yours first I'm out of practice." He unlatched Emmanuel's stall. "You're welcome to join me."

"I planned on it." She disappeared behind the patient cow, but he could hear Nettie's soft voice as she spoke low to the animal. A bucket clanged and soon a ping, ping of milk hitting metal filled the air.

Birds chattered overhead as Hank hefted the horse collar from the tack room. The collar smelled of freshly washed leather as he slipped it over his shoulder. Emmanuel stood placidly cross-tied in the aisle. He kept a curious eye on Hank, but sniffed the collar and then accepted it. Bessie proved much easier to handle.

He hitched the team to the mower and, with Sam on his shoulders, headed the team out past the cornfields and the tattered wheat to where grass grew wild and heavy. Rich green stalks, already turning gold beneath the sun, fell at the cut of the mower's blade. The machine made a contented humming sound not quite loud enough to drown out the chirrup of grasshoppers, the buzz of dragonflies, and birdsong.

The sun felt good on his back. It slanted low in the horizon. The long fingers of light peered over the jagged majesty of the mountains. The sharp, high scent of fresh-cut grass filled the air and lifted on the breezes.

Those gentle winds weren't cold yet, but he could feel summer's end closing in. He was glad he was here to help. Nettie was a strong woman, but the harvest would be a quick one. He could feel the threat of autumn's storms, even if the morning sky was clear.

Yes, Nettie needed help, and she wanted him. It felt damn good. Remembering the love they'd made, the happiness he felt doubled.

He'd never thought she would want him that way. He never thought he could be this lucky. Life had never been this good. He had his land back. He'd made amends with his brother. He'd found a woman to love.

Sam wanted to ride Emmanuel, and Hank stopped the team with an easy whistle. The big gelding gave a low-noted nicker of welcome when Hank settled Sam on the horse's broad back.

Little hands wound into the bay's dark mane. Emmanuel whipped his head around to give Sam's boot a sniff, then a lick. All was well, and Hank, holding the reins in one hand and keeping a hand on Sam's knee, walked beside the team through the peaceful morning.

He felt a prickle against his back and he turned. He saw nothing but the wind through the tall grasses and a hawk circling far overhead.

Jake kept to the low cut of the creek bed, to stay out of sight, and walked along the mud and rocks instead of riding the horse he led. Mud sucked at the soles of his boots and slowed him down. His stomach curdled because he knew Callahan was spending his nights in Nettie's house and probably in her bed.

That bastard had everything Jake had ever wanted. A rich patch of land instead of the rocky spread he'd been tricked into buying. The topsoil was poorer on the far side of the creek, and that smart-talking banker, Callahan's father, had told him it was a prime piece of farmland. He'd just married Abby, and he was so taken with her that he knew he had to do right by her, find her a house, and provide for their future.

She'd liked the view of the mountains and the grove of cottonwoods, tall and sedate along the tiny creek that went underground all summer long and froze throughout the winter. She'd wanted that land, and the price was right. Still, he'd borrowed heavily against it over the years.

He figured he was far enough out of Callahan's sight and swung up on his gelding. Through heavy grasses he could just make out her house. Dressed in a pair of Richard's trousers, a shirt and an old sun-bonnet to hide her curls, she skipped down the steps and circled around back.

Judging by the basket she carried on one arm, she was taking breakfast out to Hank and Sam in the fields. She looked happy. He knew now for sure that she was sleeping with Hank.

Hot rage claimed him. Callahan had beaten him one too many times. He'd been the one to find Sam, which had won him a place in Nettie's bed.

His guts soured with disappointment. He thought Nettie was better than that. He'd always liked how good she was, pure as an angel, as if she were above anything petty. And yet now he saw her through different eyes. She'd made her choice and turned against him. He wouldn't forget that in the times to come.

Hank might have the upper hand this time, but it wouldn't last. That sheriff had nearly arrested him for the theft at the McCullen's ranch, and Jake had made damn certain old McCullen would think Hank had done it. Callahan would be out of the way soon enough. And if it cost Hank his life, that was even better.

A dead man couldn't talk.

Happiness poured through Nettie at the sight of the big broad-shouldered man and the little boy mowing her fields. A hat shaded Hank's face from her view, but she could just make out the cut of his strong chin. Memories of kissing that chin and all the passion they'd shared last night stirred longing deep in the core of her. She blushed, remembering.

A finch buzzed by on the wind, lifting above the stalks of corn. A few blackbirds fed on the ripening ears and she shooed them away. They landed not three yards from her, cawing angrily. She would have to remember to load the rifle with buckshot and spend a few hours this afternoon scaring off the birds.

"Mama!" Sam met her at the edge of the long swatch of cut grass.

He wanted to look into the basket and see what she'd brought, so she let him lift the lid and peer inside. He chattered on about working with Hank and bringing in the hay. Excitement flickered in his dark eyes and pride drew up his chest.

"I was hoping you wouldn't leave me starving for too long." Hank's slow smile greeted her. A dark shock of hair fell over his brow, just above his eyes, and the way he looked at her made her feel higher than the sun.

"I brought a feast. I want to feed you well because I intend to work you hard."

"I thought you did last night." His lips grazed her cheek, and it was such a tender gesture. Hope gathered in her chest. It felt so right. The snapping gleam of his eyes told her it wasn't only tenderness he felt. "Maybe you want to work me hard again tonight."

"Behave," she whispered, although she didn't want him to. Never had she found such ecstasy as in his arms, wrapped around his body, joined with him. A shaky, silvery feeling rippled through her stomach.

He helped her spread out the light blanket she'd brought, and they laughed together when the wind snatched it from their fingers and sent it flying. Hank caught it, and with Sam standing in one corner and the basket holding down the other, they managed to spread it out in the fragrant grasses.

Nettie unpacked the food and handed out plates.

Sam climbed up on her lap to eat. She cuddled him close, and they laughed and talked. Had she ever been this happy? She couldn't remember.

Hank sat near enough to touch, his sparkling gaze stroking her with hot, sweet brushes. The air buzzed between them with their need to touch, but he never reached out. The smile tugging at the left corner of his mouth let her know he was thinking about making love.

She shivered. There was another night ahead to spend in his arms, tasting passion and joining together as one. She couldn't wait.

They had finished eating when Emmanuel pulled at his picket rope, lifting his head over his shoulder to stare back at the house. His nostrils flared as he scented the wind. Nettie's fingers slipped off the edge of the plate and it clattered to a noisy rest inside the basket.

Hank stood, his jaw clenching into a hard line. He moved with a predatory power away from their intimate circle and headed toward the corn rows. His hand covered the gun holstered at his hip, but he didn't draw. Back straight, he strode to the edge of the hay field.

Tense seconds stretched by. Then Hank's voice rumbled above the drone of the grasshoppers and the rush of the wind. "Sheriff, what can I do for you?"

Nettie set the last of the flatware inside the basket and closed the lid. She stood, brushing Sam's crumbs and bits of grass from her lap, just as the sheriff emerged from the tall cornstalks.

"Ma'am." The lawman tipped his hat, then turned to face Hank. "We've got a complication."

Nettie watched Hank knuckle back his hat. His broad shoulders straightened, and he looked confident and invincible. "What's the problem?"

"Those stolen horses of McCullen's were found in your barn on your land." The handcuffs hung on the lawman's belt and refracted the light. "Now, that's enough evidence to bring you in. I'm getting pressure from the marshal's office to wrap up this case. It's taken a long time to turn this frontier into a ranching community and chase out the lawless troublemakers. We want to keep it that way. You understand."

Hank rubbed his jaw with one hand. "Are you going to arrest me?"

"I'm only interested in the real thief." The lawman gazed off in the direction of Hank's land and the McCullen ranch. "Seems interesting to me that Harv Wheaton's place juts right up against the back of your ranch and that he's the one who said he saw some strange goings-on from the road. That's how we found the stolen horses."

"That interests me, too." Hank's jaw tensed.

"Now, I'm not making any accusations, but I've noticed Wheaton and Beckman spend a lot of time gambling in town. They get in trouble now and then, and I'm called in to establish the peace."

Harv was in on this, too? Nettie's throat felt dry and gritty with sorrow for her friend. She wondered if Maude suspected her husband was earning money on the wrong side of the law, and stealing from people she called friends. She remembered how sharp Maude had been lately and vowed to stop by the Wheaton ranch with a treat for the family, maybe fresh corn and a batch of cinnamon rolls. The times ahead would not be easy for Maude.

"I suspect that Beckman is your man, Sheriff. If you want, I can—"

"Leave this in my hands, son. Catching the horse thief is my job, so let me do it." The lawman rubbed one graying temple. "Don't worry, we'll catch him, but it's going to take some time."

"What about the marshals?"

"I can handle them, and let me know if you have any more problems." The lawman looked grim. "One thing—keep away from Beckman. And watch your back."

The sheriff tipped his hat and left, striding with a brisk, long-legged gait through the mowed grasses. Then he was gone, hidden by the tall stalks of waving corn.

A bad feeling shivered through Nettie and she gazed off at the horizon toward Hank's land. Jake had tried to turn Hank in to the sheriff for a hanging offense, but he wouldn't turn violent, would he?

Hank swept off his hat and let the wind tousle his hair. He raked his hand through the thick locks without saying a word.

He pressed a kiss to her mouth. "C'mon, let's get this grass cut."

She pulled up Bessie's picket rope, but the brightness of the sun seemed dimmer. There was no smile on his mouth and no sparkle in his eyes.

Watch your back, the sheriff had warned. She shivered and drew Sam close.

CHAPTER ELEVEN

The sheriff's words lingered in Hank's mind all day. When Emmanuel lifted his head and scented the wind, Hank dropped his pitchfork. Determined to race trouble head on, he marched across the freshly turned grass and kept his hand on his revolver.

Edmund Johnson stepped into view. "Callahan, I tried the house but you weren't there. I heard your mowing machine and followed the sound. Hi, Nettie."

Nettie called out a hello after she halted the team. She swiped at her brow and headed in, tugging Sam along by one hand. The soft denim trousers she wore were too big, but shaped her legs nicely. The tan muslin shirt hid the curves of her breasts, but there was no mistaking her beauty. Hank's blood surged as she breezed close, smelling of sunshine and new-cut grass.

"I was wondering if I could borrow a blade. I was in the field when I hit a rock." Johnson knuckled back his hat, looking Hank in the eye first, then Nettie. "It's set me back a couple of hours already, and a trip to town would cost me the rest of the day. I need to get this grass cut before the wheat is ready."

"I have an extra blade in the barn." Nettie's smile was a gentle one. "Thanks again for pitching in when Sam was missing. You took charge of everything, Edmund. It really made a difference."

"I'm just glad the little fellow is all right." The rancher looked tired, although he managed a genuine smile. His strong shoulders stooped a bit. Times had been tough, and the thefts had obviously made it tougher.

She also wondered why he was mowing alone. The neighbors had always worked together, moving from ranch to ranch during the harvesting. Maybe she wasn't the only one who hadn't been included this year.

"Thank you, Nettie. I'll replace the part just as soon as I can make it to town. If it's all the same to you, I'd like Callahan to walk me in. There's some-thin' I need to talk over with him."

Hank could read the note of uncertainty in her eyes. The sheriff's warning had scared her. He longed to reach out and pull her against his chest. To comfort her and kiss her and tell her not to be afraid. He would protect her and Sam at any cost.

"I'll bring some cold water back from the well." He grabbed the water jug by the small handle.

Sam wanted to go, too, but Nettie said no. Hank promised to bring him back a surprise from the kitchen. That seemed to satisfy the boy.

They headed through the rows of fragrant corn. He sensed Johnson's hesitation, and Hank wondered what the man had to say.

Finally, Edmund cleared his throat. "I always thought you were a good neighbor, Callahan. I remember how you pitched in and helped me dig a well. You just came by and offered, seein' that we'd just come all the way out from Missouri in one wagon. There wasn't a drop of water on my land and it was the heat of high summer. You were the only one who helped me, and that wasn't the only time."

"I do what I can for my neighbors."

"Folks are sayin' all kinds of bad things about you, Hank." Johnson gazed off at the road where a thin cloud of dust smudging the view told of an approaching rider on the main road, out of sight, but coming fast.

"Sometimes that's all people have to do—spread gossip."

"Well, this time people are getting riled up. Even though Mrs. McCullen got her horses back this morning, folks are angry. They're blamin' you. So what I'm about to ask you ain't easy but here it is. I'd like to ask your help with the harvest. Two men working together can do more than a man alone."

"I think we can bring in a good crop before the good weather breaks." Hank led the way into the cool barn.

"You sense it, too?" Edmund hooked his thumbs in his back denim pockets. "I can feel it in the wind. Winter's comin' early and hard."

"Then the faster we get this done, the better."

Birds flew noisily overhead. The babies were now airborne and a little clumsy. One glided all the way to the ground, and Hank had to stand between it and a barn cat until the little creature found its wings and took off. He tugged open the storeroom and dug for the right mower part.

"We'll do Nettie's fields first," Edmund offered, "since you've got more to cut than I do. I'll bring over my older boys and they can help."

Hank dusted off the new blade and handed it to his neighbor. He walked Johnson to his horse.

Yes, he could feel it on the wind—a change of weather was on its way, for better or worse.

They stopped haying at midnight. Acres upon acres of mowed grass lay in the silvered stardust and scented the night breezes. Nettie took care dousing the lanterns while Hank promised to show up at the Johnson's by first light.

Edmund and his boys left, dog-tired and dragging. Sam slept, safely bundled in the wagon bed, lost in little-boy dreams. He looked like an angel with his bow-shaped mouth slack and his round face innocent. She lifted him into her arms, careful not to wake him. His head bobbed against the crook of her shoulder, and she carried him to the house.

Hank led the team, pulling the mower. A coyote yipped in the distance. An owl hooted from the barn roof. The house was dark, and Nettie hesitated on the top step to watch Hank unhitch the horses in the yard. The bull raced around the corral fence, investigating Hank's work.

She pushed open the screen. She caught the faint scent of cigarette smoke, just a trace. She knew Johnson smoked, and he had been in the house to fetch more cider from the cellar. Still, it didn't feel right. She stopped to light a lamp, awkward with Sam heavy and slack in her arms.

She walked through the house, but nothing was amiss. The sheriff's warning still bothered her, that was all. She remembered

Jake's hard-edged rage as he'd tried to take Hank in as the horse thief, and she shuddered. She was glad Hank was here and a better man than Jake, and not just in strength and character.

During all the years she'd known Jake, she'd never felt an attraction to him. He'd always felt like a friend, and she'd blamed her lack of sexual interest on her grief. She'd figured one day, when she was ready, those feelings would surface. Now she knew she'd been spending time with the wrong man.

Footsteps knelled on the porch, and she recognized Hank's gait, still uneven from his healing leg. She tucked the sheets up to Sam's chin and closed his door.

"Did he wake up?" Hank turned the bolt. "I owe him a story."

"It can wait until tomorrow." She ached with want for him. She also ached with exhaustion from the hard day in the fields. He held out his arms and she walked into them. She laid her cheek against his iron-hard chest. His arms enfolded her close, and she shut her eyes. Her muscles ached with overwork.

"Come, let me put you to bed." Hank's fingers twined around hers. His voice was cello-smooth and pure temptation. He stopped to turn down the wick, and darkness flooded the room. He led the way into the moon-dusted bedroom, where he closed the door and guided her to the bed.

"You mowed those rows like a seasoned rancher." His eyes were dark and deep. The brush of moonlight in the room lengthened the shadows, and she could hardly see him although he knelt right in front of her.

His fingers cupped the heel of her left boot and pulled, and then he did the other. He rolled down her socks. His fingers brushed the curve of her ankle and then again at the arch in her foot. Want curled low in her belly, hot and keen. Her skin tingled.

His fingers tugged at her buttons, and the placket separated all the way down to her waistband. Warm air skidded across her ribs and breasts. Hank's hands brushed the garment from her shoulders and slid it down her arms. He dropped it to the floor with a whisper of muslin.

He loosened the belt and tugged off her trousers. Her drawers slid down, too, and she shivered when he took her hand and guided her to the mattress. The sheets felt cool against her skin. The pillow felt soft and rustled as she sank into it

It was too dark to see much, but she watched him circle the

bed, unbuttoning his shirt. Fabric parted to reveal the hard plane of his chest and the bulge of his erection. He slid off his clothes and climbed into bed beside her. The feather tick gave beneath his weight. The ropes groaned in protest as he stretched out.

His arm brushed hers and she felt his heat. He rolled over and stroked his fingers through her hair. Anticipation pooled in her stomach and chased away her exhaustion. She felt alive every place he touched her. Her skin sizzled wherever his kiss brushed.

She moaned when he drew her nipple into his mouth. Her breath grew ragged as his hands parted her thighs, and he filled her in one long thrust. They moved together in a slow, sweetly agonizing rhythm as the moon hid behind clouds and the stars disappeared one by one from the sky.

* * *

Nettie snapped awake at the sound of Bessie's alarmed neigh. Sleep-bleary, she shrugged off the sheet and sat up to listen. The mare neighed again, sharp and urgent.

Something was wrong. She reached out in the dark and laid a hand on Hank's chest.

He started awake just as Bessie's call rang out a third time. He swore and bolted out of bed. He stepped into his denims. "Stay here with Sam."

"I'm coming with you." She reached for her dress, hands trembling, and pulled it over her head. "If it's the horse thief, then you'll need help—"

"What I need is for you to stay in the house." He tore open the bedroom door. "Bolt the door. I'll find out what's going on."

Bessie's squeal intensified.

"No." She crossed the dark room in four strides. "This is my responsibility too—"

"No, listen to me. I want to know where you and Sam are, in case I have to shoot." He launched down the hallway, anger harsh in his voice. "I couldn't bear to make another mistake like I did once. My conscience is burdened enough. I couldn't live if I hurt you, Nettie."

Her chest tightened as he lifted the gun from the pegs above the door. She could just see the line of his shoulders in the dark, bunching powerfully as he checked the chambers. She didn't want him going out there alone. Bessie neighed again, and Hank bolted outside, shutting the door behind him.

She pulled back the curtains. The clouds overhead blocked all light from the sky. The night was so dark she lost sight of Hank. She wrapped her arms around her waist and wished she could follow him. And, remembering his words, knew she couldn't.

I couldn't bear to make another mistake. My conscience is burdened enough. Is that why Hank was here? To try to ease his conscience? Is that why he was cutting her hay and helping her with the harvest?

There was so much silence. Worry hammered in her heart and pounded in her blood. She hated waiting. She laid her hand on the bolt several times, but drew back. Hank was right. He needed to know where she was in case he had to shoot.

Nettie padded back to the window, the wooden planks smooth against her bare feet. The crisp ruffled curtains brushed her hand as she gazed out into the darkness. Where was he? She saw blackness and shadows and the shape of the wild rose bushes sprawled across the ground outside.

But no sign of Hank.

Then she heard the thud of his boots on the outside steps. Heart bumping, she flew to the door and flung it open. Hank stood framed against the ebony sky, brushed in shades of the night.

"I've got to run over to Johnson's," he growled, abrupt with anger.

"Why?" The hair on her arms stirred, and she knew something was wrong. "Is Bessie gone? And Emmanuel?"

"Yes."

"Oh, Hank." She glanced over his shoulder into the dark yard. "Can we track them? That team is old. They aren't worth much."

"They took your prized bull, too. And he let all the cattle out of the pasture."

"But the crops—"

"I'll get Johnson to help me round up the animals." His voice boomed low and dark. "You stay here with Sam. I just wanted to tell you where I was going."

"I'm not your wife, Hank. And I'm not helpless. I won't sit back—"

"You have Sam to protect." He held up one hand, stopping her. He sighed, a frustrated release of air. "Look, if you want your horses back, I have to go and fetch the sheriff now while the tracks are fresh. And if I do, that means gunfire. I can't risk your getting hurt."

She heard the catch in his voice, betraying his emotion. He did care for her. Or was it the weight of his conscience? "I can leave Sam with the Johnsons—"

"No, Nettie. I'll be back." His hand cupped the back of her neck, holding her still. His mouth slanted over hers, lips parted. He kissed her with a fierce tenderness. "My revolver is hung on the bedpost. I want you to keep it, in case you need it. I don't think there'll be any more trouble tonight."

Her knees gave out beneath her. Nettie grabbed hold of his arms. "Promise me you'll be careful."

"That's a promise I'll try to keep." Hank brushed his lips across her knuckles. "I'll be back."

He loped down the steps and into the dark. They must have taken his horse, too, because she heard no jangle of a bridle or the clop of hooves against the earth. Only the drum of Hank's gait.

She closed the door and locked it. Her knees were still trembling, and she leaned against the solid wood. Had Jake done this? A man she'd once called a friend? He knew what these losses would mean to her. She had little savings left. What if she had to sell the land? Or take out a mortgage against it just to make ends meet?

She lit a lamp and headed back to the bedroom to dress. Hank would return with the sheriff. Johnson would be over to round up the cattle. She pulled on a pair of Richard's old denims and a clean shirt She tied her hair back and when she heard horses approaching the house, she told herself she could handle this, too.

She met Edmund and his sons at the door, and handed out enough lanterns for them to find their way through her fields. She could see at once the devastation the cattle had made. After first stampeding and now milling around helping themselves to the sweet cobs of ripening corn, the cows had taken down half the field. *Half.*

Between the loss of this, the wheat, and her animals, she was just about ruined.

The sheriff brought even more bad news. Five ranches were hit, and Harv Wheaton and his family were one of the victims. They lost their best workhorses, and Harv swore he saw Hank riding away from the barn. It didn't look good, and the marshal was getting impatient to make an arrest.

Hank looked exhausted as he swung down from the borrowed

horse. The sheriff searched the barn by lantern light He and a deputy took off following the tracks, refusing Hank's help, even though he'd asked to accompany them.

The Johnsons had rounded up the last of the cattle—only three head were missing. Probably lost in the dark fields, and Nettie vowed to try to find them come morning. They were the only income she had left.

By the time Hank pushed open the cabin's front door, dawn was glowing golden peach against the eastern horizon. His boots knelled on the floor, ringing with a sharp authority. She set down the empty milk pail and it clanged against the table.

When he turned his gaze to her, his eyes looked haunted. "You took some heavy losses last night. The corn is ruined. All of it."

"All I care about is that you're safe." She took the hat from his head by the brim and hung it up on a wall peg. "Sam and I are safe."

He closed his eyes. "I feel like I failed you."

"Failed me?" Was this about the past? Or just about the losses. "You didn't steal my horses and my best bull. You didn't send the cattle stampeding into my fields. And you couldn't have stopped it."

"Not in time." The downward tug of his mouth looked grim. "This happened because I'm here in your house and sleeping in your bed. It isn't fair that you've stumbled into the middle of this battle between Jake and me. Do you blame me?"

"How could I?" Only affection gleamed in her eyes. "The sheriff will take care of this. He knows you're innocent."

"It didn't save me last time." Hank headed for the bedroom.

He didn't want to feel what ached like an old wound in his heart, but he had to face it. He had to look at it. He couldn't keep living with himself if he didn't—or with Nettie.

He heard her step behind him. "Times have been hard for a lot of people around here. And with these thefts, that's just made it harder. Good work animals are expensive to replace, and look at Johnson. He had to borrow a team from McCullen because he couldn't take out more debt against his land."

She made no sound, but he felt her presence like a burn to his back. So much churned inside him, and yet all he wanted to do was take her in his arms and lay her down on that bed. If he made love to her, maybe he could find again that peace he'd lost long ago.

"Why don't you get some sleep? You were out riding most of the night." Nettie's hand settled on his arm, warm and sustaining and with the promise of hope.

Heat sparked across his skin and his groan tightened. "I'm too exhausted to sleep."

"Is that so?" A smile played at the corner of her mouth, a wicked one that promised pleasure. "It's early yet. Sam won't be up for another half hour." The soft thin light of dawn dusted a rare glow across her face. "Maybe an hour."

"A whole hour."

Hank needed what she was offering him. He reached out and tugged open one button at her throat and then another. Rain began to drum at the window, and thunder rattled the panes. But he didn't stop.

He liked undressing her. He liked watching the cotton fall away to reveal her creamy skin and the shadowed dip between her collarbones. Two more buttons, and the shirt slipped aside to reveal her smooth breasts, small and full and pink-tipped. He leaned forward and snared a pebbled nipple with his mouth.

Nettie moaned and tipped her head back. He rolled his tongue around her nipple, first licking, then suckling. Her hands curled around the back of his neck, holding him there. She rained kisses along his brow.

She tasted like temptation, and he could never get enough. He traced his fingertip down her abdomen and felt her shiver. He latched onto her other breast, and she arched into his touch. He heard the catch in her breath.

She ran both hands over the spread of his shoulders. Hank closed his eyes in pleasure and released the last button on her shirt. The garment slid down to her waist, and he eased it to the floor. He disposed of her denims the same way. Only her drawers and his trousers separated them. He found the tie at her waist and heard the cotton whisper down her smooth thighs. His groin tightened.

Her fingers tugged at his waistband. She loosened the denims with one hand. His shaft sprang free and into her palm. Air trapped in his lungs at the feel of her gentle squeeze. He caught her chin in his hands and claimed her mouth with his. She felt like liquid fire—soft as satin, hot, and undulating. She writhed against him, and her hand gently stroked up and down his shaft until he could take no more.

He guided her to the bed, and he arched over her, never breaking their kiss. Her breathing came shallow and she rocked her hips upward, eager to take him inside. At the first warm-wet feel of her, he groaned. Want and desire shook through him, leaving him weak and vulnerable. He thrust deep into her gloving tightness, his troubles forgotten. All that mattered was Nettie—pleasing her and loving her and joining his life with hers.

Release crashed through him, and they cried out together in a rush of pleasure and need and love. He held her close and kissed her tenderly.

In her arms, he found a sleep without dreams.

A crash woke him. First he thought it was the storm, but it wasn't the sound of thunder. It was a gunshot that pierced the air. Then another.

"Come out, Callahan." Even through the barriers of wood and distance, there was no mistaking the venom harsh in that voice, ringing with the same dark fury of a bullet.

Hank sat up, realizing he was alone in the bed. The sheets were rumpled and pulled out from the bottom of the mattress, a testimony to their urgent lovemaking.

Nettie. Where was she? Fear washed over him. She hadn't stepped outside the house, had she? He sprang out of bed, pulled on his trousers and yanked on his shirt. His Colt hung in its holster over the bedpost, and he grabbed it.

The bedroom door flew open and Nettie burst through the threshold, the fear in her rounded eyes unmistakable. Relief filled him at the sight of her. He wrapped one arm around her shoulders and trapped her hard against his chest.

He closed his eyes and breathed in the scent of her hair and savored the soft but substantial feel of her body against his. He was glad she was safe. He wouldn't be able to bear it if anything happened to her.

"There's a mob coming down the road." Her voice wavered, and she burrowed harder against his neck. "I've bolted the door."

"A mob?"

She was scared. He could feel her trembling. He brushed his cheek against her dark satin curls. He didn't want to let go of her, and his stomach fell at the thought.

A mob. He knew what that meant—it wasn't the first time he'd come face to face with a crowd of irrational people. "Make sure

Sam doesn't see any of this. I want your word, Nettie."

"What are you going to do?" Her fingers curled into the loose fabric of his shirt and held on tight, as if she were afraid to let him go.

"I'm going to face them."

A knock pounded at the door.

"Mama!" Sam dashed down the hallway, toy horses in hand. Worry crinkled his face. "Mama!"

He hid in her skirts, seeking comfort.

"Stay in here and lock the door." He released her, his gait heavy. He didn't want to leave her side, but she was safer here behind a closed door.

"Hank, I won't let you face them alone."

"I know, but you have a little boy to protect." He pulled the door shut, his gaze lingering over her as if this were the last time he would ever see her. "You're all he has, Nettie. He needs you to look out for him."

"He has you." She whispered the words, and tears filled her eyes. But they didn't fall.

Another bang against the door rattled the hinges. "Callahan, I'll break down this door if I gotta."

Beckman. Hank cinched his gun belt tight. The corridor felt too long. He heard the din of voices outside the door. He stepped into the front room and saw the crowd through the window. Mostly men and their older sons milled in the rain, guns in hand. Cold and calm, he opened the door.

Beckman filled the threshold. Fury made him powerful, and he reached out to grab Hank by the collar.

Hank stepped back. "Watch it, Jake. This is Nettie's house. Whatever you boys have planned, don't do it here."

"Nettie's made her bed, and now she has to sleep in it." Jake ground the words out. Tension hardened his jaw. His eyes glittered with cold hate. "The good folks in these parts just ain't gonna put up with a criminal in their midst. Callahan, you're a dead man."

Nettie heard Jake's threat. It echoed down the hallway, dark and ugly, like black poisonous smoke that choked all the air from the room. Her stomach churned and she set Sam to the floor. He stumbled, trying to look past her skirts to see what was happening between Jake and Hank.

"Why's he so mad, Mama?"

"That's what I have to go see." She pushed open the door to his room. Toys littered the floor and a window offered a view of the leaden skies and silver rain. She led him to his bed and sat him on the edge of the mattress. "I need you to stay in your room."

"I wanna see Hank." Sam's eyes filled.

"Hank wants you to stay here." The sounds of the angry mob filtered through the house, leaving a residue of anger and ugliness that made her shiver.

Sam gave a little nod, and Nettie wrapped him in a hug. He was a gentle boy, good hearted, just the way Richard had been. She was proud of that—that her son carried most of what she treasured of his father. She didn't want him to see the ugly crowd outside. Neither did she want Hank to be alone with those men.

"Our crops are ruined and now we don't even have our horses," one voice rang out, harsh as a newly sharpened blade above the other men's threatening shouts. "It's five miles to town."

Nettie closed Sam's door tightly. Her knees gave out beneath her. She grabbed the wall and leaned against it. She knew the sound of a lynching party, she'd heard it before when she was young and the law had less of a hold in this part of the territory. She'd heard it the night Richard had died.

One man couldn't fight a crowd. And even if Hank wanted to fight, he wouldn't risk a gun battle. She already knew he was too noble for that. A stray bullet could ricochet into the house and harm them. Fear gathered into a hard knot in her chest; she willed her legs to stop trembling and headed down the hall.

She couldn't see Hank. Cold air breezed through the open door, and the threshold was empty. She could see the wet boot prints on the covered porch, and then the sheen of rain on the steps. Maybe twenty men marched through her roses and trampled her cut lawn following Jake. She recognized his black hat Hank was beside him, bare headed, already wet with rain.

"If the sheriff won't hang him, we will." A red-faced barrel of a man shook his rifle in the air. He wasn't someone she knew.

"Get the rope, Harv," Jake bellowed above the sounds of wind, rain, and fury. "We're gonna have justice today. If he puts up a struggle, then we take from Nettie what he took from us. She's got enough cattle left to reimburse us for our losses."

"No!" The protest tore across her lips but was battered away by the wind.

The band of men marched straight to the tall cottonwoods shivering in the cool wind. She watched in horror as Jake dumped Hank on the ground beneath a sturdy-branched tree.

How could she stop this madness? Nettie reached above the door and grabbed the Winchester from its pegs.

A gust of wind blew cool drops through her clothes to wet her skin. Her skirts tangled around her ankles. She grabbed a corner of the hem with one hand and sprinted down the steps. Panic drummed in her heart. Could she stop them? Water collected in puddles on the ground, and she splashed through them, slipping in the mud.

"Stop it! Jake, let Hank go." She skidded to a stop behind the intimidating wall of hard-faced men who turned to study her, guns drawn and ready.

The hardship of the past year lined their faces. She felt the unforgiving harshness of their gazes as she stood with gun drawn.

"Nettie." Hank's voice, ringing with courage. "Go back to the house."

"How can I?"

"You couldn't stay out of this, could you, Nettie?" Jake motioned to Harv, who stepped forward from the safety of the crowd and tossed a coiled rope to the muddy ground.

"How can I? You seem determined to trespass on my land and appoint yourself judge and jury." Her grip tightened on the Winchester. "I wonder why that is?"

"Because I'm not afraid to stand up for what's right."

"What's right? You don't have the authority to do this." She thumbed back the hammer.

"I don't expect you to see things our way." Wariness pinched the corners of his eyes when he studied her hard, as if trying to read her intentions. He knew she wasn't afraid to fire the gun and he knew she was an accurate aim. "Besides, you've been listening to Callahan. You've been sleeping with him and believing his lies. I expected better of you."

A man standing in front of her hissed. Judgment glittered in his hard eyes. "You ain't no respectable woman, not now. So don't interfere where you're not wanted. No one respects you here."

"See, Nettie? Now put down the gun and go back in the house." Jake tossed the noose end of a rope over a sturdy tree bough. "No one's turned against you yet, but these are desperate men."

"He's innocent and you know it, Jake." Rage tasted acidic on her tongue. The wind battered her and the drumming rain tried to drown out her words, but she spoke loud enough for them all to hear. "You're doing this to cover your own guilt."

"My only guilt was helping you out all these years because Richard died." Jake checked the strength of the knotted noose.

"Go back to the house." Hank's command rumbled with unmistakable dignity. And a hidden plea. He didn't want her to see him like this. He'd been hurt. She could see him well enough to notice the fresh blood on his bottom lip and the puffy swell above one eye.

"Bring that gelding over here," Jake instructed, and Harv jumped to obey.

She couldn't take her eyes off Hank's calm strength. He faced death and unjust hatred without a rage of his own. He was not weak—no, he was the strongest of all the men here. He was not petty, and he was not afraid.

Nettie watched in horror as the two men lifted Hank into the saddle. They treated him roughly, and he looked in pain. "I'm not going to let you do this, Jake. Put him down."

"You aren't going to shoot." Jake turned his back on her and placed the noose over Hank's head and drew it down over his face.

"Nettie, please, go back in the house." Hank's plea was nearly drowned out by the cheers of the crowd, determined to do the work they believed the sheriff had refused to do.

Her finger leaned on the trigger. Alone, she didn't have a chance of stopping these men, but she had to try. "I'm going to ask one more time, Jake. Then I'm going to start shooting."

"You're just one woman—"

"No, she isn't." Edmund Johnson halted his gelding behind the crowd, his rifle aimed and cocked. His sons did the same, flanking him.

Nettie's heart soared at this show of courage. She saw other men circling around the cottonwood grove, guns ready.

"You know what a damn good shot I am, Jake." Old man McCullen closed the half circle. "I almost put a bullet in you for stealing my wife's horses."

"Cut him down, Beckman. You've riled up these men until they're salivatin' at the mouth," Johnson called out above the now quiet crowd. "Nettie, go up there and get your man. Anyone who stops her will have to deal with us."

Nettie kept the gun loaded and watched the crowd part and make room for her to pass. She held the gun so tightly, her hands shook. Would there be trouble? She didn't know. But she sensed Jake's hold on the group was waning.

As if he sensed this, too, Jake swatted his hat against the gelding's rump. The animal shot forward, and Hank swung out of the saddle by his neck. His hands gripped the rope over his head, and muscles corded against the wet muslin sticking to his arms like a second skin. Hand over hand, he started climbing the rope.

Shots rang out, and Nettie fired. The Winchester kicked hard against the ball of her shoulder and knocked her to the mud. The bullet severed the rope in two, and Hank tumbled to the ground.

She raced through the milling crowd. "Hank!"

He climbed to his feet, peeling off the thick noose. Bruises scraped against his throat, but other than that he was unharmed. She flung herself into his arms and held him with all her might.

The mob was dispersing, racing off as the sheriff and two deputy marshals rounded the grove of Cottonwood trees with McCullen's grown son. On a shout, they were riding hard, trying to bring down the true horse thief.

"Jake tried to get me riled up to join these clodheads," McCullen explained as he holstered his rifle. "I sensed trouble and sent my son for the sheriff. I remember how Jake started this up last time, when your husband was killed. Hank, I can stay to make sure you two are all right."

"Thanks for all you've done." Hank stood strong and tall. Strength knelled in his voice, but his eyes were shadowed.

Nettie laid her hand on his arm, and thanked the men who'd ridden to their rescue. Words seemed so inadequate when compared to what the McCullens and Johnsons had risked today—their lives and their reputations.

She watched Edmund's brothers and sons and the McCullens ride off after the crowd to make sure there was no more trouble.

Hank's hand cupped her shoulder, and she knew by his touch that something had changed inside him. Together they went to check on Sam, who was sitting quiet and afraid on his bed where she'd left him. The little boy ran into Hank's arms and held him so tightly, it looked like he was never going to let Hank go.

THE RANCHER'S RETURN

Nettie hoped Sam would never have to.

CHAPTER TWELVE

Hard, hot anger burned in Hank's chest. He could hardly draw air into his lungs, there was so much of it. The more the sheriff talked, the more Hank felt that fury spread like a sickness through his body.

A rage that reminded him of his father.

As if she sensed it, Nettie curled her fingers around his. Her skin was cool and soft, a contrast to his red-hot rage. He sat in the chair by the crackling fire struggling to control it.

It seemed Jake had eluded the lawmen—Beckman knew the backcountry well, and their horses had lacked the stamina after a hard gallop from town. But the marshals were still on his trail. Beckman's mortgage was in foreclosure, and by the month's end he would lose his land.

And that wasn't all. Heavy gambling debts at a few saloons and gaming halls in town all proved Jake needed the fast, ready cash that came from selling stolen horses. Wheaton was in jail right now, awaiting questioning.

"You're within your rights, Nettie, to file charges against the men who threatened you today." With elbows propped on his knees as he sat on the sofa, Sheriff Larson thumbed the brim of his dark Stetson in his hands.

"I couldn't." Her fingers withdrew from Hank's and she settled down in the rocking chair on the other side of the hearth. "Think of the hardship it would place on their families. I wonder if they hadn't been drunk—"

"Beckman and Wheaton were getting some men riled up in a bar in town. According to Wheaton." The lawman stared hard at his hat, forehead furrowed with thought. "With the weather ruining the crops this year, most ranchers are in tough straits. It's not unusual that men commiserate together in the saloon over whiskey. I think that's what happened. Their judgment was a little impaired, and Beckman was there to convince them Hank was behind the crimes."

"Beckman didn't do this only for the money." Hank felt anger pulse at his temple and gather in the muscles of his jaw. "It's vengeance. He's made no secret about it."

"You can file assault charges, Hank." The sheriff stood. "Don't worry. The marshals are going to track him down. If he's smart, he'll be across the border into Oregon or Idaho by now. Neither territory is more than a few hours' ride."

Hank bolted out of the chair. He knew the lawman had done his best and shown a rare sense of fairness. "Thank you for giving me the benefit of the doubt. Or I'd probably be paying for Beckman's crimes."

"I have no doubt that's what he intended the minute he saw you'd come back to town." Larson tipped his hat, then plopped it on his head. "Ma'am, thank you for the coffee."

Nettie nodded, and her hand curled into fists at her side. Her knuckles turned white. Her hair had come loose from its single braid and now spilled down her back and over her shoulders in rich molasses splendor. Curls shimmered in the lamplight as she turned to pick up the empty cups.

The wind caught the screen door and slammed it against the wall. Hank waited until the sheriff had mounted up before he retrieved it, latched it tight, and closed the door.

Sam ambled down the hall, rubbing his eyes. He'd been playing in his room during the sheriff's visit, and now he looked tired. "I wanna cookie, Mama."

"I know, but it's your naptime, fella." She set the three enamel cups on the table with a clink. "I'll get you a cookie and you can eat it on the way to bed."

"I don't wanna nap." Sam dug in his heels.

"You take a nap every day." Nettie lifted the crock with graceful ease and withdrew a cookie. Molasses scented the air. She bent at the waist and presented it to him. "It's your favorite."

He took the cookie, but his bottom lip protruded. "I don't wanna nap. Hank don't take one."

"Hank is a grown man and you're not" She laid a hand on his shoulder. "Head on down the hall, young man, and go pick a story."

"I don't wanna." That lip looked fatter. Tears gathered in his eyes.

Hank felt that defiance feed his temper. He squeezed his eyes shut and faced the window. Rain fell in heavy sheets from sky to earth. It dripped from the eaves and puddled on the ground and turned dust to mud. The leaden sky looked as bleak as his heart. He could still see the churned earth where the angry mob had gathered.

How did Nettie do it? Find forgiveness? Look at the world through eyes of compassion?

He heard Sam start to cry, and closed his eyes. His memories weren't far from the surface these days. Nettie's voice came calm but firm. Sam sounded unhappy all the way down the hall. The fire popped like the blast from a gun, and Hank startled. An ember was smoking on the polished floor. He crossed over to flick it back into the stone hearth.

He heard the low mumble of Sam's voice and a sniff. Hank's heart felt cold as he strode down the hall. Nettie sat on the bed, her son in her lap. Sam leaned against her chest, snuggling beneath a wool afghan. He rubbed his tired eyes and still looked a little belligerent.

Hank knew just how he felt. "Have you started reading yet?"

Nettie looked up, and her smile was tentative. Shadows clung to her eyes and fatigue had drained the pink glow from her cheeks, but she was beautiful. Dark curls shimmered in the light, drawing his gaze. His blood heated just looking at her.

"I don't wanna story. I don't wanna nap." Sam stuck his fist up to his mouth and chewed on his knuckles.

"Do you know what, partner? I'm really sleepy. Do you want to take a nap with me just this once?" Hank knelt down before the bed. "I would really like a story."

Sam's lip shrank two sizes. "I getta pick the story?"

"Sure."

Sam flew into Hank's arms. His tiny fingers dived around Hank's neck. Warmth flooded his chest. The troubles Hank faced simply melted away. He cradled Sam in his arms as he stood. Nettie smiled up at him, her eyes alight with an affection so bright he could not look away.

With her trailing behind them, he carried Sam to their room. She'd straightened the bed and hurried to pull back the quilt and top sheet. Hank lowered Sam onto Nettie's pillow. He hated letting go.

"Read, Mama. Please." Sam clapped his hands, enjoying this rare treat.

Nettie melted. Hank had never seen anything more beautiful. Emotion swam in her dark eyes, and happiness played along her mouth. She loved him. It hit him hard, and his healing leg nearly gave way. He sat on the edge of the mattress to catch his balance and his breath.

Nettie began the story of a toad along a road. Like music, her voice soothed. Rain tapped at the window and drummed on the roof like a different kind of music.

Hank shucked off his trousers and crawled between the covers. He'd barely had a chance to sleep last night, and it felt good to lie back in the feather-soft tick and smell the line-fresh sheets and see Nettie's face brushed by the lemony lamplight.

He closed his eyes, and not all his dreams were good ones.

Nettie gave her skein of yarn a few good tugs, and a long string of blue coiled like a snake in her lap. The fire snapped in the grate, near to where Hank sat, book propped open in his hands. Sam was in bed asleep, and the clock on the mantel chimed nine times.

Unlike his reluctance at naptime, Sam had gone to bed tonight without any fuss. Hank had spent the late afternoon working in the barn fixing a few leaks in the roof and the walls. Neighbors had come by to offer their support over what had happened, but the morning's vigilante justice still tainted the air.

Anger still simmered in her chest. It would be a long time until it faded. Hank had been so quiet, she feared how it had affected him. Her knitting needles clacked in a fast rhythm as she pearled and knitted, row by row. The heat of the fire felt good and made her drowsy. Rain still pounded the roof and dripped off the eaves.

Her gaze met his over the top of *Life on the Mississippi*. Need for him bolted through her. Seconds ticked by as she forgot to breathe. She could read the same need in his eyes. She laid down her knitting, tucking the tips of the needles into the yarn ball, and stood.

He closed his book and held out his hand. His skin felt warm from the fire's heat. Anticipation fluttered in her stomach as she stepped into his arms. She lifted her hands to his shoulders and tipped her head back, ready for his kiss. His lips swept across hers, igniting a tingling pleasure.

He caressed and nibbled, and she opened her mouth to him. His tongue stroked like velvet heat across hers. Her fingers curled around the back of his neck, holding on. His arms encircled her, supporting her as her knees grew weaker.

"I'm assuming you're ready to go to bed." His words whispered across her lips, and his smile became hers.

"Yes, Hank, I'm ready."

His lips brushed her brow, and his hand cupped her shoulder. He waited while she turned down the wick, leaving the orange-red glow of the fire to light their way across the room. The hallway was dark, and need shimmered inside her—warm and delicious and thrilling. She stepped into the bedroom and he closed the door.

She curled her fingers around the quilt's top edge and pulled it down over the bed. It had been a tough day, and she needed to feel his arms around her and his weight over her and lose herself in their love.

His hand settled on the back of her neck, sending sparks shooting down her spine. She knew in that span of a heartbeat that Hank needed the same kind of comfort. She turned and unbuttoned her bodice.

"Oh, Nettie." He groaned, his mouth a whisper's touch on hers.

Darkness cloaked them, and she felt his fingers bump against hers. He tugged open the last of her buttons. His hands brushed the dress and the straps of her chemise from her shoulders, and the garments slid to her ankles. Cool air breezed over her breasts, but Hank's hands covered them and warmed them.

"Undress me." His whisper came rough and needy. His kiss grazed her lips. His fingers squeezed.

Pleasure stretched like a band through her abdomen, straining tighter. She plucked at the buttons on his shirt. She loosened the buttons on his denims. She could feel his hardness through the fabric as she worked. The garments slid down his hips and the hard heat of his erection sprang forward. She curled her hands around his thickness. He pressed a kiss to the hollow between her shoulder and her neck.

His hands caught her by the elbows and guided her back to the bed. She stretched out on the cool muslin and shivered. But Hank settled at her side and drew the blankets over them. His skin was hot and male-rough.

His hand splayed across her throat as she reached up for his kiss. Her eager fingers explored him. He was all steely lines and sculpted muscle. She ran the flat of her hand across the washboard ridges of his abdomen. On a groan, his hands kneaded and caressed her breasts until they felt heavy and tingling and her breath came short and rapid.

His hand swept over the curve of her stomach and across her thighs. His hand nudged her knees apart, and his fingers parted her, circling and gliding until white-hot fire licked through every inch of her body. Her hand swept lower, too, and curled around the hard thrumming length of his shaft.

A moan rattled low in his throat. Her fingers squeezed. He pressed his heated mouth to her breasts and slid his fingers into the hot dampness of her body. She squeezed tight and looked up at him. She could see him in the dark, his eyes lustrous with passion and his mouth swollen from her kisses.

"I need you now, Hank." The words felt hoarse and scratchy on her lips. "Now."

"I know it isn't considered polite to make a lady wait." His lips brushed hers, and his kiss was fiery hot and driven.

She felt him rise up over her, and her skin prickled with the anticipation of his touch. His gaze snared hers as he settled between her thighs, and she opened up to him. He filled her with one long thrust.

Her head tipped back and she lifted her hips, taking all of him. She clenched around his hard shaft, and fine, thrilling quakes rattled through her body. She folded her arms around his back and held tight. He brushed his lips across hers.

Love welled in her chest, filling up all the shadows and empty places, leaving her whole. She couldn't move; she only wanted to hold him. He must have felt the same, because he remained inside her, taut and breathless.

His tongue laved her right nipple, sending heat across her skin. His mouth clamped over the aching peak with agonizing sensation. Nettie arched her back, offering more. Desire strummed tight inside her, and she savored the pleasure. She arched her hips. He responded with a hard thrust, setting a wild rhythm that drove her past the edge of control.

Release rolled over her with wave after wave of thrilling pleasure. Tight, hard, clenching pleasure that left her breathless and aching and weak. She clung to him as he bucked, his own release breaking through him. He was still holding her tightly against him when they fell asleep.

Hank woke with a start. He sat up in bed, heart drumming, but he heard only the tap of the rain. Nettie slept beside him, the quilt to her chin. The damp night felt cool, so he grabbed his denims along with his drawers and tugged them on.

Nettie still did not wake, lost in dreams, a touch of her smile shaping her mouth. The truth landed like a hard punch to his chest. He loved her, truly and completely.

He'd stayed to keep her safe from Jake Beckman. He'd stayed because it was the right thing to do. And along the way his guilt over the past had eased, and now he was sleeping every night in her bed.

He shut the door behind him and ambled into the front room. Dying embers flickered in the hearth and cast long eerie shadows across the plank floor. He brushed the curtains aside and stared out the window. Beckman was out there somewhere, desperate and hunted by the law. A smart man would head for another territory and keep on riding, but Hank couldn't fight the notion that Beckman hadn't headed to Idaho.

Jake had been stealing Hank's horses the night Richard was shot. He'd been in the barn—it only made sense. Maybe Jake had had doctor bills to pay; his wife had lingered for some time before succumbing to fever. Maybe he'd just needed a way to work off the anger of her death, and taking from others did that.

Hank closed his eyes. Jake had witnessed Richard's shooting, and instead of stepping out of the shadows to help save the man's life, he'd run like a coward to protect himself. Maybe that was what explained Jake's violent hostility. Or maybe all he wanted was to cover up his crimes.

Either way, Hank would do what it took to keep Nettie safe from Beckman or anyone else. And what of the other neighbors who still doubted his innocence? What if they posed a threat?

He leaned his brow against the cool glass, his heart troubled. What about Nettie? She loved him, he knew, with the kind of lasting affection he'd long ago lost faith in. He thought of Sam's gentle innocence and how much both mother and son needed to be protected from any more ugliness and heartache.

Hank remembered his dreams, nightmares from his childhood and his father's violence. He'd lived his life intentionally trying to be different from his father, but in the end he'd taken a man's life. He wasn't sure he could ever make peace with that. He feared the violence that had haunted his father could be in his heart, too.

He stared out into the night and watched the rain fall. The storm ended toward dawn, when exhaustion claimed him and he could sleep again.

Sam tugged away from her hand at the sight of the kittens tumbling over one another in the straw-strewn aisle. The barn felt enormous and empty. Muffin mooed from her pen, alone and unhappy about it Nettie ran her fingers across the bridge of the cow's nose.

Hank stood in the weak sunlight that spilled in through the open back door, hands on his hips, shoulders braced, and legs apart. He looked distant and powerful and confident. He'd hardly said a word over breakfast, not that he was gruff, but he was certainly preoccupied.

She wished she could do more to comfort the pain inside him. The vigilante hanging hadn't exactly been the most neighborly of acts. But others had stood by him, and that gave her hope. She wished she knew how to make things right for him and for them both. She wished she knew how to pull him back when he felt a thousand miles away.

Her shoes tapped on the hard-packed earth, but he didn't turn around. She shoved her hands in her skirt pockets. "It feels lonely in here without Emmanuel and Bessie."

"It sure does." His back straightened at her approach. "The sheriff says that now that Harv gave them the name of the horse trader, they might have a chance of getting the horses back. We'll see."

"Harv sold his own team to try to make you look guilty." Nettie held out her hand, then drew it back. "I need to drive over and see how Maude is doing. I'm afraid the same people who turned on you might give her grief, and she's not to blame."

Hank didn't turn to face her. "I'm going over to my place, since it's too wet this morning to work in the fields. The Wheaton spread is just behind mine."

"Is that an invitation?"

"I guess so." He turned, and the sadness in his eyes struck her the most.

She'd felt his need for her last night in the dark— the tender urgency in his loving had been unmistakable. Now he looked so distant and hard, it didn't seem like he could be the same man. "You want to check and see if any damage was done to your place when Jake left the horses?"

"Something like that."

Something lingered unsaid, and her pulse thudded with the feel of it. A tight cold sense of unease banded around her midsection, and she wrapped her arms there. Something occurred to her. "Are you thinking about moving over there?"

"I'm considering it." He lifted his chin, and there was no softness in his blue eyes and no warmth in the taut line of his mouth.

She tried to keep the twist of pain she felt out of her voice. "Is that what you want?"

"Maybe it's the right thing to do."

"You want to leave because of what happened." Nettie felt an old anger and an old fear. When he didn't answer, she felt her heart crack. "I need you. It's as simple as that. I don't care who doesn't like it. You and Sam are all that matters to me. But if you *want* to leave—"

"You need me?" He didn't sound as if he believed it.

"More than I've ever needed anyone."

He ached to fold her against his chest, to hold her hard and place his faith in her. But he couldn't. "These problems aren't going to go away, Nettie. The doubts are going to linger for a long time. Maybe it's better for you if I go."

Pain filled her eyes, and she held herself so still. "Better how? I don't have doubts about you."

He heard the pain in her voice. He didn't want to hurt her. He fisted his hands against the pain tearing through his chest. He wished he knew what to do. "I'm not sure I can give you what you want."

"What do you think I want?"

"I think you want a husband."

"Only if you want to be one." She lifted her chin, looking so dependent and strong, as if she didn't need him. But she did. He could read it in her beautiful eyes.

Should he go? Even if it meant she would be safe? His lonely life stretched out behind him, and it held no joy. But here, living with Nettie, he knew what his future could be—days working in the sun-swept fields and nights made sweeter for the love he'd found in her arms. "I want to do my best by you and Sam. That's what I've meant to do ever since I woke up with a broken leg in your bed."

"You make it sound like duty." Her voice sounded as brittle as dried grass. "Or a jail sentence. That's not what you mean, right?"

A wagon rattled up the driveway before he could figure out how to answer. Nettie spun away with a twirl of light gray skirts and headed out of the barn. Sam trailed after her, his kitten clutched in his hand.

He heard her voice, low like autumn rain. "Hello, Maude. I was just thinking of calling this afternoon."

Maude's response came as a murmur, and he turned away. He leaned one shoulder against the back door and stared out at the trampled corn and the ruined wheat. The rain had broken the sun's hold on the land, and new green shot through the bunchgrass waving in the wind.

"Maude asked me if I would take her to town tomorrow. She is catching the afternoon train back east." Nettie hesitated, shoulders back, an invisible wall between them. "She wanted to know if you would be needing a team of horses."

Hank managed to nod. He stepped outside and faced Mrs. Wheaton's red-eyed scrutiny. But it was a brief one, and she bowed her chin. It looked as if the news of her husband's wrongdoings had been hard for her to bear.

He checked over the animals—not high quality, but not bad either. He offered her a high price, and he saw the gratefulness in her eyes. He promised to have the money waiting for her at his father's bank by tomorrow morning.

"I'm going over to help Maude pack up." Nettie caught his elbow, her touch as cool as the wind. Her hands were cold, and he realized she wasn't wearing a sweater.

Sadness stood between them, but their problems were not as great as the Wheaton's. Hank pressed a kiss to her knuckles. He took Sam's kitten in one hand and lifted the boy up into the wagon with the other. Sam waved as the vehicle rolled away, and he waved back.

But it was Nettie's gaze that knocked the air from his lungs and the strength from his spine. He could see it in her face, before she turned back around on the wagon seat and the vehicle bounced down the road. He'd hurt her.

The road home was overgrown and almost unrecognizable. Bunchgrass and wildflowers thrived in the center hump and tumbled over the wheel tracks, disguising them from view. Hank nosed his mount through the grass and away from the sun, where fields gone wild shivered in the wind.

The house faced him when he crested the last rise. Sun glinted in the windows as he approached. He saw the drying tracks from horses—the sheriff and the marshals had been here. He checked his barn, but it was empty.

He strode up on the porch and pushed open the door. He expected the place to be a mess, but it wasn't. Just several fresh sets of muddy boot prints tracked through the dust on the floor. Someone had used the kitchen table. And laid out a bedroll on the floor.

The skin on his neck crawled. Jake Beckman had hidden here.

Hank drew his revolver and searched the house, but he was alone. Tracks headed off in the grass. Hank mounted back up and rode to town. The hair on the back of his neck prickled all the way to the sheriff's office.

Larson and a deputy marshal rode back with him. The sheriff said they'd found Nettie's team of old draft horses. They were being held at the livery in an Idaho border town. Hank knew Nettie would be glad.

Hank wanted to go with the lawmen following the fairly fresh trail, but the marshal advised against it. So Hank watched them ride off with a sinking feeling.

Beckman was out there somewhere—and it wasn't far away. Hank could feel it.

Those marshals thought they could catch him. Jake sat back in the grass and plucked the roll of papers from his shirt pocket. He'd been evading the law half his life. Truth be told, when he married Abby, he was ready to put his lawless ways behind him. But then her death had forced him back into them.

If only Nettie had married him . . .

Well, she'd made her choice.

He was careful to keep hidden, and had left his horse tied up back in the gully out of sight of the house. He'd trailed through the grass for hours, and then rode the creek until there was no way those marshals could find him. They wouldn't think to look right under their noses.

All he had on his side right now was luck and his Colt .45s. But his luck wouldn't last forever. It never did. When the marshals came to take him in, Jake wanted to know one thing—that at least Callahan wasn't going to be able to identify him to a jury.

Jake was going to make sure his only eyewitness was dead. He finished his cigarette and then checked the chambers in his Colt. Satisfied, he ducked through the grasses and circled around to the back of the house.

The wagon jostled over the rough road with loud creaking protests. The matched bays, heads down, trudged through the thigh-high grass with obedient indifference. Maude had asked Nettie to go ahead and take the wagon and horses today, before the buyer that the bank sent arrived. He would be making a blanket offer on furniture, livestock, and property.

There wasn't much packing to do, for they would only take a few trunks on the train, but Nettie knew Maude needed an understanding friend. They had sat and drank tea while the children played, but when mealtime came, Nettie said she had to get back to Hank. Maude apologized for all the harsh things she'd said about him.

Autumn scented the breezes. Wildflowers waved with the grasses as the house came into sight. The log house, two stories and snug, crested on a small rise and faced the Blue Mountains. Nettie wondered if Hank thought of this place as his home.

She pulled the horses into the shade and halted the wagon. She set the brake. The front door swung open and Hank strode across the porch. He looked better than she'd ever seen him. His tan shirt was open at the throat, and his sleeves were rolled up to expose his sun-browned forearms. His dark locks were tousled from the wind, and no hat shaded the snap in his blue eyes or the easy smile on his face.

The doubt of earlier this morning had faded from him. He walked with a relaxed confidence that drew her gaze and sparked heat in her blood. She remembered last night's lovemaking, slow and tender and then wild and passionate, over and over again. Desire curled low in her belly, and she melted when he cupped her face in his big hands and brushed a kiss to her lips.

"Lemme down!" Sam demanded, arms spread wide for Hank to catch him.

Hank's chuckle rumbled across her mouth. "Okay, partner, jump and I'll catch you."

Sam launched forward off the seat, and Hank caught him easily, flying him in a wide arc before setting him gently on the ground. Sam wrapped both arms around Hank's leg and held on with all his might.

Her heart gripped as Hank lifted the little boy into his iron-strong arms with so much gentleness and with so much care, she began to believe that maybe, just maybe there was happiness ahead, after all.

"Need some help?" She followed him across the porch and into the house.

"I was wondering what you thought of this place." Hank balanced Sam on his hip and closed the door behind them.

"It's beautiful." She brushed her finger across the carved mantel. "Did you do this?"

"I did." A touch of pride flickered across his face. "I could change anything you don't like."

"What do you mean? It's your house."

"But maybe you would like to live here."

"With you?"

"Yes." He felt as if he were standing on the edge of the Columbia Gorge, looking down hundreds of feet to the churning river below. He took a deep breath. "I want you to be my wife."

She took a step back, and her hand flew to cover her mouth. Big, happy eyes stared up at him. "You want me to marry you?"

He swallowed. Now he felt like he was falling, hurtling toward that mighty river and certain disaster. How could he tell her what she meant to him? Words of love and need and dreams wrapped around his heart. "It's the right thing to do."

"The right thing? I see." The brightness faded. Her hazel eyes lost their luster and pinched in the corners. "I just lost my crop. Is that why you're asking me now?"

A terrible, silent whirlwind began to roll in his stomach. "I never thought that. No, I—" He didn't know what to say. He thought she'd be happy.

"Do you truly want to marry me?" Pain shimmered in her eyes. And she twisted away. She covered her face with her hands. "Are you asking because you think it's the right thing to do?"

"I want to marry you because I want to be with you every day and every night for the rest of my life." He felt as if he'd crashed into the river and struck bottom hard. His chest hurt so that he couldn't breathe.

"I love you, Hank. But after what you said—" She paused, truly troubled and torn. Her eyes shimmered with emotion and she looked so sad. "I will only marry you for love."

"Why else would I ask to marry you?"

"You're a man of honor, Hank. I know you've never forgiven yourself for taking your friend's life—and my husband's. But until you do, there's no way—"

The back door banged with a burst of wind, echoing through the house. Had he locked that door? He couldn't remember, but he had closed it. The wind wasn't gusty enough to have blown it open.

Hank unstrapped the revolver and cocked it. "Take Sam upstairs and stay there. I need to know you're safe."

Her eyes widened with fear. Her gaze flicked from the revolver he held to the little boy trying to climb up on a dusty chair, and she didn't argue. She knelt to pull him off the upholstered cushion and swung him onto her slim hip. She hurried past him, quiet as a breeze, and climbed the stairs.

Determined to protect her, he edged around the corner. He saw the sun-filled kitchen and the door swinging open with a lazy creak. He scanned the floor and the corners and under the table. The cabinets on the back wall were coated with dust and cobwebs and looked untouched.

But Jake was out there somewhere. Hank could feel him

waiting. He eased into the dining room. The un-curtained windows stared straight out at the backyard. Hank could see the slanting sunlight and the endless fields of waving grass and wildflowers, but no sign of Beckman.

He took no chances. He ran through the room in front of the window.

Gunfire shattered the glass and bullets whizzed through the air at his back, trailing him across the room. Bullets sprayed through the wood wall at his side. He dropped to the floor, and a bullet grazed his back. He felt the burn of raw skin, but that's as deep as it went

Hank trained his eyes on the door and aimed. Beckman probably thought his bullets had found their mark. He didn't make a sound, straining to listen for the faintest footfall outside the door.

It wasn't long in coming. Grass crackled beneath the pad of a boot, then another. Hank figured Beckman was close to the steps. Leather brushed against wood, and he was on the bottom step, then the middle, then the top. Hank held his Colt steady. He could see Jake through the glass in the top half of the door. Hank climbed onto his knees and fired.

Glass shattered, and Jake dropped from sight. Answering bullets plowed through the door, and Hank rolled out of the way and sought safety around the corner. Bullets dug into the wall where he'd been, and he breathed a sigh of relief. He would have been a dead man if he hadn't moved.

"Give it up, Callahan. This is one thing you can't beat me at."

"Says who?" Hank knew Beckman was buying time as he reloaded.

A good time to strike. He took a breath, steadied his hand, and dived around the corner, firing. He squeezed off three shots, and sent Jake back through the door. Hank thumbed bullets into the chamber and raced through the kitchen.

No sign of Beckman. The door swung open, offering a peaceful view of the countryside. Shards of glass crunched beneath his boots. He leaned against the wall, thumbing the last of his bullets into the chamber, and spun it shut.

Maybe the sound of their gunfire would bring the sheriff and marshal. Hank could always hope. Sound traveled for a long way over these flat plains. Then again, he couldn't count on help arriving. He had to protect Nettie and Sam and bring in Beckman, and he had only six bullets left.

He had two choices—to stay in the house or go after Beckman. Hank thumbed back the hammer. He wanted this over and done with. He didn't want to have to worry about his family's safety again.

He dared to cross the threshold. A movement against the outside wall caught his eye and he spun.

Beckman was faster. The hard, hot nose of the revolver burned against Hank's jaw, and he froze.

"Say your prayers, Callahan." Jake's finger brushed the trigger. "You've got one more second to live."

CHAPTER THIRTEEN

Beckman kicked the gun from Hank's grip. Anger surged in his chest, and he knew he had only seconds to act before Jake pulled the trigger. In a split second, he swung fast and hard, his fist connecting with Jake's hand. Jake's revolver tumbled to the ground.

It fired wildly, and a window broke upstairs. Glass rained from the second-story window, and all Hank could think about was Nettie and Sam. What if that bullet had hit either one of them? Black fury blinded him as he fisted his hand and slammed it against Jake's jaw.

Beckman's head rocked back and smacked the side of the house. His second revolver hit the ground. Jake rebounded off the wall, blood sluicing over his chin, and sprang, fist balled and flying right at Hank's face.

All Hank could see was Nettie helpless against Jake's rage, and he focused all his strength in his arm. He curled his hand and drove it straight toward Jake's belly.

His fist drove knuckle first into Jake's diaphragm. The impact knocked the tall man to his knees. As Hank drew back for another blow, Jake cursed and grabbed Hank's ankles.

He fell with a heavy, breath-stealing blow. The back of his head hit something hard as rock. Pain exploded through his skull. He tasted blood on his tongue. The blue sky circled overhead, and he struggled for air. He couldn't pass out Nettie and Sam's safety depended on him.

He fought to sit, but Beckman's hand slammed against Hank's chest, sending him back to the ground. Pain sluiced through his head. Hank read the black rage in Jake's eyes, as lethal as his own.

Beckman grabbed his revolver and thumbed back the hammer. The night Richard was killed flashed through Hank's mind. Jake had been responsible for setting the events in motion the night that resulted in a good man's death. That resulted in the years of Hank's guilt and self-banishment, and Nettie's grief.

His rage became a hard, dark hatred and it drove him forward. He heard the gunfire and felt the bite of a bullet dig into his side. It didn't stop him. Before Jake could cock his gun for another shot, Hank's fist connected with his jaw. He heard a bone-breaking crack and Jake tumbled to the ground, his hands to his face.

Hank grabbed his gun and cocked it. He towered over the injured man, who writhed with pain. His grip on the revolver tightened. His hand trembled. He wanted to vent his blinding rage and to make Jake Beckman know how it felt to be hurt. To make him pay for all the harm he'd caused.

Hank froze. He recognized that the dark rage burning inside him was like his father's, tottering on the edge of control, thinking he had the right to inflict pain and punishment.

"You broke my jaw," Jake accused, blood sluicing between his fingers. "You son-of-a—"

The drum of horse hooves interrupted, and the sheriff and deputy crested the close rise, loping into the yard.

"Need any help, Callahan?" Larson swung down from his saddle.

"I could have used it ten minutes ago." Hank released the hammer and holstered his gun.

"Looks like you did a good job." The sheriff's boot caught Jake's arm and pushed the criminal back onto the ground. "You aren't goin' anywhere this time, pal."

"Nowhere but the jail." The marshal tugged a set of handcuffs from his belt. "There's a few crimes in Idaho and Oregon we'd like to try you for, too, Beckman."

Hank trembled—from fear or unreleased rage, he didn't know which. He turned, ashamed of what he'd seen in his heart.

"I've got to go check on Nettie." He crunched across the

broken glass and tipped his head back to look at the shattered window. He wiped blood from his lip as he headed inside.

Glass was everywhere. Bullets had driven holes through the outside wall. Bullets had embedded themselves in the dining room wall. Remembering how close he'd come to dying, he headed upstairs, heart pounding.

The silence was so loud it hurt his ears. And made him afraid. Maybe that stray bullet had hurt Nettie. He dashed up the stairs, his boots ringing like thunder on the wood steps.

"Nettie!" His voice boomed in the hallway.

A door shot open. Sunlight spilled through the room and over the woman who emerged from the threshold.

His weak leg nearly gave out. "Thank God. You're all right. I can't believe it."

"I wasn't sure if I'd see you again." Tears wet her cheeks, and she ran into his arms.

She felt like an angel, slim and graceful against his rough strength. Her silken curls brushed his jaw. She smelled like spring. He pressed a kiss to her hair and gathered the courage to step away.

He saw Sam hesitate in the doorway, eyes wide with fear, but unhurt. Hank's throat ached with the knowledge of what he could have lost today. "I caught him. The sheriff and marshal are here."

"I hated not knowing—" More tears brimmed her eyes, not weak tears, but tears of happiness. And that cut like a knife through his heart. "I was so afraid I'd lose you, and yet I had to keep Sam away from the gunfire. If I'd had a gun—"

"You've saved me often enough." He wound his forefinger around a lone loose curl. "It was my turn."

"You're hurt."

"I'm fine." He pressed his hand to his side. It was nothing compared to what he'd seen of his soul today. "I've got to ride in with the sheriff. Please, head home. A little boy needs your care right now."

Nettie held out her hand, and Sam wrapped his fingers around hers. "Will you be coming home?"

Home.

The single word tormented him and his heart broke as surely as an ax cleaving it in two.

"I'll be back." It was a promise, but it was only that.

THE RANCHER'S RETURN

He would return, but not to stay.

* * *

Two weeks. It took him two weeks to head back to Nettie. He'd had to have his side stitched up from Beckman's bullet, fetch the horses, and decide what to do. Although he already knew in his heart what was right.

A light frost crisped the ground and chilled the air. Winter was coming hard and fast. He stopped to speak to Edmund Johnson to offer him the Wheaton's team and pay him, although the man first refused, to plow under Nettie's fields for her. Johnson wished him luck and was sorry Hank didn't feel like he wanted to stay.

That wasn't the problem. As the cold wind burned his face, Hank realized he wanted nothing more than to have the right to love Nettie for the rest of his life.

But when he remembered the rage that roared to life when he'd fought Beckman, it humbled him and scared him. Violence lived in his heart, like it had in his father's. And for the first time in his life, Hank had nearly lost control.

Gray smoke curled from the stovepipes, lifting into the foggy morning. Golden light shone in the window, a warm beacon luring him closer. He rode his palomino into the barn and swung down. The two draft horses, reins tied to his saddle horn, gave happy nickers, glad to finally be home.

Emmanuel and Bessie looked the worse for wear. Both had been ridden hard to Idaho and treated shabbily when they arrived. Word was the trader was figuring to sell them to slaughter. Hank rubbed his hand along Emmanuel's neck, savoring the velvety warmth of his coat and the power of the animal. Gentle as a lamb, the big gelding lipped his shirt, asking for more candy.

Hank broke three pieces off the sticks in his pocket and handed one to each horse. He led the palomino into a stall, filled it with soft straw, and forked the manger with hay. Then he did the same for the draft horses.

The garden had been brought in; only the big squash and pumpkins remained on their vines— bright yellows and oranges against the white fog and frosted earth. How did he face her? How could he leave her?

His boots crunched on the frosted step. The curtains were tied back, and he could see a slice of the parlor. A wall hanging of quilted fabric flowers brightened one wall. He saw a corner of the built-in bookshelf and the chair near the fire where he used to read.

The door swung open and Nettie filled the threshold. Her hair was down, shimmering like satin over her shoulders. She wore a russet dress that complemented her eyes. She looked pale, and he wondered if she'd worried about him. And that cut him to the core.

"Hank!"

He eased his saddlebags to the floor as she flew into his arms. He held her tight, and it felt good. He breathed in the scent of her—roses and wood smoke and cinnamon—and memorized how slight she felt against him and how warm.

She stepped back, her hands falling to his forearms, looking him over as if she couldn't get enough of him. "Goodness, you look half frozen. Come in, I've got the fires going."

"I'm used to colder weather than this." He closed the door behind him with a click, and it felt good not to have to worry about a lock. The country was safe again, like it should be. "Up at my shanty, it dips well below zero for most of the winter."

Nettie's quick fingers flicked at the buttons on his jacket. As he shrugged out of the garment, pain shot up his side. He winced. He'd forgotten about those healing stitches from Jake's bullet wound.

"Are you all right?" Alarm brought out the green in her eyes. Love, as gentle as starlight, shimmered in those depths. And that love made him want to forget his past and the black rage he'd felt in his heart.

"The wound is almost healed." Hank ducked away from her concern and hung his jacket up on the peg by the door. He swept his hat off and hung that up, too.

"Hank!" Sam raced down the hallway, dropping his wooden horses with a clatter. A kitten dashed across the room and dived under the table as the little boy sprinted straight into Hank's arms.

He swung Sam up into a warm bear hug. Hair ruffled as always, Sam planted a wet smacking kiss on Hank's jaw.

"I missed ya lots."

"I missed you, too, partner." Hank's throat ached at those words. "I brought you something. Go ahead and look in my pocket"

Sam's finger plucked at Hank's shirt. His eyes beamed at the sight of that familiar white sack. "Candy."

Hank swung the boy down. Sam reached into the small sack

and pulled out a red-and-white peppermint stick.

"Sit down and lick it quietly." Nettie laid her hand gently against the back of the boy's head and steered him toward the chair. The kitten leaped up on his lap.

"Go warm yourself by the fire." She pressed another kiss to Hank's stubbled cheek. "I'm glad you're back."

He watched her disappear into the kitchen. He hesitated by the door. He wouldn't be staying long.

Nettie reached down the hand mill from the top shelf above her work counter. She moved with a willowy grace he wanted to memorize. He wanted to watch every movement of her delicate hands, every tilt of her head, every slow stretch of her smile. He never wanted to forget the smallest detail. The winters were long, lonely, and cold in the mountains.

His boots knelled on the floor, but she didn't look up from her work. She poured a handful of coffee beans into the grinder. The fragrant beans rattled inside the chamber, and she latched the lid. She turned the handle, and the grinding sound grated through the kitchen. A spark popped in the stove. He breathed in, smelling cinnamon and coffee and lemon wood polish.

"I rode down to fetch your horses."

"Emmanuel and Bessie?" The sparkle of pleasure drew pink across her cheekbones. "Thank you, Hank. I wondered what took you so long to come home."

She abandoned her grinding to wrap her arms around his neck. Her hair tickled his ear. Her wool dress felt soft against his exposed forearm. "You truly are a good man."

Her luminous eyes shone with a bright, unmistakable belief. He felt overwhelmed, because that was the way he loved her. Beyond anything he'd ever known. Beyond the value of his own life or happiness.

"No one could find the bull. Jake probably sold it to a rancher along the way for a good price. He's not saying."

"Jake." Her mouth compressed in a hard line, and she stepped out of his arms. "He was stealing your horses the night Richard was shot, wasn't he?"

"Yes." Hank's chest felt near to bursting. "He's been covering his tracks or blaming other people for years."

"I'm glad you were the one to stop him." She poured the ground coffee into the pot. "You did that, Hank."

He looked out the window at the world of grays and whites. He looked so distant. He didn't look as if he'd slept the entire two weeks he'd been away.

Maybe coffee and a hot meal would make a difference, and he could sleep the morning through. She'd feared he wouldn't keep his word to her—that he wouldn't return.

But he'd come back to her, and they could try to pick up where they'd left off—with his marriage proposal and offer to live in his beautiful house. To start a new life together, free from the past.

But what did he feel for her? Love or a sense of responsibility?

She set the coffee to boil and grabbed a plate of cold leftover pancakes wrapped in cloth. They took just a moment to warm, the same time it took to fry up a couple of eggs.

He turned from the window, staring at her as if he'd only just realized she'd been cooking breakfast. "I'm sorry, Nettie. I hadn't realized—" He paused and rubbed his jaw.

She saw the dull, dark smudge of a bruise almost gone crowning his jawbone. Jake had put that there. She set the plate on the table, then brushed her hand over that waning bruise.

He truly was a wonderful man.

"I should have made it clear when I walked through your door." His words sounded dark and bleak and cooled the house like a bitter wind. "I don't plan to stay."

"Stay?" Her hopes plummeted. Maybe she was wrong. "You mean you're heading over to your own house."

"No. I'm going back to my shanty in the mountains."

"The mountains? I thought—" Emotion bunched in her throat. "You asked me to marry you, and I—" *Hoped there was a chance you loved me.* She kept back the words that would leave her heart too vulnerable.

He'd chased away the loneliness in her life. He'd made her feel love and happiness and passion. He'd given her a future to embrace, one spent at his side.

"Why are you walking away from your ranch?" Her hands trembled as she set the flatware, butter, and syrup on the table. She couldn't look at him. "Whatever happens between us, you love ranching. I know you do—"

"It isn't a matter of what I love, damn it. I couldn't live there and not think of you every minute." His throat corded. He stood tall and invincible, but he looked so alone. So very alone. "I lost control for the first time in my life, don't you see? I wanted to beat Beckman into a bloody pulp, even when he was injured and unarmed."

"But you didn't."

He stared down at his hands, loosely fisted and iron-strong. She didn't understand. He didn't expect her to. He had to fight to keep from reaching out and pulling her to his chest and into his arms. He wanted to feel her mouth move against his, taste the heat of her skin, and feel her writhe beneath him. He wanted to love her every day for the rest of his life.

But he didn't have that right. Not now.

He drew himself up straight. "I have to go, Nettie. I wanted to leave you some money—"

"No, Hank, I—"

"I know you won't accept it." He reached for her hand. Even though the room was warm, her skin felt cold. He pressed his lips to her knuckles. "I don't want to insult you, just help you."

"I'd rather have you love me."

He had to leave now before the pain in her eyes made him stay.

"Explain to Sam for me." He turned, striding toward the door. It took every bit of willpower he possessed to lift his coat from the peg. He grabbed his saddlebag and hat without turning around.

He gripped the door and hauled it open. Cold air and meager daylight swept into the room.

"Do you know what I see when I look at you?" Her voice called him back.

He froze on the bottom step.

"A man who risked his life to protect my son. A man who showed me that I could love again. You've stood beside me and showed me what true honor is."

He squeezed his eyes shut. Her beautiful words touched his heart, in the place where he wanted to believe he could be the best, not the worst.

The fog lifted like a veil of white, and he crunched across the cold ground. He felt the tug of her gaze, and he knew she was hoping that he would turn around and walk back into her arms.

He forced himself to keep walking. He forced himself not to look back. He mounted up and guided his palomino out into the rutted road.

The first snowflake tapped to the ground in front of him. The second clung to the brim of his hat. More fell, and he rode on, fighting the pull to turn the mare around and head home. Flake by flake the snow kept falling, making the world new.

Nettie stood on the porch and stared at the empty road. Wind twisted her skirts and tangled her hair. Snow fluttered to the ground, one flake at a time. He'd ridden away from her and away from their love.

No, he'd never said he loved her. Not once. She closed her eyes, but she could still see him riding his golden mare down the driveway and out of sight.

It took all the strength she had to let him go. He'd only been here to protect her from Jake's threats, that was all. That was the only reason he'd been here.

Or was it? Too much pulled at her heart. She wanted to run after him and fight for him; she wanted to let him go if that's what he wanted.

"Where's Hank goin'?" Sam huddled in her skirts.

"To town." She took her son by one sticky hand and ushered him back into the house.

Shivering, she shut the door and added fuel to both fires. Sam kept asking questions. When was Hank comin' back? What was he gonna do? He ended up in tears. Nettie calmed him the best she could.

Cool air seeped through the window, and she watched the snow fall. Slowly it began to accumulate on the frozen ground and turning trees. Golden leaves fluttered to the ground when the breeze kicked up.

Why did it feel as if her heart had been cut right out of her body? Because she loved him.

Pain cracked in her chest and deep in her soul. She eased down onto the sofa's soft cushions and felt the tears sting her eyes.

She'd lost a love before, and she'd survived. But it hadn't been easy.

Darkness had settled over the town. A white blanket of wet snow glistened beneath a half moon, blanketing roofs and streets and the fields beyond the city blocks. The streets below were quiet. Everyone had gone home for the night. Hank let the curtains fall. The whiskey bottle felt cold and smooth in his hand. He sloshed the liquid around, then drank. Hell, he was lonely. And hurting.

Walking away from Nettie had been the right thing to do. Hadn't it?

Hank rubbed his brow. Pain throbbed in his head. Alone in his hotel room, he couldn't help thinking of her. She would have put Sam to bed by now and would be sitting near the fire in the cozy front room, knitting needles clicking together with a soothing rhythm.

He missed her. He didn't want to be alone. He cradled the bottle in both hands, staring into the golden depths. The potbellied stove in the center of the room puffed as the wind blew and the door rattled. His stomach burned.

He capped the bottle and set it aside.

By morning, Hank had figured out what he was going to do. He'd given his word to the sheriff he'd stay for Beckman's trial. That was a few weeks away. No sense in heading off to the mountains yet, just to turn right back around. And he wasn't a man who could sit idle in a hotel room.

He thought of Nettie and wished he could be the one turning her fields. He wanted to wake up in her bed every morning. He wanted to make her life better. His heart cracked. It was better not to think about her.

He stepped out onto the street and into a bitter wind. Snow crunched beneath his feet as he crossed the road. A horse-drawn wagon rattled by, and Edmund Johnson called out a hello. Hank returned it and knew he would miss this friend and neighbor.

He tugged open the bank's ornate front door. The warm lobby drew the cold from his face and hands. He unbuttoned his jacket, thinking of how much money he might need.

"Hank. I wondered when I might see you again." Barnaby Matson's hand shot out in welcome. They shook. "Robert was in a little bit ago. Said he'd seen you. I'm glad you've stayed around. I'd been hoping you would come back and lift some of the burden from my old shoulders."

"I just came to withdraw some money. I won't be staying long. Just until the Beckman trial is over."

"Oh." Some of the brightness faded from the old man's eyes. "I thought—well, I thought you'd come back to work."

"Work? I'm not looking for a job."

"I don't understand." Barnaby drew his wrist across his forehead in a brief, troubled swipe. "I've been patient, you know, waiting for your decision. Robert said you would come around, that you just needed time."

"Time for what?"

"Surely the lawyer contacted you." Barnaby drew the chair out from behind his desk and eased into it. "Your father left his share of the business to you, Hank. I think he felt bad in the end, that he hadn't believed in you."

Hank buried his face in his hands. A sharp thudding began at the hollow behind his left eye. "I didn't know."

"It's a chance to start over. You have a head for numbers, Hank, and for business."

"And you've been running this place alone."

"I couldn't let it go to ruin." Wise eyes studied him. "You came in here to withdraw some funds. Tell me what you need."

Hank did, and Matson hurried away to fetch the money. Hank rubbed the back of his neck and gazed around the lobby. He didn't want his share of the bank. He didn't want anything of his father's.

Matson returned, and Hank made a decision. He would see Father's attorney and give his share of the bank to Matson's son.

He thanked the old man and headed out into the snow, feeling more free than he had a right to.

CHAPTER FOURTEEN

"I couldn't believe my wife when she said you dropped by the house." Robert swung down from his horse. "You're fixing up the place, I see. Does this mean you're staying?"

"No. I just couldn't leave it like this." Hank hooked the hammer in his tool belt. He'd put a lot of himself into this house, hours of contented work. "I can't let winter destroy it. I wanted to hire someone to put in the windows, but I've got some time on my hands before the trial."

"What happened with Nettie?"

"I'm the man who killed her husband, that's what." Hank knelt to grab another shard of the shattered windows from the grass.

"That was an accident."

"Well, I held the man while he died. And I had a life after his was gone." Hank strode across the grass to the back door.

"If Nettie can forgive you, then you should forgive yourself." Robert's hand lighted on Hank's shoulder. "Need some help with that window?"

"You aren't much of a carpenter." Hank grabbed one end of the wooden frame and waited while his brother grabbed the other.

"No, but I guess I can learn. Maybe I have a hidden talent."

"Let's see if you do."

He and Robert lifted the heavy wood frame and settled it into the big hollow in the outside wall. Robert held it steady while Hank nailed it snugly into place.

This is what he liked—working with his hands. The scent of freshly sawed wood in the air. The wind at his back and the satisfaction of building something of worth. All that was missing was Nettie.

"Why don't you and Nettie and her son come join us for Thanksgiving?"

"I can't do that." Hank's fingers fumbled and he dropped a nail. "I don't belong with her. Besides, after the trial, I'm leaving town."

"Why are you so intent on leaving?" Robert's frown deepened. So much gleamed in his eyes and passed over his face. "I had thought we could be brothers again, but this time real brothers. The way it should be."

Hank positioned a nail and drove it in. "I won't lie to you. I would like to stay. With Father gone, everything's changed."

"You're afraid you're like him at heart, aren't you?" Robert clipped his chin, a thoughtful gesture, and his face hardened with difficult emotions. "Is that why you've left Nettie and her son?"

"I've made up my mind. I'm going back up to my claim. It's the right thing to do." Hank felt as if his world had been turned upside down. He closed his eyes and saw the shattered glass littering the ground and Beckman writhing in pain, at his mercy. "I'm capable of wanting to kill a man. I wanted to pull that trigger, Robert. I'm not proud of myself."

"If that man had tried to harm my wife and children, I would have pulled the trigger." Robert's hand lighted on Hank's shoulder, a touch of brotherly understanding that came from a shared past. "You're a better man than me. You let him live. You let justice be served. That's the sign of an honorable man, not a violent man. No matter how angry you got, you made a good choice and the right one."

It didn't seem that way. He hadn't liked what he'd seen in his heart. Hank's chest twisted so tight he couldn't breathe. Robert understood and said no more. They worked together as the day lengthened until the windows were snug in their casings. There was something sad about an empty house, made of shining wood and glittering glass and waiting rooms. He would never have a family to fill this place with laughter and memories. Or could he?

His gaze strayed westward to the rise of hills marking the property line. Dusted with lingering snow, Nettie's land glistened like gemstones for miles.

As the early December storm battered the north side of the house, Nettie set the bean pot into the not-too-hot oven. The beans would be done in time for supper. Already the sweet molasses smell warmed the kitchen and made the cold day seem less bleak. She closed the oven door and straightened.

"Mama." Sam curled his fingers into her skirt and tugged. "Mama, I'm awful hungry."

"You are? You ate up all your dinner."

"Yeah, but I need a cookie."

Nettie ruffled his hair. There hadn't been a lot of smiles since Hank rode away from them, without so much as a good-bye. Sam's heartbreak remained, but he was doing better. And so was she. This little boy was enough to fill up her entire heart. She didn't need Hank Callahan. Or, at least, that's what she told herself. "Maybe we both better have a cookie."

"Goody." Mischief twinkled in those dark eyes.

Laughing, Nettie swept him up in her arms and held him up to the counter. She dragged out the crock and lifted the lid. Sam pulled out two cookies. "Why don't you find Pumpkin and give her a few bites? I bet she likes molasses."

"Okay." The instant she set him down, Sam stormed off. His shoes striking the floorboards made an awful racket. Luckily the small kitten had grown used to such noise or Sam would never have been able to catch up to her.

Nettie grabbed a dish towel and rescued the coffeepot from the stove. She filled a tin cup and added a touch of milk and sugar. She nibbled on the edge of the cookie and sat down at the table. Alone.

She had hoped Hank might change his mind. For nearly a month now she'd listened for the sound of a horse coming up the driveway or the knell of his boot on the outside steps. She went to sleep at night in her empty bed, missing him at her side. Now, she'd finally stopped listening and waiting for his return.

The courtroom hummed with anticipation. The judge banged his gavel, signaling the start of the trial. Hank took his seat behind the prosecutor, his hat in his hands. He didn't like being here, but he had to face Beckman one last time. Beckman had been in the barn that night, but Hank had still taken a man's life. Accidental or not, it was a thing that hurt him still.

Now, he'd come full circle. Jake would pay for the crimes that led to the shooting. But Hank wasn't looking for absolution. He'd taken the life of his friend that night, and for the past handful of months had been living in Richard's house, loving his wife, caring for his son.

Beckman looked bowed by his capture. He sat, chin down, shoulders slumped during the opening statements. Finding an impartial jury had taken time, and the trial had almost been moved to another county. The room behind him felt hostile. Many people had been hurt financially by Beckman.

Jake looked over his shoulder and their gazes met. Hank read the man's blame and hatred, as if Jake held Hank personally responsible for his crimes. He learned their defense would be to claim Jake was innocent, that Hank had been the true criminal. The first day ended, and Hank watched Beckman being led out of court in chains.

As the courtroom cleared, he searched for Nettie. He saw no sign of her. A part of him hungered to see her. He thought she might come today.

Edmund Johnson and McCullen and sons walked him out. Sunlight glistened on snow as a crowd of people moved from the courthouse to their waiting sleds, sleighs, and horses. Voices buzzed in the cool air, and boots crunched in hard-packed snow. Amid the colors of coats and jackets, Hank caught sight of a dark wool coat and a flash of molasses curls. He excused himself from his friends and wove through the crowd.

Nettie was untying her team from the hitching post. A blue hat crowned her head and matched the blue hand-knit scarf at her neck. Emmanuel recognized him first and nickered, tossing his mane in welcome. Nettie looked up and the brightness eased from her eyes.

"Hank!" Sam raced across the ground and into his arms. "Mama said you don't live width us no more."

"That's right." He couldn't help the kick in his heart when Sam wrapped him in a hug. He savored the sweetness for a long second before he set the boy down. He avoided looking at Nettie. He dreaded the look on her face as Sam clung to his gloved hand. "I sure miss you, partner."

Sam held tight. "You gonna come home now?"

"No."

He had thought how hard it might be for Sam. His throat ached with unspoken affection for this boy. His heart had hurt, missing him. And he could feel the same hurt in the tight, unyielding hold the boy had on his fingers.

Nettie's boots crunched in the snow. "I came just for today. I had to see that it was real and make my peace with what Jake has done. Even the role he played in Richard's death."

It hurt to look at her. She was beautiful with the cold wind brushing pink across her cheeks and nose. Her eyes shone with the gentle luster he'd come to love. He read no accusation there, but he could see her hurt.

"I was hoping I'd run into you, but I couldn't see you in the crowd." She swiped at a flyaway curl with her mittened hands. "When you left, you didn't take time to pack your things. I have all your clothes in the sled under the seat."

"I'll get them." He moved past her, saving her the trouble. He couldn't bear to have Nettie do one more thing for him. He wanted her with a force that thundered through him. It took all his strength to turn away from her.

He found the old pillow slip with the laundered, neatly folded clothes inside, and the book he'd been reading at her house at night by the fire. He slung the bag over his shoulder.

"I heard you were working on your house." She settled Sam on the sled's seat.

"I had to fix the windows. I didn't want the weather to cause any damage." He had so much he wanted to tell her. Like how he saw her when he walked through his house. That now and then he imagined them living as husband and wife, as a family, there in the home he'd built. Both of them free from the past.

"You shouldn't head up to the mountains." She climbed into the sled, avoiding the hand he offered, and took the reins in both slim hands. Even after he'd hurt her, there was gentleness and caring in her voice. "You love ranching. It's wrong for you to give up what you love just because of what Jake did to you. Because of what he made you feel. You're the gentlest man I know."

She released the brake and snapped the reins gently against the horses' rumps. The runners squeaked on the hard-packed snow. He watched her join the traffic in a long line waiting to turn out onto the street. Sam looked over the top of the seat and waved.

Hank waved back.

He looked again in the pillow slip, scented from Nettie's soap, and saw his billfold. He knew without looking that the money he'd left her long ago was there. She'd returned it.

She may have welcomed his help, but that wasn't why she'd let him stay. He could see that now. She'd forgiven what he'd done long ago. If only he could do the same.

Bereft, he watched her turn out onto the main street and disappear from his sight.

The moon brushed the curtains with a watery glow, and Nettie rolled over in bed. She couldn't sleep, not after seeing Hank today. Her gaze had caressed his handsome chiseled face and the strong line of his shoulders. He'd looked haunted, and she'd heard in court as the defense attorney spoke, that Jake still intended to try to prove Hank was to blame, just as he'd done the night of Richard's death.

She had been torn ever since Hank had left her. She hadn't known if he loved her. He was so intent on doing what he thought was right that she'd feared he looked at her and saw duty. That he wanted to care for her out of a long-standing sense of honor. But today, when he'd looked at her, there had been unmistakable love shining in his eyes, tender and abiding and real.

The bed beside her was empty, and no matter how she tried, she couldn't sleep. She slipped out from beneath the covers and brushed open the curtains. Pale light sheened the frozen expanse of earth. The world felt so peaceful. She felt so alone.

She thought of the letter she'd picked up in town today. Maude had arrived safely in Vermont. She'd settled in with her mother, who was ailing and needed care, and Maude said the change was for the best. She was happier than she'd been in a while.

Nettie had started a letter this evening and left it halfway written. She didn't know what to say about the trial. Or Harv, or Hank.

She closed her eyes and she could still see him standing in the crisp winter air, the silver-white sky above him, handsome in his dark suit. The love in her heart still burned. She missed him, how she missed him. He was gentle and strong, protective and honorable. And she would always be grateful she'd had the chance to love him.

She hoped Hank would find the peace he was looking for. The peace he deserved.

The prosecutor, over the course of the two-week trial, destroyed Jake's defense. It was long and arduous. Hank dreaded taking the stand, but he went when called. Jake glared with hate, his eyes hard and face twisted, and Hank was surprised to find the black rage that had driven him to pull a gun and contemplate firing it, had faded now.

He told his story. Of the night he'd shot Richard in his barn. His life had changed that day. He'd lost friends, family, his reputation, and nearly his life when he'd been run out of town. Beckman had almost cost him those same things a second time.

He told of the fight out at his ranch. His voice echoed in the silent courtroom as he told of how Jake had tried to kill him and did manage to put a bullet in his side. He recalled how the gun had fired and broken the second-story window, and how he'd feared Nettie or Sam had been hurt. He spoke of the rage that had driven him and how he'd overpowered Jake.

And he realized then, as he heard the lingering echo of his words, that he hadn't lost control after all. Robert was right. It was Jake's threat to Nettie and Sam that had sparked his blinding rage. He'd acted out of the need to protect them, that was all.

A lifetime of burden lifted from his shoulders. Emotion knotted in his throat, and it grew harder to talk. He saw his brother in the second row look at him encouragingly. They were true brothers now. They had become friends.

The jury reconvened days later to announce Jake's guilt. Hank listened to the verdict. For the first time in three long years, he was free.

Snow trickled from the sky, collecting on his hat brim and the front of his coat as he crossed the street. Robert had tried to talk him out of leaving for Idaho, and Hank didn't know what he wanted to do. Everything was changed now. He felt changed. He thought of his house and his ranch and hope filled his heart.

Town was busier than usual. Wagons and horses and buggies jammed the main street, and he wove between them to reach the mercantile. Women bustled along the boardwalks from store to store, accompanied by small children.

Frustrated by the madness, Hank managed to weave around the wide hoop skirts and children lingering at store windows, and pushed open the door of the mercantile. A merry bell above his head jingled.

He stepped aside to allow a woman loaded down with packages to pass. Then he stepped into line at the counter to hand in his list of winter supplies.

"I saw you at the trial." A voice startled him, and he recognized the woman standing in the aisle.

He hadn't seen her in years. He felt gut-punched and straightened his shoulders. He read the shadows in her eyes and noticed the hard-set line of her mouth. "Mother."

"I heard you were staying with Nettie Pickering." A muscle jumped along her fine-cut jaw, and she laid a hand there, as if distressed or trying to figure out what to say to him. "How is she?"

"I don't know. I'm not living there anymore." He took a step back, not knowing what to expect.

The hard lines bracketing Mother's face eased a bit. "That's too bad. I thought you might be buying Christmas gifts for them."

"Christmas gifts?" The words caught in his throat.

"Tomorrow's Christmas." Mother gestured to her bulky load. "I decided it's a grandmother's right to spoil her grandchildren. I bought some toys for Nettie's son. I had just assumed that Robert invited you, and that you would bring her and Sam."

"You bought gifts for Nettie's son?"

"You should marry her, Hank. And no, this time I'm not worried about my reputation." Dignity lifted Emmalouise's plump chin. "I want you to be happy. I think you deserve it. I watched you at the trial, and I saw a man I didn't know—strong and brave and honorable. You aren't like him, and I was wrong to condemn you the way I did. I should have stood by you. I should have taken you in when you were injured." Tears glistened in her eyes. "After all, you are my son."

Hank bowed his chin. He could feel the people in line around him listening. He stared down at his list, and he didn't know what to say.

Mother's voice fell to a low whisper, maybe aware that others could hear. "It took a stranger to see in my son what I could not. But I can see it now."

"You spoke with Nettie?"

"No, but she took you in when you were injured, and did what no one else had the compassion to do, and that opened my eyes." Mother turned to go. "Will I see you at Robert's tomorrow?"

"I can't say." He watched her leave, and something broke apart in his chest, leaving him completely vulnerable. He handed his list to the clerk at the counter and paid for delivery to the livery. He had a sleigh waiting.

But as he pushed out the door and stepped onto the busy street, he didn't know what to do. Nothing was the same as it had been—and all because of Nettie. She'd changed his entire world.

The hope in his heart grew, shimmering like a star at twilight. Faint at first, then strengthening as night deepened, giving it substance.

Hank's gaze fastened on a set of wooden train cars in a display window. He stopped, staring at the brightly painted, intricately accurate engine and freight cars and caboose. And the yards and yards of track. The perfect gift for a little boy. For a son.

Hank stepped into the store. His hands trembled as he reached for the train set. He had been a good father to Sam. He had been a good man to Nettie. He had protected them, risking his own life to do so. The past was over. Talking about Richard's death in court had set him free. Of guilt. Of obligation. Of the fear that he was as destructive at heart as his father had been.

Nettie's words rang in his mind, words he refused to believe when he'd been so determined to walk out of her life. *Do you know what I see when I look at you? A man who risked his life to protect my son. A man who showed me that I could love again. You've stood beside me, and showed me what true honor is.* She saw a man she loved, a man she could count on, a man to raise her son.

He was that man.

"Mama?"

"Yes, sweet pea." Nettie looked up from rolling her pie dough. Sam stood with his hands jammed in his little trouser pockets and his blue flannel shirt untucked, his sunshine-gold hair standing up on end.

"I need a string." He gazed up at her with wide, button eyes that never quite smiled completely. Even though so much time had passed, he still missed Hank. "I'm playin' with Pum'kin."

"I have one in my apron pocket." Nettie slipped her floury

fingers into the deep pocket and searched through the various shapes and textures buried there. She located the familiar woolly bit of yarn and pulled it out. "Here you are."

Sam wrapped his little fingers around it, but his eyes lingered over the dough. "I getta help?"

"Yep. As soon as I get the cookies cut." This was her second batch this morning. Sam's fingers were already stained red and green from the decorating sugars he'd helped her sprinkle on the previous batch of cookies.

"When do we getta eat 'em?" he asked eagerly.

"We'll sneak some as soon as they're out of the oven." She brushed a hand over his unruly cowlick but to no avail. "Remember to keep Pumpkin away from the fire when you're playing."

"I remember." Sam pounded off, his shoes striking the floorboards.

He halted at the braid rug where the kitten was dozing. He dangled the red string and the kitten came to life, reaching out with a lightning-fast paw. Sam giggled, and the chase was on. He raced down the hall, yarn trailing, kitten pouncing.

She returned to her sugar cookie dough. She wondered if Hank had headed for the mountains, like he'd told Mr. Johnson. Edmund had gone to the trial's closing arguments and said he'd seen Hank there. She hadn't gone back after that first day. She hadn't wanted to see him and wish for what would never be.

Well, enough of sad thoughts. Christmas would be festive this year with just the two of them. She wanted Sam to enjoy the holiday. She had presents hidden and stockings hung. The little tree in the corner was decorated with cranberries and popcorn and paper snowflakes.

She was preparing a feast—half of it was already covered and crocked down in the cellar. There was only the turkey left, and after she finished with these cookies, they would take the sleigh to town and fetch it from the butcher.

"Mama?" Sam ran to the table, the red length of yarn crushed in one little fist. "What's that?"

"What's what?" Nettie reached for the cookie cutters and dropped them in the flour bowl.

"That noise." Sam cocked his head.

Nettie's hand stopped in midair and she listened. The wind

whistling against the outside wall had a silver, jingly sound to it. "I don't know." She wiped her hands on a towel and crossed to the only window.

Falling snow obscured her view. Then she saw a golden horse pulling a fine-looking sleigh lope around the corner of the cottonwoods and into her yard. Sleigh bells jangled a merry tune.

"I wonder who . . ." Then she recognized the broad-shouldered man wearing the dark Stetson as the sleigh sped by.

At the barn door, the horse stopped and Hank climbed out of the vehicle. Snow clung to the dark wool of his coat as he pulled open the door to stable the mare inside.

"Hank!" Sam's breath fogged the window before her. The chair he stood on toddled with the shift of his weight. She put a hand on the back of the chair to steady it.

It couldn't be, but it was. He'd said good-bye and left them, and even in town he hadn't wanted her back, he hadn't said one word to make her believe . . .

Winter had come, and she'd gone on with her life.

"He came. Mama, he came." Joy beamed across Sam's face.

"He sure did." Nettie tucked away her hopes, because she had no idea why he'd come. Maybe to check and see how they were doing. He felt an obligation to look after her; she'd figured that out by now. "Hop down off of that chair."

"But I wanna see Hank."

Nettie held out her hand. "Go climb up on the sofa, this once. It's safer."

"Goody!" Sam hopped to the floor, dragged the chair back to the table and dashed across the room. He climbed up onto the horsehair sofa and propped his elbows on the windowsill. "He's comin'!"

She heard his boots on the steps and crossed the room to open the door. Wind and snow rushed into the house, and Hank emerged out of the storm. He closed the door behind him. Her heart skipped a beat just looking at him. She'd never seen him look this good. His face was relaxed, his eyes bright and without shadows, his smile untroubled. Snow clung to his hat brim and to the broad line of his shoulders.

"I'm making a mess." He swept off his hat.

"That's what a broom is for." She tore her gaze from the sight of him before hope lit her up like a Christmas tree. She grabbed the broom and held the worn-smooth handle in her hand and waited for him to take off his jacket

Snow plopped to the floor and she swept it toward the door. The work kept her busy and she didn't have to look at him, but she felt his gaze like a touch as she worked. Sam was chattering away about decorating the tree and popping corn and his kitten, and it was all Nettie could do to put the broom away.

She heard his step and felt his presence. The kitchen's temperature seemed to increase, and she felt hotter than before. She forced her eyes to meet his gaze. He stood with thumbs hooked in the pockets of his denims, unflinching and as strong as steel. His gaze caught hers and held.

Her heart skipped another beat.

"It smells mighty good in here. Is that cookie dough?"

Nettie bit her lip. "Sam and I were going to decorate them later."

"It would be polite to ask me to join you." Hank folded his arms across his wide chest. How substantial he looked with his hard-won confidence.

"Maybe I'm not feeling too polite." Nettie's fingers fumbled as she grabbed a greased cookie sheet from the counter.

"Would saying I'm sorry help?" Apology warmed his voice, tender and loving, and it was the sound of his love for her, rich and warm and forever, that made her look up.

"What do you intend to apologize for?" She turned her back to him and plucked the star cutter out of the flour. She punched it into the cookie dough. "For leaving me? Or for not meeting all your obligations to me?"

"That's not fair, Nettie." Hank's fingers curled around her shoulders with the familiar ease of a lover. "I had to straighten out some things."

"And now are you going to leave?" Her chin trembled, and she didn't want him to know how she felt. How much she loved him.

"Leave? No." The heat from his fingers licked through the fabric of her dress. "Why would I ever leave again? You're the woman I love."

Love. The image taunted her. She'd dreamed of cozy evenings spent together in front of the fire, of warmth and laughter and waking up every morning at his side.

"I asked you to marry me once, Nettie. And I'm here to ask you again." His fingers gently squeezed at the tension in her shoulders. "You said you wouldn't marry me until I was clear why I was asking you."

"That's right I don't want your charity. I couldn't stand for that to be the basis of our marriage."

"It isn't. This love I have in my heart is for you, Nettie. Honest and true. It's for the woman who saved me in the road that day, who tended my wounds and healed me. You gave me your love, and now I'm here to give you mine. Please be my wife."

She twisted around to face him. Love shone in his eyes, as true as the north star, as deep as the sky. Unmistakable and real and all for her. His eyes sparkled, and his mouth quirked into a smile, and she was weakening. Her heart was breaking and she was falling in love with him all over again.

"Let me be a father to Sam. Let me be the man you need for the rest of your life." He pressed a kiss to her brow, tender and sweet, a promise of a life of passion to come. "It was always you, Nettie. Everything I've ever done or will ever do is because I love you."

The past was gone. There was nothing standing between them but their future. She laid her hand in his, happier than she'd ever dreamed of being. He'd come back to her, he'd come home. "I love you, Hank. I'd be honored to be your wife."

His arms wrapped around her, and his mouth closed over hers. His kiss was tender and claiming, and heat sparked in her blood.

"Too bad the table's crowded." Wicked humor flashed in his eyes. "I have very fond memories of that table."

"There's always tonight." She kissed him, long and hard.

"Mama." Sam tugged on her skirt. "We gotta make the cookies now."

Hank chuckled and lifted Sam in his arms. Joy warmed the room and drove away the sounds of the storm. Nettie pulled up a chair knowing that this happiness was just the beginning. A lifetime of love reached out before them. Hank pressed a kiss her brow, and she knew he felt it, too.

Maclain's Wife

"Pa, is today the day the stage is comin'?" Emily MacLain flipped twin ponytails behind her thin shoulders and ignored her steaming plate of pancakes.

Ben set the tin of maple syrup on the table. His heart warmed as always at the sight of his daughter's happy anticipation. Her eyes sparkled. A broad grin lit her face. How Emily was looking forward to meeting her new mother. "Yes, today is the day."

"*Finally*. It's taken *forever* to get here." Emily sighed with deliberate drama, then stabbed her fork directly into the pancake pile.

"Miss Curtis only agreed to our proposal last month." Ben grabbed the blue enamel pot and grimaced. He'd over-boiled the coffee again.

Looked like he wasn't the only one who would be happy with a woman in this house. Maybe, if he could cook worth a darn, he wouldn't have to get married. But he couldn't cook anything but pancakes, bacon and eggs—and those not very well. His stomach hardened at the sight of the fried eggs congealed at the bottom of the blackened frying pan.

Yes, it was a good thing Pauline Curtis arrived today. He couldn't take one more meal of his own cooking.

"I hope Miss Curtis is nice. And laughs a lot just like Adella's ma." Emily took a big sip of fresh milk. "And I hope she knows lots of songs and sings all the time."

"I hope so, too." *Please, be all that Emily needs.* Ben hoped Pauline Curtis was a kind woman, not dour and sour. Little Emily deserved a mother who would love her, a mother who would stay.

Polly Brown rolled her eyes at the skinny stick of a woman dressed in ruffles and frippery. Not that she usually spent time in the company of such people, but crammed in the confines of the stagecoach, she had little choice. She sneezed again at Pauline Curtis's sweet, high-scented perfume that hung in the air like fog. Even though she tried not to watch, her gaze kept straying back to the young woman who dabbed at huge, continuous tears with her expensive lace handkerchief.

What on earth did a woman like that have to cry about?

Polly knew darn well that she was being uncharitable. Heck, maybe she was even a little bit envious. After all, she wore only a pair of men's trousers and a cotton shirt, rolled up at the sleeves. Her boots were worn and scuffed. And her hair, well, there just wasn't much she could do with her shoulder-length brown locks.

She wasn't a golden blonde or a striking ebony-haired beauty. Nor would she ever be. She was just plain Polly Brown, the daughter of an outlaw, who could outshoot nearly every man she'd ever met. She was not in the same class as delicate Pauline Curtis.

"Roland said he wasn't ready to get married,"

Pauline sniffled into her handkerchief. "And I loved him so."

"Well, with the babe in your belly, you'll need a husband soon," the old matron beside her whispered. "Be grateful your father knows of a decent man who will take on a woman, sight unseen. He's desperate, he is. Says there's not a marriageable woman in the whole of Montana Territory. And him with a little daughter to care for."

"I just wish Roland would marry me." Pauline burst into sobbing tears. "I don't want to be with a rough, uneducated sheriff."

Polly pushed her hat over her eyes and sank back into the seat. All that heartbreak made it too noisy to take a nap. Good thing she made up her mind a long time ago never to bother with love and marriage. Look at all the tears it required.

No, she was content with the choices she'd made, content that her only companion was a six-shooter strapped to her right thigh. If only she wasn't running for her life, everything would be perfect

Gunfire popped outside the stage. Polly snapped open her eyes and sat up. Across the aisle, proper Miss Pauline Curtis let out a shriek.

"Road agents! Indians!"

What use was a female who got scared at every little thing? Polly had been handling ruthless robbers and rampaging Indians for as long as she could remember. All it required was a six-shooter and a little bit of attitude.

"We never should have come," Pauline whined.

Really. Maybe Miss Curtis didn't have everything after all. She could use a bit of backbone and some common sense.

Polly always kept her gun loaded, so all she had to do was unsnap her holster and wrap her hand around the comforting walnut handle. "Keep quiet," she advised the others.

"Nana, she's got a gun!" Privileged Pauline gasped in horror, her eyes widening as if she'd seen a two-headed serpent.

Polly kicked open the stage door and cocked her revolver. She saw three saddled horses tied to a low pine bough. None of the horses were breathing hard nor sweating, so they had not been ridden hard. She heard men's voices up ahead and climbed out of the coach, keeping careful watch.

"It's just a fellow talking with the driver." She released the hammer but kept the gun in hand in case there was some trouble. Maybe the man just needed a ride to the next town, but maybe he wanted something else.

"Women carrying guns. What's next?" Pauline sniffed as she climbed out of the cramped stage, lifting her nose as she passed.

Polly bowed her chin. Fine, she wasn't a high society lady, not even a pretty, normal kind of woman. How could she be? Her ma had died when she was just a child. And Pa had been busy with his work. He was a rough man and hadn't known anything about little girls—and hadn't wanted to.

Well, if she had been raised right and could wear pretty dresses, she would not be mean like Miss Pauline Curtis.

"Roland! It's you!" In a flurry of ribbons and ruffles, Polly watched Miss Curtis grab up her skirts and run toward the newcomer. They entwined in a tangle of arms and apologies and what sounded like wet kisses.

It just went to show how little sense a woman like that had.

Men were nothing but trouble. Polly had learned long ago that men only wanted two things. One involved getting what they wanted—money, revenge, prestige—with their revolvers. And the other involved getting what they wanted with, well, a body part she was too embarrassed to think about.

"Praise be!" The old nana tossed her thanks toward the heavens. "Forget Sheriff MacLain. Pauline will have her prince."

Personally, Polly would be thankful if the stage could get a move on. She had Bad Bart Dixon tailing her with a loaded gun and a grudge. A real big grudge. The problem with Dixon was simple—he was the one man she couldn't outshoot, and he was a gunfighter who wouldn't take no for an answer.

Yes, it would be just fine with her if Pauline's prince would hurry up with whatever it was he wanted.

"Roland has asked me to marry him instead of going to that awful old sheriff." Pauline burst into sight. "He brought horses so we can start heading home right away."

"How wonderful. After all, Roland is a banker's son." The old nana embraced her charge with great enthusiasm. "Let's hurry."

Polly holstered her revolver. It didn't look like she was going to need it. Now the stage was empty. It might be a lonely ride, but at least she wouldn't have to keep breathing in Pauline's nose-stinging perfume.

"What about my baggage?" the pampered princess whined.

"Leave it." Roland, a strong-shouldered man wearing a bowler hat and the nicest black suit Polly had ever seen, strode back into view. "The driver is angry because I've made him late. And I didn't bring a pack-horse to carry your trunks. I'll buy you anything you want once we reach a civilized town."

"Oh, Roland." Pauline threw herself into his strong arms once again.

Polly strode back to the stage, shaking her head. If Pauline knew what was good for her, she'd give that slick-looking Roland a kick in the shins and make her own way in the world.

"Hey, you." Pauline's sharp voice sliced through the air thick with chalk-dry Montana dust. "You, gun-toting girl."

Polly spun around, spine stiff, half in and half out of the coach.

"You might as well have my things. Looks like you could use them. And a bath."

Pauline flounced off. Polly bit her lip. A bath? She was dusty, not dirty. And there was nothing wrong with her perfectly good trousers and shirt.

But as she dropped into her seat and the stagecoach lumbered into motion, her heart felt heavy. It wasn't just Pauline's words, but her attitude as well.

What Polly wouldn't give to be a fine young woman with her hair all twisted up in a knot and those frilly little curls falling all around her face. And a real dress that flounced when she walked.

Then no one would make fun of her when she rode into town. Or look down at her and say what a pity it was when women tried to be like men.

She just didn't know any other way. How could she? She never had a woman around to show her womanly ways. She'd never had anyone to help her. She was alone. Alone, making her way in a world not always kind to females.

As the morning sun rose higher in the sky, Polly started thinking about the things Pauline Curtis had left behind. There was a satchel stashed under the seat, forgotten in the hurry to be with broad-shouldered Roland. Should she look inside it?

Half of it was curiosity over what a proper sort of woman carried in a satchel. The other part was the knowledge that maybe it was something she wanted. After all, Pauline said she could have her things.

Heck, taking a peek wouldn't hurt. She knelt down and tugged the satchel out by one strap. She pulled open the unsnapped top and peered inside, then withdrew two pairs of white gloves, both spotless and brand-new looking. Another lace handkerchief. And a folded piece of paper. Now that was interesting.

Polly smoothed the parchment and studied the letters written there. She had some schooling, not much, but enough to recognize a few of the words. Why, it looked as if Miss Pauline Curtis was going to work for a sheriff in Indian Trails, the next stage stop. She was going to cook and clean for them. And a little girl was mentioned.

Hmm. Polly considered that piece of information. The sheriff of Indian Trails wouldn't know his housekeeper wasn't coming. And there was no way that sheriff knew what Pauline Curtis looked like.

Hmm. Polly leaned back in the seat. She found more beautiful things in the satchel. Pretty-smelling soap. A silver mirror and brush set. A bonnet the color of a Montana summer sky. Why, it was an awfully pretty bonnet. All blue, her favorite color.

In a snap she tossed off her Stetson. The bonnet fit right on her head, despite the lump of her ponytail. A blue feather plumed over her left ear and tickled just a little. She caught hold of the velvet ribbons and tied them in a big bow beneath her chin.

Why, she'd never worn a woman's garment in her whole life. She probably didn't look very good in it. Pa had always been honest in his comments about her appearance over the years. She knew she was no beauty.

But curiosity got the best of her and she grabbed that engraved, silver-framed hand mirror. A woman she didn't recognize gazed back at her in the beveled surface. She saw her own blue eyes, and yes, that was her face, but she looked completely different. Almost fancy, the way a real lady did.

She thought of the clothes up in those three trunks. Pauline Curds had been just about her size. And those trunks were now hers. Suddenly she knew what she would do with all those frilly garments that were probably stuffed inside.

Even Bad Bart Dixon wouldn't recognize her dressed up in a city woman's finery.

COMING SOON!

ABOUT THE AUTHOR

Jillian Hart makes her home in Washington State, where she has lived most of her life. When Jillian is not writing away on her next book, she can be found reading, going to lunch with friends and spending quiet evenings at home with her family.

Made in the USA
Lexington, KY
15 October 2013